Providence

Providence

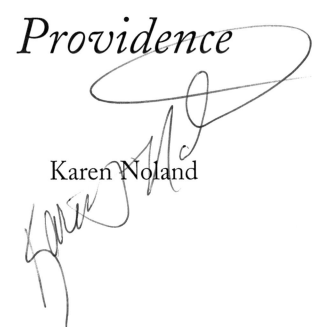

Karen Noland

Writer's Showcase
San Jose New York Lincoln Shanghai

Providence

Writer's Showcase
an imprint of iUniverse.com, Inc.

For information address:
iUniverse.com, Inc.
5220 S 16th, Ste. 200
Lincoln, NE 68512
www.iuniverse.com

This is a work of fiction. All events, locations, institutions, themes, persons, characters and plot are completely fictional. Any resemblance to places or person, living or deceased, are of the invention of the author.

ISBN: 0-595-19780-9

Printed in the United States of America

This book is dedicated to my husband Ted Noland, without whose love, support and guidance I could not have seen this through.

CONTENTS

CHAPTER I

Choking on the red dust, Kate drew another deep breath as she waited for the contraction to ease before reaching in once more as the cow relaxed. This time she felt the small hoof there in her grasp.

"Take it easy, mama," Kate whispered. She tugged, gently at first, then with ever increasing force. Icy tendrils of panic began to whirl around the edges of her mind, trying to steal her concentration. Just when she was sure it was lost, the tiny leg popped into place. With one last loud bellow the cow gave a mighty heave and the calf emerged into the light of day.

Kate gasped, sitting back on the hard Oklahoma earth. Wiping an arm across her sweaty brow, she sighed with relief. Once again the miracle of new life lay before her. The little thing was already fighting to find its legs. The big black cow lowed softly heaving herself up, as the calf struggled, gaining strength, finally finding its feet. A rough tongue ran over the calf's back and he was down again.

Kate smiled through her weariness. The freshness of new life never ceased to amaze her. "God, you are so great," she murmured aloud. "Thank you for allowing this one to live today, thank you." This daily dialogue with her Creator had become a wellspring of comfort for Kate over the weeks and months since Will had died. The solitude she faced tending to the cattle, the land, the horses, and the myriad other responsibilities left to her when she became a widow threatened at times to overwhelm her.

Cow and calf were moving away from her, the calf swaying unsteadily in his attempts to keep up with mama. "He's a nice one, going to be big and stout," Kate thought, "May make a nice bull. After all, old Casey isn't getting any younger." These thoughts ran through her mind as she watched the pair approach the herd a short distance away. This one made it, but what about the next? Only last week she watched in despair as a cow struggled to give birth to a calf hopelessly too large. She could still feel the sting of the bitter bile that had risen in her throat as she steadied her hand to pull the trigger, putting the poor cow out of its misery. Kate felt every death not only as a personal loss, but cattle were the lifeblood of her ranch, and each one lost was lost income as well.

Strands of damp hair clung to her temples, while beads of sweat trickled between her shoulder blades. It was already so hot, and only April. What would the summer bring? She reached down, running her hand through the new grass emerging to cover the prairie. Would the spring rains come? Would there be enough grass this year? So many of her cows had calved and still more were coming. How would she get them to market this fall?

"God, why? Why did you have to take Will?" His death was a raw wound on her soul though it had been almost nine months since the accident. The red dirt over his grave beneath the willow was already covered by the green of springtime, but the pain in her heart was as fresh as newly turned earth. Tears of frustration and anger welled within her threatening to spill over. Turning her face to the clear sky, she took a ragged breath searching the heavens, but there were no answers forthcoming this day, only the wide expanse of infinite blue.

Sighing, she stood and headed toward the sorrel mare waiting patiently with the reins draped over the branch of a nearby tree. Kate opened the leather pack strapped behind the cantle. Retrieving a rough rag, she scrubbed at the blood and dirt covering her arms from the recent calving. Livid scars appeared as the grime was scrubbed away, remnants of long ago pain. Rolling her sleeves back down to cover the unsightly burns, she picked up the reins, stepped into the stirrup and swung herself into the old leather saddle.

Kate looked down at the worn chaps covering her legs. Yet another reminder of Will's passing and having to adapt to running a cattle ranch alone. She longed for a hot bath and a fresh pretty dress to wear, but they just weren't suited to the work she was forced into. She smiled at the memory of the first time she had tried to round up a herd of old rangy cows wearing long skirts and a petticoat, riding the side saddle that Will had saved for and surprised her with on her birthday. It wasn't long before she decided Will's pants, sturdy cotton shirts and old worn saddle were far more suited to the job at hand. Besides, who was there to see her out here?

The mare was young and fresh. It wasn't hard for Kate to urge her into an easy ground-covering lope toward home. They steered away from the small herd, careful not to disturb the cows and calves who lazed in the warmth of the late morning sun. A golden glow shone all around, highlighting every blade of green prairie grass and gilding the leaves of early budding trees. The tightly curled blossoms of redbud and dogwood were beginning to unfurl in a riot of color. She relaxed into the saddle. Tightening the reins, the mare obediently slowed to a trot, and finally to a fast walk.

"How could anyone doubt your existence, Lord, with all this life abounding?" The mare snorted and tossed her head as if in agreement. Kate laughed. The morning's tension easing, she picked up the reins and they set off again at a trot.

✷ ✷

Climbing a grassy rise, the homestead came into full view. Will had chosen the perfect spot to build their dream, nestled in a small valley protected on the north and west by small knolls rising from the prairie. They felt God had led them to the place they dreamed about from the moment they left tragedy behind them in Missouri. A beautiful grove of trees growing along a spring in the small valley provided the backdrop for their new life in Oklahoma Territory.

Kate caught her breath at the sight of her beloved home. She checked the mare, slowing her to a walk, then reined to a stop. Head tossing impatiently, the sorrel mare pawed the ground. "I know you're anxious to get home, but just look, Gypsy, isn't it perfect?" Kate said reaching down to stroke the mare's silky neck.

Smoke drifted lazily from the chimney of the stone fireplace. Kate smiled at the memories. In the summer of 1889, her hands bleeding from quarrying and carrying the heavy native stone she had sat down in a fit of tears. "I can't do this, Will, it's just too hard!"

Blue eyes flashed as he stood above her. "I will not have you living in a soddy, Kate," he said before taking her hands and tenderly kissing the raw blisters. "Just imagine a roaring fire on a cold winter's night, you and me cuddled up in front of that great stone hearth. " He gazed longingly into her eyes, a faint smile playing at the corners of his mouth, he raised his brows suggestively, scooped her up and carried her to their makeshift tent, laughing at her feeble protests.

It wasn't long before the snug frame home took shape around that enormous hearth, surrounded by a wide porch and real glass windows. Over the eight years that marked their short life together there, other buildings were added. The barn and corrals were built with the help of neighbors. The bunkhouse adjoined the barn to house the cowboys they hired off and on. A smokehouse, spring house, and the blacksmith shop, now sadly neglected, completed the idyllic scene.

From her vantage point, Kate ran a critical eye over the place. Fences needed mending, a new hole appeared in the smokehouse roof, probably from the hail storm a few weeks ago. She sighed and said a small prayer for the strength to face the challenges ahead.

Suddenly, the front door of the main house flew open and a small red-haired figure darted across the yard into the chicken coop. Kate's heart filled with love for her small irrepressible daughter. Jolene was so like her father, full of life and filled with mischief. Jo was followed shortly by a small graying woman carrying a basket and brandishing a bonnet. Though Kate was too far away to hear the woman's words, she knew Mrs. Insley was berating the little girl for being out in the hot sun without it.

Forgetting about the chores that lay ahead and the cows behind, Kate and Gypsy set off down the hill toward home.

✶✶✶✶✶✶✶✶✶✶✶✶✶✶✶✶✶✶✶✶✶✶✶✶✶✶✶✶✶✶✶✶✶

"Mama's coming, mama's coming!" shrieked Jo. Nana Insley looked up. Shaking her head, she disappeared into the house.

"What has my little Irish rose been doing this morning?" Kate called to the small spitfire running toward her. She swung a leg over the back of the saddle, stepping easily to the ground. Securing the reins over the corral fence, Kate turned just in time to avoid being tackled and swooped the girl up into her arms.

"Where have you been, Mama? We've got breakfast waiting for you. I found six whole eggs this morning and Nana let me knead the biscuits. Later we're going to churn butter, and if I'm good Nana said that I could help her with the baking." Kate placed a finger over her daughter's mouth to stem the endless flow of words.

"It sounds like you've a busy day planned, then! I've been out checking the herd in the west pastures. Would you like to hear about it?"

"Oh, yes, Mama! Nana said that Jonathan should be home today with Papa Insley. I've missed them. Do you really think they'll be home today? Maybe Jon will play with me." As Jo paused for a breath, Kate set her down when Mrs. Insley appeared on the back porch with a basin of warm water and a clean towel.

"Thought you looked as though you be needin' these." She set the basin on a bench near the kitchen door, draping the towel over a rail above the bench.

"Thank you, I do, Mrs. Insley." She gave the older woman a grateful look as she climbed the steps to the porch, followed by her constant red-haired shadow. "Jo tells me you expect the men back today."

"Aye, that I do, two days to city, a day to load provisions, and two days back. They best be rollin' in here by this afternoon, no less!" She stated firmly, standing arms akimbo at the open kitchen door.

"Well, that's one thing to look forward to. I've sorely missed them these last few days," Kate said.

"Humph."

Kate took off the soiled hat she wore, handed it to Jo, and pulled loose the ribbon that held her hair up. A mass of dusty brown curls fell over her shoulders. Dipping both hands into the warm water, she let it cascade over wrists and arms, splashed it up over her tired, dirty face. The cleansing flow was exquisite. Kate lingered briefly praying the water would wash away more than just the dust—wash away the scars, the fear and anger, the loneliness and the frustration of the last few months. She breathed deeply letting the relaxation seep through her entire body.

"Look at me, Mama, I'm a cowgirl!" Jo's voice cut through her reverie, bringing her back to a full realization of time and place. Jo was wearing the old felt hat and riding the porch rail, holding on with one hand, the other flung high in the air.

"Jo, stop that! Get down from there this instant!" Kate snapped at the girl.

"But, Mama, I just…."

"I don't care what you just—Get down now! Do you hear me?" Kate's voice was sharp.

"Yes, ma'am." Jo answered meekly. Giving her mother a wide-eyed stare, she slipped by and ran into the kitchen, seeking refuge in the arms of her Nana.

Trembling, Kate closed her eyes and took a deep breath, "Oh, dear God, forgive me, but I was so scared." She finished washing quickly, hung the towel to dry on the rail and entered the kitchen. The smell of fresh biscuits and strong coffee enveloped her. In spite of the fear, her stomach growled reminding her just how hungry she was. Jo was sitting at the table watching warily, tears streaming down her rosy cheeks.

Kate knelt and opened her arms. "Honey, come here." Jo ran into the outstretched arms and Kate hugged her. They were both crying. Tears of grief streamed down Kate's face, mingling with the tears of pain from Jo. "I am so sorry, Jo, I didn't mean to frighten you. But when I saw you like that…"

"I know, Mama, Nana told me, I didn't mean it, honest I didn't. "

"I know you didn't. I love you. "

"Love you, too, Mama," Jo sniffed.

"Why don't you hop up to the table and we'll all eat a nice hot breakfast together. How's that sound?" Kate stood the girl up and gave her a tap on the bottom sending her to the big plank table.

In the instant that Kate had turned to see Jo riding that rail, the little girl had looked so much like Will, wearing the same beat up felt hat with red curls peeking out, a hand thrown up in the air as Will had always done when breaking the colts. As he had done breaking the last colt. His last ride. In that one instant, Kate had relived the entire horrifying moment. She saw Will again riding the colt to the ground, the horse falling, Will crushed beneath the thousand pound animal, his neck snapped in an instant. One minute so full of life and dreams, the next no more than a shell; a limp, lifeless body lay crushed and broken on the ground. Her world had changed forever in that moment.

Kate joined her daughter at the big table set with a heaping platter of warm biscuits, a crock of freshly churned butter and the last of the honey from the fallen bee tree they had found last autumn. Mrs. Insley carried over plates with fried eggs and slices of cured ham, while Kate poured two mugs of strong hot coffee and a cup of milk for Jo. Truly a feast for the three women of the ranch. As Mrs. Insley took her place on the far side of the table they joined hands while Kate asked a blessing on the food and the safe return of the men.

At first, the meal was enjoyed in silence. The everyday sounds of farm life drifted in through the open door. The bellowing of a bull, a shrill neigh from a mare to her errant foal, soft clucking from scratching hens, and the ever-present drone of flies and honey bees filled the morning air.

"Mama, how are the cows doing today? Are there any new calves? I want to feed one like last year. Are there any that don't have mommies?" Jo asked between bites of biscuit, honey dripping down her small round face.

Kate reached over and caught the golden drop from Jo's chin just as it threatened to mar her clean white collar. "I had to help one this morning, Jo, but I'm happy to report that cow and calf are both doing quite well. No orphans so far this spring, thank God." Kate took a bite of ham, savoring the rich smokey-sweet taste. "I counted forty-two cows in the west pastures with our brand. At least twenty had healthy calves and I'm certain that a dozen more should calve in a week or two. And there were over thirty steers in the far valley on that side. If the herd on the east side does as well, we should be able to send a fair lot to market. "

They had separated the herds some years earlier when Will was determined to improve on their native longhorn cattle by introducing a new strain he had read about. The bull he brought back from Kansas with him, Casey, was big and black and had no horns at all. He said it was called an Angus, and should serve to produce superior calves with better weaning weights and earlier maturation. Along with Casey had come ten mixed blood cows, mostly black and only a few with horns. To Kate it had all seemed Greek at the time, but she grew to like the look of the bull, and his calves certainly were larger and more prepared for market than the others.

"T'would be a welcome thing here." Mrs. Insley added.

"Yes, that's the truth. Since we only sent the forty steers last year, well…" Kate was interrupted by a commotion in the yard.

"The men are here! Jonathan's home!" Before Kate could react, Jo was out the door and barreling toward the wagon approaching from the north.

✳✳✳✳✳✳✳✳✳✳✳✳✳✳✳✳✳✳✳✳✳✳✳✳✳✳✳✳✳✳✳✳✳✳

Kate stood and walked to the open door. The men were indeed home. A deep sigh of relief escaped her before she even realized how tense she had been. Jake Insley's buckboard drawn by his two blonde draft mares approached the main yard of the ranch. Kate's mare, standing patiently at the corral gate whinnied a greeting, answered by the lead mare of the team. Jo had climbed the garden fence to gain a better view of the proceedings. Jonathan's faithful cow dog, Smokey, followed the wagon at a brisk trot with his tongue lolling to the side.

"Whoa, easy there Rosey; hold up there now, Ginny." The wagon rolled to a stop between the house and the barn under the competent hands and gentle voice of Jake Insley. Jonathan jumped down from the high seat, as his grandfather set the hand brake. He held his jacket close to his side and a bit awkwardly as Jo regaled him with a monologue of happenings on the ranch. Kate was busy going over the stores and provisions visible in the wagon with a quick and calculating eye. Jake tended to the team, as he watched her meticulous inventory.

"What did you see, Jon? What did you do? Was it fun? What's Guthrie like? Did you bring me any candy this time?" Jo was relentless as she approached her only playmate. Though ten years her senior, he was patient and caring, and always had time for the little girl he thought of as his baby sister.

"Well, I s'pose you could call her Candy if you like," he said slowly. "Hadn't rightly thought of a name for her yet." Jon held out his faded gray coat to the little girl who looked at him with curiosity. Just then the coat wiggled, nearly jumping from the boy's hands.

With a delighted squeal, Jo grabbed for the now squirming bundle and discovered a small fawn colored pup with four white feet. "Oh, Jonathan!" Jo gasped. Then she and the pup were sprawled together on the new spring grass, a jumble of flying paws and petticoats.

"Jolene Rose Shaughnessey!" Rang out a stern warning from the back porch.

Jo froze instinctively. Turning toward the voice, Jo's face broke into a dazzling smile as she held up her new-found treasure. "Oh, Nana, look! Isn't she wonderful? Jon brought her for me." The sheer delight shining from the girls eyes was enough to melt a heart of ice.

"Well, I s'pose it can stay then. But on the porch, not in the house. "

"Oh, Nana, you're going to love her. She's the most wonderful gift ever." Jo scooped up the pup and headed directly to her room in the loft followed closely by Jonathan and Smokey, leaving Mrs. Insley shaking her head and muttering quietly about dogs in the house.

✶✶✶✶✶✶✶✶✶✶✶✶✶✶✶✶✶✶✶✶✶✶✶✶✶✶✶✶✶✶✶✶✶

"It's most all here, Kate. What with prices risin' like they are in Guthrie, and such, I had to do some sure bargaining and all to get what we did." Jake spoke without apology.

"I know you did right, Jake. You know I trust you." Kate sighed as she looked over the meager supply of stores that would have to see them through the seasons ahead until they could send the steers to market properly this year. "Did you get the seed you'll need for planting this spring?"

"Yes'm. Me and Jon, we figgered we could do that same forty in wheat again, produced pretty well last time. And I was going to do ten acres in corn, and at least ten in oats again this year. You think we did all right on the oats this last time?"

"I do. There's still a few bushels left in the granary. "

"Um-hmm, I thought so as well. "

Kate hesitated, then asked the question that had been on her mind since they left, "Did Mr. Johnson give you the rest of the money from last fall's steers?"

The older man looked at the ground, standing silent for a moment in the warm Oklahoma sunshine. The light breeze stirred his sliver hair; a bird chirruped in the stillness. Kate stared at him waiting for his answer, trepidation building within. Finally looking up, Jake reached into his inner breast pocket and withdrew a yellowed envelope. He handed it to her without comment, his flinty eyes saying far more than words ever could.

She took the envelope and opened it, withdrawing eight twenty-dollar bills and a receipt. She looked at the collection of papers in disbelief. "A hundred and sixty dollars? But there should have been at least six hundred dollars here!" Her heart sinking, she leaned against the buckboard for support.

"The fine gentleman says that prices are down for beef, and what with losses along the way, and his 'expenses,' and all, why, what he has given you is more than fair. Oh, and he'll be very happy to oblige you with this fall's steers as well." Jake's mocking tone left no doubt as to his feelings toward the offer.

"I'll bet he would!" Kate seethed.

Matthew Johnson was one of the largest ranchers in the territory. He had helped Will improve the herd by introducing him to selective breeding practices, and Will had sold him one of the Angus bull calves born that first spring. Matt made no secret of his desire to buy their claim when she and Will were struggling through the early years, but Will was determined to make their dreams come true, and the Lord had provided for them during those hard times.

"Providence," Will always said. "The Lord will provide our needs. "

He truly did provide for their needs, and so much more. Through careful management, they were able to buy and acquire land, until the ranch was expanded from their initial homestead claim of a hundred and sixty acres to six hundred and forty. The cattle prospered, and they began to raise quality working horses as well. And so they began to call the place Providence. It was a secret name between Will and Kate, until one day she had the sign maker in Guthrie carve a beautiful wooden sign with the word *Providence* intertwined with vines, leaves and small clusters of grapes.

Tears flooded Will's deep blue eyes the evening she presented it to him. He tenderly caressed her cheek. Drawing her into his arms, he kissed her sweetly, professing his undying love for her. She surrendered her heart to him completely that night, finally shuffling off the last of her scars and pain, accepting his love as unconditional, at last she was truly home and safe. He hung the sign between two rough timbers, spanning the road leading into their ranch the very next morning, the morning of the accident. Providence.

The old man and the young women stood together quietly, each wondering what the future would hold. Kate swallowed hard again, "What about the colts I sent with you?"

Jake's face brightened considerably at that and a sly twinkle came into his eyes. "Well, now I couldn't very well give those fine beasts to such a man as Johnson, could I?"

"So?"

"Oh, he saw them all right, and said what fine animals they were. Asked did they come out of your black stud there. For all his faults, that man has a fine eye for the horseflesh, he does. 'Yes,' says I, 'and some of the finest mares in Oklahoma Territory, too. But Mrs. Shaughnessey has promised these three to Mr. Van Buren up yonder.'"

"I did no such thing!"

"Well, Mr. Johnson didn't know that now, did he?" Jake's eyes twinkled all the more.

"Jake…."

"He paid one hundred fifty for that bay colt, and fifty dollars apiece for the fillies," smiled Jake, holding out a second envelope. "I probably

could have got a bit more had they been broke to saddle." He said raising an eyebrow at her.

Kate took the envelope shaking her head helplessly as tears of mirth
and relief streamed down her cheeks. She had intended those colts to be
sold at the local blacksmith shop for twenty dollars each, the going rate
that most cattle punchers of the Territory would pay for unbroke stock

"It isn't all you had expected to get, but we come a might closer this
way." Jake laid a comforting hand on her arm and smiled. "We will make
it, Kate." She smiled up at him, and mutely nodded her agreement.

"Now, let me round up Jon, and we'll get these stores put up right."
Jake stepped off to call his grandson, but Kate reached out a hand to
stop him.

"Jake, I just want you to know how grateful I am for…"

"Hush now."

"Well, at least go in and see your wife. You and Jon get some decent
food in your stomachs. You know Nana Insley won't let you go to work
without it!" She waved him toward the porch, "Now go. "

✶✶✶✶✶✶✶✶✶✶✶✶✶✶✶✶✶✶✶✶✶✶✶✶✶✶✶✶✶✶✶✶✶

The oil lamp cast its golden glow across the open ledger on Kate's
desk. Shadows danced across the dark walls, as the fountain pen
scratched quietly over the paper. Distant thunder boomed occasionally.
The rest of the house was still and silent. The four hundred and ten dollars Jake had given her that morning was safely locked in her desk until
a trip to the bank in Fallis could be planned.

"April 2nd, 1897, born one black, polled bull calf. Received $160 as
balance of payment due on sale of steers. Received $150 in payment for
one bay stud colt, aged two years. Received $100 in payment for two
sorrel fillies, aged two years each." She dutifully recorded the sale of the
colts, the birth of the calf, and the income, limited though it was. Next
she enumerated the many purchases and their costs.

With a deep sigh she laid down the pen and ran a hand across her weary brow, flinching at the roughness of it. Looking at her work-hardened hands in the flickering light, tears spilled down her cheeks. The money was barely enough to keep the small family through the next few months, and if she wasn't able to find some hired help soon, she would have to seriously consider Matt Johnson's offer to buy the ranch.

Closing the worn green ledger she placed it in the bottom drawer of the old oak desk. Reaching beneath it, Kate pulled out a small leather bound volume and placed it before her. Opening the front cover, she read the words that were a constant source of comfort to her soul, especially in such troubled times.

"To our beautiful daughter, Kathleen Rose Dover,
from your loving parents, David and Amanda Dover,
on the day of your birth March 12th, 1870."

She ran a finger lightly over the words so beautifully inscribed in her mother's flowing script, as though in caressing the words, she could once again feel her mother's healing touch. Below, in the same loving hand, her mother had set out a biblical promise that had sustained Kate through the years....

But they that wait upon the Lord shall renew their strength; they shall mount up with wings as eagles; they shall run, and not be weary; and they shall walk, and not faint.

Isaiah 40:31

"Lord, I could sure use some of that renewing strength right now," she whispered into the still night. Reaching out a tired hand, she turned down the wick of the lamp until darkness enveloped her. Standing and stretching her weary body she walked to the window on the far wall. Lace curtains blew in the soft evening breeze drifting through the open pane. The air was laced with the faint scent of honeysuckle blossoms. Kate turned her face to a black velvet heaven in which a thousand points of light twinkled merrily. The distant rolling boom was growing fainter, there would be no life-giving rains here tonight. Perhaps tomorrow would bring the renewing strength they all longed for.

CHAPTER II

As the last of the cattle were sorted, counted and loaded into the holding pens of the Rock Island rail yard, the cowboys turned toward the small town of Addington. "I'm going to the post office, see if any letters came. Where will I meet you?" Joe asked.

"Try the hotel. You go get your letters; I'm going for a hot meal." Luke suppressed a grin, but the mirth in his eyes was evident.

"Aw, you educated city boys are all alike. Proper meals, heck, you'll probably be in a bath tub by the time I git there!" Joe taunted.

"Yeah, and you'll be all doe eyed over some love letter!" Luke retorted with a grin.

"You wait, Luke, someday you're gonna meet someone and be lookin' for those letters from home like a lovesick puppy dog, too!" Joe strode off whistling toward the gray frame building that housed the post office. Luke shook his head with an indulgent smile and turned to the new brick hotel that advertised hot meals for fifty cents.

A city boy he may be, but this life suited him far better than the schools and seminary that his father had selected for him. Less than a week after his mother died he had struck out for the Indian Territory and a new life away from the yoke of oppression he felt under his father's stern bearing. It had been four years now, four long years, and still he wasn't certain he had found what he was searching for.

The sun was already lowering in the western sky. They had been on the trail for the better part of the last month moving over four hundred head of fractious cows and steers to the new railhead here in Addington. It was a far cry from the herds that had moved across the Chisholm Trail less than a decade ago, but it still provided gainful employ for men that were game to try it. Luke Josey was one of those men.

The last month had proven a true test of the men on this drive. They were a small band to start with, only five punchers; the trail boss, Joe; and a cook. They faced a snowstorm less than two days out. One of the men had taken sick and they made him a bed in the back of the cook wagon. He died three days later, and was laid to rest beneath the broken sod of the prairie. How many men lay in unmarked graves, wondered Luke, without so much as a prayer nor even a memory? Is that my destiny?

The remaining men had been pressed into even greater service over the next few weeks. Freezing winds buffeted them from the north. Every hour in the saddle seemed an eternity. They hunkered down in their coats, wild rags drawn up over their faces and hats tilted low against the onslaught of the bitter wind. The cattle were nervous, milling and low-ing, trying to break at every opportunity. It was all they could do to keep them moving on. Then just as suddenly, the temperatures rose, the snows melted as fast as they had come, and the run off swelled the rivers to overflowing.

By the time they reached the ford on the Red River, it was a madly rush-ing torrent. They knew once the herd started across they had to keep mov-ing. This ford was notorious for the quicksand that lay all around. They made camp, and waited two days for the river to subside enough to make a relatively safe crossing. On the morning of the third day, the sun shone forth from the east in a blaze of red and gold, the river shining in the light. Joe decided that it was now or never. Luke rode ahead with the cook wagon to meet the first of the herd as they emerged.

The rest of the men gathered the cattle into a tight bunch and with loud shouts and cries from all around they ran them into the swiftly

flowing waters. At first, the herd stayed together, moving through the
water. The lead cow found her footing on the far side and mounted the
steep bank with little trouble. With more and more cattle dragging
themselves from the water and clambering up, it was soon a hopeless
mire of churned mud. A large brown and white cow started up but
slipped down, buried to the chest in the sticky black ooze. Others tried
to go over and around, cowboys shouted a warning as the cattle began
to split into two columns around the struggling cow. Others became
entrenched in hidden bogs. Luke, joined by Joe, circled the portion of
the herd that made it to the far side, trying to keep them calm and in
one place. The old lead cow, far enough from the commotion at the
ford, calmly dropped her head and started to graze on the new spring
grass. The others, though nervous, followed suit.

"Stay with the herd, Joe, I'm going back," Luke called out. Joe began
to protest, but realized that his first responsibility was the safety of the
herd, and most of them were now here. He reluctantly agreed and
watched as Luke rode off on his large gray gelding.

Arriving at the ford, Luke assessed the situation. Two of the men had
followed the cattle up the far bank and were each working the remnants
of the herd, gathering them slowly and methodically back toward the
main herd. Glancing at the river, he saw the cow still struggling feebly in
the mud.

"Phillip?" He called. There was no sign of the young, fresh-faced
cowboy that had started out with them that morning. "Where the devil
is that blasted boy?" He looked east down the river and saw a hat caught
among the branches in a small eddy under the bank where a grove of
trees overhung the muddy water. Fear gripping his heart, he turned his
gelding and galloped to the spot. Swinging down and dropping the
reins he scrambled down the bank into the swirling torrent. Reaching
down into the icy water, groping frantically, praying to a God he wasn't
sure existed, "Please, Lord, let me find him." He waded a bit further out,
one hand anchored firmly to a low hanging branch, the other still

searching blindly below the water. His fingers passed fruitlessly over rough boulders, while from all around he was struck by limbs and debris carried by in the wildly rushing deluge. His arm ached from trying to maintain a desperate grip on the anchoring branch. He knew that if he lost his grasp, they would both be done for. There! At last he felt what could only be Phillip's head. Grasping a handful of hair he pulled. Muscles straining, heart pounding, still praying, he pulled. At last Phillip's head rose above the level of the brown swirling waters. With a last mighty effort he heaved the unconscious boy to dry ground, following as quickly as he could. A fallen tree lay nearby. Draping the limp body face down over the trunk he pushed against his back over and over. "Come on, man, get it out, come on." Until the water came flowing from the boy's lungs in a muddy rush, he gasped, and sputtered, coughing, finally taking a ragged breath on his own. Luke fell back, drained, breathing heavily, as Phillip fought for breath and life.

✶✶✶✶✶✶✶✶✶✶✶✶✶✶✶✶✶✶✶✶✶✶✶✶✶✶✶✶✶✶✶✶

Coming out of his reverie, Luke found himself standing before the door of the Hotel. A sign in the window proclaimed,
"Hot bath and shave, twenty-five cents;
Good home cooking, fifty cents;
Rooms one dollar a night."
He opened the door and stepped into the dim lobby. His food on the trail had been free, but the smell of bubbling stew, hot bread, and fresh coffee made it seem almost worth the fifty cents. A tall gaunt man sat quietly behind the desk surveying the activity in the busy room. A pretty blonde girl, not more than sixteen scurried between tables with a blue ironware coffee pot held in one hand, a dingy white cloth protecting her fingers from the heat. A stack of dirty pewter bowls and spoons in her other hand tottered precariously, threatening to tumble to the floor at any moment. Just then a rough hand reached out from one of

the tables attempting to grab the girl by the waist. She deftly side stepped the unwanted attention, but the bowls lost their fight with balance and crashed to the floor in a jumbled mess, eliciting a coarse laugh from the offender.

"Sarah, what have you done now?" Called a terse voice from the open kitchen door.

"But, mother, I…" Sarah started, tears welling up in her bright blue eyes.

Luke strode quickly to the girl, scooped up the errant dishes from their resting place on the wooden floor. With a quick wink and a conspiratorial shake of his head at the frightened girl, he called out as he made his way toward the open door, "I'm sorry, ma'am, I must have knocked these from the table. I am such a clumsy oaf. I hope you can forgive me."

The rest of the conversation was lost as Luke disappeared into the kitchen. He emerged a short time later, somewhat cleaner, and very hungry. Sarah's mother had indeed forgiven him, and provided him a towel, soap and wash basin. Sarah stared openly at her erstwhile savior, then hurried to find him a seat and provide him with a well-deserved meal.

The steaming stew wafted a rich meaty aroma, the bread was soft and fresh, the butter creamy. Luke was certain that heaven couldn't be any sweeter than this. He ate heartily and well, being constantly attended by the grateful Sarah.

The hotel door opened. Luke looked up expectantly as Joseph entered the lobby. His warm smile of welcome faded to be replaced by a frown of concern as Joe made his way to the table.

"Joe, what is it?" Luke asked.

Joe laid a small stack of papers on the table before his friend. One was the pay envelope containing their wages for the past month, nothing unusual there. Another was a letter from Zora, Joe's wife back in Rush Springs, it was dated March 1, 1897, and hadn't yet been opened. The last letter was opened, and crumpled. Luke picked it up and began reading.

"March 28th, 1897. It is with great despair that I must write to inform you that your wife Zora and your young son, Samuel, were both taken from this world on the 25th of March. They suffered only briefly with the cholera that has become epidemic in this region. Burial will be made without delay. Please come as soon as you can. Your loving sister, Annie."

Luke felt as though a hot knife had been thrust into the depths of his heart. Zora was a vibrant, black-haired beauty, so full of life. She and Joe truly loved one another with the carefree spirit that youthful love engenders. And Sam, that bright star their love had created. A charming boy with his father's open, adventurous spirit, but his mother's dark good looks. How was it possible that they were gone?

He put the paper down and smoothed the wrinkles mechanically with his fingers. "Joe, I don't…." He swallowed hard, the words sticking painfully in his throat.

"I'll be leaving at first light. I'd be grateful if you'd see to it the men are paid." Joe stated woodenly.

"I'm going with you."

"No, I couldn't ask you to do that."

"No one's asking, I'm going." Luke stated firmly. He gathered the papers, placed a dollar on the table, walked over to the man at the desk and paid for a room in advance. Striding across the lobby, he called, "Sarah."

"Yes, sir?" She appeared promptly at the kitchen door.

"See that my friend there gets a good meal, then take him up to our room." He handed her a key and two dollars.

"That I will, but this is too much…" she began. He held up his hand. The look in his eyes told her that he would accept no protest, and that this was a most serious task he had set her to do. "Yes, sir."

✶✶✶✶✶✶✶✶✶✶✶✶✶✶✶✶✶✶✶✶✶✶✶✶✶✶✶✶✶✶✶

Assured that Joe would be in good hands until his return, he left the hotel quickly and headed toward the livery where he knew he'd find the rest of the boys. The sun was sinking rapidly in the west painting the heavens with vibrant shades of pink, purple and red, the azure sky darkening towards the deep violet of night. A few bright stars already shone like diamonds against the varicolored background. An early group of revelers sang drunkenly on the wooden plank sidewalk in front of the largest saloon. Shopkeepers were busily closing up for the night in anticipation of returning home to hearth and family. The everyday sights and sounds struck a note of discord in Luke.

Entering the livery through a small side door, he was struck immediately by the earthy aroma that was so familiar and comforting. The pungent odor of manure overlaid by sweet smelling hay mixed with the rich scents of oiled leather and horse sweat was almost like a balm applied to his soul. He stood for a moment breathing it in, and listening to the myriad sounds, horses contentedly munching hay, the buzzing of a few early flies, a snort, a soft answering nicker from a distant stall.

All too soon, the drone of conversation caught his attention. He made his way through the dim barn to a small room at the back. Here he found the other three men he had shared the trail with this last month. Entering quietly, he was met with hearty greetings from the gathered men. They had formed a close bond over the last few weeks, and all regarded Luke as one of their own, while respecting his quiet authority, and answering to him as readily as they had their trail boss, Joe.

The small lantern in the middle of the room cast a golden glow across the assembled men. Luke hesitated, hating the task at hand, then slowly began, "I've brought your pay. You're free to go as you please, though I'm sure the ranch would welcome any of you back. Me and Joe, well, we'll be leaving in the morning."

"Where ya headed?" Asked Phillip, eager to continue on wherever they might lead.

Luke paused for a long moment, looking hard at Phillip, then at each of the men in turn. Silence fell heavily upon the small group as they waited intently for Luke to continue. "Zora and their boy, Sam, they…they died last month." Shocked disbelief filled the room. "I'll be ridin' home with Joe."

A palpable silence filled the room; the sounds of the livery and the gathering night beyond filled the void. Finally Phillip spoke, "I 'spect, I'll head back to the ranch," he said softly. The others nodded agreement. "You'll be comin' along, after, won't ya, Luke?" He asked earnestly.

"I don't know." Luke replied with a sigh.

✼ ✼

There was a chill in the early morning air as the two men started out for Rush Springs, the bedrolls and saddle bags tied tightly behind their saddles contained all they would need for the short trip, indeed all they really had. The forty miles to their destination could be done in a couple day's hard riding, but the horses walked slowly over the well worn trail, and neither man chose to push them any faster.

The miles rolled by uneventfully. The red Oklahoma earth was dotted sparsely with trees in this region, and the new spring grass just beginning to emerge, painted the plains with the lush green life that would sustain the cattle herds. A gulf of silence lay between the two men. Joe could find no words to voice his grief, and words of comfort were foreign to Luke.

Joe muttered irritably under his breath as his bay mare stumbled and nearly fell. They came to a stop and Joe dismounted. Picking up her left front hoof the reason for the misstep was obvious. The iron shoe that covered and supported her hoof was loose and a large chunk of hoof wall was torn from the quarter. Without stopping to reset the shoe, the little mare would end up lame.

"Why don't you let me take care of that?" Luke always kept a set of tools in his saddle bags, a hammer, clinches, sole knife, nippers and a rasp, a few spare nails and one or two shoes. A good horse was more than just a means of transportation, and keeping one sound was an ongoing concern to any cowboy. He laid out the tools and set to work.

Joe held the mare's reins while Luke placed her hoof between his knees. He removed the old shoe and tossed it to the side. Evaluating the injury with an experienced eye, he determined that the hoof was not too badly damaged and set about trimming the wall. Rasping it smooth, he nailed a new shoe in place. He set her foot down gently and walked over to the discarded shoe, picking it up, he placed it absently in the pocket of his jacket.

"Hungry?" Asked Joe, holding out a thick slice of bread and some seasoned jerky.

"Yeah, as a matter of fact, I am." Luke replied taking the proffered meal. They sat down with their backs to a large outcrop of rocks and ate their sparse meal in silence. The horses grazed contentedly a short distance away.

"Hey, Rio, get back on over here." Luke called as he noticed his big gray gelding drifting further away. Rio's head popped up and he obediently trotted over to his master, nosing Luke's arm and waiting patiently for his share of the bread. "You old rascal. Here. Are you satisfied now?" Rio took the chunk of bread that Luke held up, devouring it in a single bite, shook his head and walked a few steps away to graze again.

The horse had been sort of a gift from his father many years ago. Luke remembered the night his dad had hauled him out of a warm bed into the chill night air to witness the birth of this foal. The mare had been down, laboring hard for too long. One small hoof and a small black nose were all that could be seen of the foal. There should have been two hooves, one a few inches in front of the other with that little nose on top of them. Something was dreadfully wrong. The mare pushed and strained, but made no progress.

"You sit at her head, Luke, and talk to her. I need you to keep her just as calm as you can." His father was rolling up his long white sleeves as he gave the instructions to Luke.

"Pa, what are you going to do? I don't want her to die, pa, please!" The boy pleaded. The small oil lamp cast a feeble glow against the dark. He could barely see his father's expression, but he knew in that moment there was little hope. Luke's heart sank, even as he watched his father reach inside the tired mare.

"The foal's other leg is back. I don't know if I can pull it forward or not. If I can't, we'll lose them both for certain. If I can, there's a chance the babe can make it. Luke, I don't know if we can save the mare or not." His father was always forthright and plain spoken; that was always the image Luke had of him. He could not remember a single time his father had shown any real emotion, except at his mother's funeral. The image of that large stoic man standing at the open grave with tears streaming down his otherwise stony face was seared forever in Luke's memory.

"I can feel it. It's coming, I think…there. Now, Maggie, push girl." As if on cue the mare gave a last valiant effort and the small foal made his entrance into the cold night. Unfortunately the effort had proved too much for the old mare. The mal placed hoof had torn her uterus, and she died the next day from blood loss.

His father had wanted to put the colt down as well, saying it would be too hard to raise an orphan foal, but Luke had pleaded with him, and the old man relented, placing the raising of the foal squarely on the shoulders of the boy. If they survived the ordeal, the colt was his to keep. They had been inseparable from that day forward.

✶✶✶✶✶✶✶✶✶✶✶✶✶✶✶✶✶✶✶✶✶✶✶✶✶✶✶✶✶✶

The sun was high, warming the air around them. Joe sat hunched over lost in his own thoughts. Luke reached into his pocket absently fiddling with the lost shoe. Pulling it out, he contemplated the u-shaped slab of iron. Funny how forging such metal could make it stronger and more malleable, yet if you heated it further, to a molten state, then let it cool and harden again, it became brittle, prone to shatter rather than bend. Struck by a sudden insight, Luke spoke, "Joe, have you ever watched a blacksmith make one of these things?"

"Well, yeah, I s'pose I have." Joe replied a little taken aback.

"He takes a shapeless bar of metal, heats it red hot, then beats it, and shapes it, over and over until its just so. When he's done its no longer a useless piece of iron, but an incredible tool that helps to keep that beast over there sound." Luke said tossing the shoe to his friend.

"Yeah." said Joe eyeing the thing suspiciously.

"You'd think the fire and the pounding would weaken the piece, but it strengthens it, makes it ready for service." He paused for a moment as though considering, hesitant to continue. At last he took a deep breath and said, "Those whom God would use, He also strengthens."

Joe's eyes narrowed as he stared at the distant horizon, silent. After a long pause he shifted his gaze back to the man beside him. "Why Zora, why Sam? If this suffering is supposed to make *me* stronger, then why did *they* pay the price?" He asked bitterly.

"Well, Joe, from everything my pa tried to get through my thick skull, I'd have to say, they're in a better place right now than you or I could even dream about. It's not them that are suffering, Joe, it's those of us left behind."

"Yeah? I thought you didn't believe in God."

Luke sighed, looking at the ground, studying every detail of the blades of grass at his feet. "I never said I didn't believe, I'm just not sure what He has to do with me."

CHAPTER III

Kate's eyes flew open. It was dark, the faint glow of approaching dawn just visible beyond her window. She lay motionless in the chill morning air listening intently for the sound that had awakened her. There it was again, a faint calling of night birds. Why did this bother her? Something about it seemed wrong, out of place.

Stealing from her warm bed, she grabbed the clothes that lay in a heap on the floor. Dressing as she walked to the table, she fumbled for the oil lamp and the matches in the drawer. Striking the match against the rough wood, Kate lit the lamp and turned the wick to adjust the glow of the light. With the lamp before her, she made her way to the kitchen. The big wood-burning stove glowed warmly from the banked fire. Opening the iron door, she stirred the coals with a long black poker. She placed a few of the larger pieces of kindling into the fire box, and held her hands out to the warmth as the small flames leapt into life.

Kate opened the larder at the far end of the kitchen and found some cornbread from last night's supper and a chunk of ham. Placing these into a small cloth, she tied the corners together to form a bundle. Amidst the preparations for her early morning ride to check the fence lines for needed repairs, she could not shake the vague uneasiness that had awakened her. Frowning, she peered out the window into the darkness that surrounded the house.

Sighing, she was about to turn back to the kitchen when a movement near the garden fence caught her eye. Fear gripped her stomach as she stared out the window in a vain attempt to make out what it was that moved so stealthily. Trying hard to convince herself that it was only a deer walking down the fence looking for tender new shoots, Kate turned back to her task. She froze instantly at the soft knocking on the kitchen door.

Kate's eyes darted about looking for a weapon, anything to protect herself and her family from the unknown visitor at their door. Her eyes lit upon Jake's old shotgun. Mrs. Insley always left it in the back corner behind the pantry. Kate had no idea whether it was loaded or what it might be loaded with, but it was the only thing to be had. Reaching for the gun, her eyes never left the door. With the weapon safely in hand, she cautiously approached the door, still hoping against hope that it was no more than the wind blowing an errant shutter against the house, but knowing in her heart it wasn't.

Praying that Jolene would stay fast asleep in her bed, she reached toward the latch. Steeling herself and steadying the gun over one arm, she cautiously opened the door. The apparition that met her eyes took her breath away. Two young men with long dark hair, clad in tall leather boots, leggings and woolen trade coats held another man limply between them. One of the men had a gun, but it was slung back over his shoulder. They appeared tired, their eyes held a haunted look, and one of them was obviously badly injured. Kate's heart raced. She had seen Indians at the fort and in Fallis, but never had one appeared at her door.

"Please, you will help?"

Without stopping to think, Kate opened the door wide and beckoned them into the warm kitchen. "Put him on the bench there." She commanded, though quaking inside. "What happened?"

The men laid their companion on the bench she indicated, looking at one another warily. They glanced around as though searching for something. Finally, the older one spoke, "We are hunting. Our ponies were stolen or run off. You have seen them?"

"No, I haven't seen any stray horses near here," replied Kate. "Your friend, he needs help." Though she was fearful, something told her that these men meant no harm, her tension eased slightly as she spoke.

"Yes. Gunshot. You can help?"

"I don't know. I can try." She knelt beside the bench and for the first time realized that this was a mere boy, perhaps ten or twelve at the most. Her heart went out to the injured child. Dried blood stained the coat a deep crimson and brown. "I'll need help getting his jacket off and the wound cleaned." She glanced around making a mental inventory of what she would need, thanking God that her mother had taught her basic medical skills. Though she had never treated a gunshot, surely she could cleanse the wound to help stop any infection. "Can one of you build a fire in the fireplace? He'll need to be kept warm. I want to make a pallet for him on the floor, he'll be more comfortable there. There are blankets in the trunk by the wall, and I'll need some towels from the cupboard next to it."

Neither of them moved, as they regarded her silently.

"Well, what are you waiting for?" She demanded. "Do you want me to help him or not? I can't do it all by myself!"

Still they hesitated. After a moment, the one who had acted as spokesman thus far said something in a guttural language to his companion, and they each set about the tasks she had outlined. Sighing with relief, Kate started a pot of water heating on the stove, and found the leather bag that contained her meager store of healing herbs and medical supplies.

The boy was laid on a pallet of blankets before a crackling fire that glowed warmly in the hearth. His jacket was removed and placed on the back porch to be cleaned later. Kate rolled up her sleeves and heard a muffled gasp from behind her. Feeling the heat suffuse her face, she glanced briefly at the livid scars trailing up her bare arms. Shaking her

head to clear her thoughts, she dipped a towel in the warmed water and
began to clean the area around the gaping hole in his arm. The wound
was not fresh, perhaps a day or more old, but the bullet had thankfully
gone clean through. As best she could tell, no bones had been broken,
and for that she said another small prayer of thanks. He had lost far too
much blood, that was obvious, but the flow had diminished to a small
trickle, and was now easy to staunch. She dressed the cleansed wound
with an herbal poultice of goldenseal and echinacea, bandaging it with
strips of clean cotton rags.

✳✳✳✳✳✳✳✳✳✳✳✳✳✳✳✳✳✳✳✳✳✳✳✳✳✳✳✳✳✳✳

Tochoway watched as the woman worked on Nocona. Could this small
white woman heal Nocona? A white man had fired the gun, perhaps the
Great Father wanted a white healer to mend him. When the woman had
begun to give orders, the men were confused. Women were meant to serve,
not command. The firelight flickered across the pallid face of the young
boy, danced over the rich brown hair of the woman as she knelt before
him. Why did she pause? Was she praying to God for guidance?

Mahseet sucked in his breath as the woman rolled up her sleeves.
"Puha." He whispered under his breath.

Tochoway followed Mahseet's gaze and nodded his agreement. This
woman was marked with a sign of puha, great power, enabling her to
perform supernatural healing. So the Father *had* led them here. Nocona
would surely recover.

✳✳✳✳✳✳✳✳✳✳✳✳✳✳✳✳✳✳✳✳✳✳✳✳✳✳✳✳✳✳✳

If she could get some nourishment into him, let his young body
begin the healing process, he might recover in time. So many things
could go wrong, though. If he had lost too much blood, if infection set
in despite her best efforts, if the bone had been chipped, he might lose
the use of that arm, so many possibilities. What would the other men

think, what would they do if he didn't recover? The thought made Kate weak and sent chills up her spine. Still kneeling before the injured boy, she bent her head in earnest prayer for his life to be spared and his body to be made whole. Taking her strength from faith, she rose to face the waiting men.

✶✶✶✶✶✶✶✶✶✶✶✶✶✶✶✶✶✶✶✶✶✶✶✶✶✶✶✶✶✶✶✶✶

Jake Insley woke with the dawn as he did every morning. Nana was already awake, busy putting coffee and bread, butter and jam on the small table in the corner. Jon was still asleep, Smokey curled up at his feet.

"Still don't cotton to dogs in the house." Nana Insley said firmly.

"Nana, we've had the same conversation 'most ever' day for the last two years." Jake replied grinning, his eyes twinkling at his stern wife. In the thirty years they had been married, he had grown to love the gruff nature that covered her large and loving heart. "You know how he feels 'bout that pup. 'Sides, I seen you sneak ole Smoke a treat now and again, haven't I?"

"Humph!" Nana turned back to her tasks, smiling to herself.

The small soddy that the Insleys occupied was set back against the side of the knoll west of the Shaughnessey home, close but not visible to the main ranch. When the Shaughnesseys and the Insleys had left Missouri for good and made the land run back in '89, they had agreed to find two quarter sections right together, and combine their efforts to really make a go of it in their new home.

Jake Insley had been a freighter, carting goods between the forts and the stage stations in the Indian Territory. He knew the land well, had seen the rich fertile ground and knew that this was truly a land of opportunity. As Jake brought these stories home, his friend, Will Shaughnessey and his pretty new wife, Kate were excited about the prospect of a new life. Convincing Nana of that had proved to be the challenge. She was set on staying put in Missouri til the end of her days.

"I'll not be moved to a land of savages, Jake Insley. My girl is buried here, and this is where I'll be buried as well," had been her final word on the subject.

Their only daughter Hannah, had died giving birth to Jonathan. Her husband had disappeared the next day, filled with grief and unable to care for a small son. Jake and Nana grieved the passing of their daughter, but her place in Nana's heart had been stolen by the helpless creature that lay in the old wooden cradle that had once held Hannah herself. In the sixteen years that ensued, Jon became their son and their joy.

"Wake up you sleepy head!" Roared Jake good naturedly.

Jonathan rolled over sleepily, then stretching, rose from his warm nest of covers. "What's to eat, Nana?"

"All you ever think about these days is that stomach of your'n! Here." Said Nana thrusting a bundle into his hands. "Bread, ham and the last of the dried apples. You be sure to get yourself down to the big house for breakfast proper after you milk them cows!"

"Yes'm."

"We'll be plowing the wheat field today. I'm headed to the barn now to hitch up the girls and make sure the plow's ready," added Jake.

"Aw, papa, Miz Kate said she was goin' to ride the fence lines this mornin', don't you think she'll be needin' my help?" Jon implored.

Jake looked at the boy's earnest face. "We'll ask Kate does she think she'll need you. But I'll be depending on you for plantin' tomorrow."

"Yes, sir, papa." Jon's face beamed at the prospect of mending fences and tending the herd. Jake watched him leave, Smokey bounding after. He shook his head, knowing that the boy's heart lay with ranching, not farming. Sighing, he took his own snack from Nana, kissed the top of her head, and left to make his way to the barn.

✶ ✶ ✶ ✶ ✶ ✶ ✶ ✶ ✶ ✶ ✶ ✶ ✶ ✶ ✶ ✶ ✶ ✶ ✶

The sun was just rising above the hills in the east, bathing the land in reds and pinks, lighting the few wispy clouds with a golden glow as Nana approached the kitchen porch. Something caught her eye. A jacket, not one she recognized, lay draped over the outer rail. On closer inspection, she could clearly make out blood stains. Clutching her heart, she froze. Fearing to go any further, she stared intently at the windows, as though willing them to give up the secrets hidden within the house, but they remained mute, giving no testimony to what might lie within.

After what seemed an eternity, she found the strength to move. Turning she ran to the barn where Jake was busy with the horses. Gasping and nearly fainting from fear and exertion, she collapsed inside the large front door.

"What in God's name...."

"Kate—the house—a jacket...."

Not able to make any sense of her tangled words, fearing for her health, Jake knelt down trying to comfort the old woman he loved so deeply. "Nana, please, stop, take a deep breath."

"No! Go—Kate—in trouble." gasped the frightened woman.

✦✦✦✦✦✦✦✦✦✦✦✦✦✦✦✦✦✦✦✦✦✦✦✦✦✦✦✦✦✦✦✦

"Oh, dear Lord." Jake ran from the barn. As he approached the house, caution over took him. He stopped, trying desperately to assess the situation. The kitchen door opened and Kate appeared, safe. Her face ashen, she motioned him to be silent, then beckoned to him. He approached slowly, questioning her with his eyes.

Looking back over her shoulder, she spoke quietly. "There are three Comanche in the kitchen."

"But they're supposed to be down to Fort Sill. How..."

"I don't know. They said they lost some ponies, they're tracking them. One is hurt, shot in the arm. He's just a boy. I've fixed him up as best I know how, fed the others, and now we wait." Her eyes were weary,

frightened. "I've told them you'd be coming. I think it's best if we go on
with our normal routine, don't let them think we're scared; though God
knows I am."
Jake nodded.
"Perhaps you best send Mrs. Insley home?" Kate suggested.
"I believe that might be best."

✶ ✶

As Kate watched Jake head to the barn to care for Nana, a choked
scream and a series of semi-ferocious puppy growls and yips erupted
from the house behind her. *Jo! Oh, Lord, protect her,* she prayed, turning
and running to the kitchen. The scene that met her eyes gave her pause.
Jo was standing in the doorway, wide eyed, mouth gaping. The pup was
before her barking and growling in her best imitation of a watch dog.
The two men still sat at the breakfast table, now just as wide-eyed and
startled as Jo. Kate calmly strode across the room, heart still pounding,
scooped up the pup in one arm and Jo in the other.

"Jo, we have guests this morning. I'd like you to meet Tochoway and
Mahseet. Their friend, Nocona was hurt, and needed our help." Turning
to the men at the table, Kate continued, "This is my daughter, Jolene."
She said, setting Jo down. "And this is Candy," indicating the small
brown bundle that she placed outside.

Jo looked at her mother, then back to the table, and finally to the
young boy on the pallet. "But, mama, they're...."

"How about some breakfast, Jo? The men will be in from morning
chores soon, and there's a lot to do today." Kate said brightly, as though
nothing out of the ordinary was taking place.

"Yes, ma'am," the girl replied, taking her place on the far side of the
table.

Tochoway, the natural leader of the group, eyed the little girl with
mirth. "Pretty girl. You do not know any Comanche?"

Jo shook her head slowly, staring at the large man.

"Well, Jo, I believe this is the first time I have ever seen you at a loss for words," Kate smiled as she placed a bowl of steaming oatmeal and a pitcher of milk on the table for her daughter.

The men had eaten, and Kate had gotten to know a little about them during their breakfast. She learned that they were away from the reservation without permission. They were indeed trying to find three lost ponies belonging to the boy, Nocona. Tochoway had given her accurate descriptions of the missing beasts, and she knew of the Comanche reputation with horses. They were highly skilled horsemen; their horses were far more than mere possessions to them. The loss of these ponies was enough to cause these men to risk severe punishment in the quest for their return.

Pouring milk over her cereal, Jo began, "What happened to No.. Noc…"

"Nocona," her mother supplied.

"Nocona. What happened to him? Was he shot? Did a panther get him? How long have you been traveling? Where are you going? Do you live in a tipi?"

"Jo!"

Tochoway laughed, and Mahseet looked perplexed at the small girl, so full of questions. "We are searching for ponies, which were taken away. Nocona got shot, the man who shot him, too far to see." Tochoway replied. "I lived in tipi once as a boy, but I have a cabin now, like yours some."

"Really?" Jo's eyes were large and shining.

Rising, Mahseet went to sit beside the still boy. He placed a hand on the bandaged arm, and murmured quietly in the language of his people. Kate was touched by the tender concern of the man. She prayed again for God's healing upon Nocona's life.

The door opened admitting shafts of golden sunlight along with the men and both dogs. Jon seemed concerned at the presence of the

Indians, but Jake was accustomed to them, having been a freighter in the Indian Territory for so long.

"Maruawe," greeted Jake. Two dark heads turned in surprise, to hear a greeting in their native tongue.

"Maruawe," answered Tochoway, "you speak Nuumu?"

"Naw, not really, just a word here and there. How's the boy?" Jake asked, indicating the pallet near the fireplace.

Tochoway looked at Kate. Her sad eyes and pale complexion spoke volumes. "He's in God's hands now," was all she could say.

The Insley men ate a hearty meal, while Jake kept up a lively conversation with Tochoway. Jo and Jon listened with delight, Jo chattering and asking questions whenever she could. It was decided that Jon would ride the fence line, mending breaks where he was able, and determining what supplies would be necessary for the rest of the repairs, while Jake would see to the plowing. Jon's face shone at the responsibility he had been given, and Jo was filled with pride for her friend as she watched the men leave for the day's work.

Kate and Jo set about clearing the table and washing the dishes while the Indians kept watch over the boy. A slight moan caught Kate's attention and she hurried to the patient. Mahseet stroked the boys feverish head, while Kate felt for a pulse. Nocona's eyes fluttered, finally opening. They were clouded and unfocused at first, but it was a good sign. He seemed to be gaining strength. Kate stepped aside, not wanting his first sight to be a strange white woman. Mahseet spoke quietly, still stroking Nocona's head. The boy turned trying to focus on his surroundings. Mahseet soothed him, and Nocona closed his eyes again, sinking back into the warm blankets.

Kate approached again, his pulse was stronger, no longer weak and rapid. He was sleeping now, a deep and restful slumber. She smiled, saying a prayer of thanksgiving in her heart. As she turned to the waiting men, the radiant glow that suffused her tired features told them that all would be well.

✶ ✶

The rest of the morning passed quickly, Nocona continued to gain strength. Kate fed him a rich meaty broth, which he sipped readily from a spoon, though still wary of the strange woman. Jo promptly appointed herself nursemaid and companion to the young man, chattering at him and sharing with him her few valued possessions and toys. Nocona seemed to take an interest in the small red-haired vision, reaching out occasionally to touch her soft hair or take a proffered toy.

Tochoway watched the pair for a while then turned to Kate, "Your girl has a healing spirit, like her mother."

"Thank you," she said simply, also enjoying the sight of the children.

"Hallo in there! Kate?" Came a deep masculine voice. Starting, Kate stared at Tochoway, afraid for him and the others. Tochoway, motioned to Mahseet and Nocona, the three retreating to the furthest corner of the kitchen. He nodded silently to her.

She took a deep breath and opened the door. Stepping into the bright afternoon sun, she closed the door and strode to the edge of the porch. There before her, sitting on a large bay colt, was Matt Johnson. "Matt! What are you doing around these parts?" She asked in disbelief, trying to mask the fear in her voice.

"On my way to Fallis for a spell. I can see why you're reluctant to part with this place, Kate. You've a fine ranch here."

"Yes." She said tersely, seeing the avaricious glint in his hazel eyes.

"Kate, I know how hard the last few months have been for you, and I realized just the other night that I'd made a mistake in the money I gave your man last week."

"His name is Jake. You know he's not my hired man!" She bristled at the inference in Matt's voice. Just then she noticed two other men, and a string of horses in the distance.

"My men," Matt said following her gaze. "I really only wanted to stop by and give you the money you're due," he continued.

Matt's words brought Kate back to him abruptly. "What?" She asked, wondering.

"Here."

She stepped down from the porch and approached the man on horseback. Only then did she recognize the bay colt that she had sent with Jake just last week. The horse seemed spiritless, almost dull. She wondered what had happened to the fire and vigor she remembered. Taking the envelope he held out, she opened it, finding two hundred dollars within.

"Matt, I….."

"I know;" he said, holding up a hand to stop her protest. "I can't imagine how you must have felt, thinking I'd cheated you on those steers I took to market for you. I do hope this sets things to rights between us?" His hard eyes belied the words of atonement as he gazed down upon her.

She smiled uneasily, tucking the envelope safely into a pocket. "Well, thank you," she said hoping he would leave.

Matt sat watching her, his scrutiny raising new fears within her.

"I'd ask you in to coffee, but—uh—well, Jo isn't feeling well, and…" she hesitated searching for something to say. Her eyes strayed again to the waiting cowboys near the barn, widening in surprise as she recognized the ponies matching Tochoway's description.

"Those are some nice looking horses, there. Where're they from?" She asked.

Surprised, Matt looked over his shoulder at his men. "Oh, here and there. Taking them to Fallis, thought I'd sell them there."

"You know I'm always looking for good stock. Mind if I have a look?" She didn't wait for an answer but started towards the barn. Matt, turning the colt, followed her.

There were six horses tied loosely together. The three belonging to the Comanche, by far the best of the lot. Kate looked at each horse with a practiced eye, as though evaluating each individual. Finally she turned to face Matt who had dismounted and stood watching her with the same calculating appraisal she had used on the ponies. "I'd give you sixty dollars for those three," she said indicating the three Comanche ponies.

He frowned, "I couldn't take less than a hundred."

"Matt, you and I both know you wouldn't get more than twenty apiece for them in Fallis. Look how skinny they are, and that one there has an abscess in her left rear, if I'm not mistaken. I'll give you seventy-five, and save you the trouble of hauling them all that way."

"You sure you can afford to part with that kind of money?"

She knew she couldn't, but given the circumstances, she knew she had to. "You let me worry about what I can afford, and what I can't," she stated. "Is it a deal?"

"All right," he decided, motioning for one of his men to loose the ponies. She reached into her pocket, pulling out the money she hadn't known would be hers, thinking once again how providentially God always supplied her every need. She counted out the bills and handed them to Matt, flinching as his hand brushed hers.

She took the leads the man handed her, and watched as the men mounted their horses, wanting them gone. The cowboys struck off with the remaining horses in tow.

Matt waited until they had moved off a ways, before turning back to her, "Kate, there's going to be a circuit riding preacher in Fallis this Sunday. I'd be delighted if you and Jo would join me at the meeting and the picnic after."

Taken aback by his invitation, Kate flushed. "If there's to be a preacher, then you can be sure that we'll be in attendance. It will be nice to see you there as well."

It wasn't an actual acceptance, but Matt nodded, tipped his hat, and rode off at a trot to join his men.

Kate stood rooted to the ground staring after the men disappearing beyond the distant horizon. Only when she was certain they were gone, did she turn and start back to the house. As she approached, leading the three horses, the door opened and Jo dashed out, "Oh, momma, wherever did you get those pretty ponies? Can I ride one, please? Are we going to keep them?"

Tochoway and Mahseet appeared on the porch, amazement written plainly across their faces. "You truly have great puha."

"Puha?" Kate echoed.

Tochoway shook his head, clearly trying to find the English to express his thoughts. "Medicine—power—spirit—great in here," he said placing his hand gently upon her chest, just over her heart.

"I do have a wonderful spirit in there," she replied, "but that Spirit is not my own."

He nodded stepping away from her. "We'll leave now."

"Oh, but Nocona, he's too weak…"

"We must go." Taking the single feather that adorned his braid, he tucked it behind her ear. "The hawk soars above the earth and sees all, so my spirit will watch over you." He brushed her cheek lightly with the back of his hand before taking the lead ropes from her.

Mahseet was already carrying Nocona to one of the horses. He placed the boy on the pony, then deftly mounted behind him. Tochoway took the other two ponies. Mounting one, he held the other's lead. She knew he was right. It was dangerous for them to stay any longer. Her heart ached for the boy, praying for his safety, and that of the others as well, the tears slipped unbidden down her cheeks.

A quiet chanting filled the still air:

"Taa Ahpu tomoba?atu, nansuwukaitu u nahnia.
U tekwapuha pitaruibe siku sokoba?a tomoba?atu nakwu waitusu.
Numi maaka ukiitsi tabeni numu tuhkarui.
Nu tusuuna aiku numu hanipukatu. Numi tusuuna.
Keta aituku numi muhneetu. Aitukutu numi
taakonin/tsaakuan.
Taa Ahpu nansuwukai suana.
Suni yutui o."

Though the Nuumu words held no meaning for Kate, she felt a stirring in her soul, as the significance of the prayer reached deeper than mere words, "Our Father, which art in Heaven, hallowed be they name. Thy kingdom come, Thy will be done on Earth as it is in Heaven…." she began.

Tochoway's dark eyes held hers, he nodded slowly. Raising a hand in farewell, they turned their ponies to the south.

Chapter IV

The small town of Rush Springs sprawled before them just visible through an early morning fog blanketing the prairie. Wet droplets clung to the horses' manes and dripped from the saddles. The dank air muffled the sounds of creaking leather and the rhythmic beat of the horses' hooves. Many of the town's buildings were obscured by the thick grey mist, but a stark white church and the lonely graveyard beside it standing on a rise above the town were painfully visible to the two silent men.

Luke stole a glance in Joe's direction. The utter despair and grief written upon the face of his companion were almost more than Luke could bear. He remembered his own stabbing pain at his mother's death, the silence that had fallen over his father, and the rift that had separated father from son.

Lord, protect this man, let him see Your mercy and Your grace in this trying time. Let him not be torn from his family—show him the healing that you have denied me. Luke prayed fervently, bitter gall rising in him at the hatred he still felt after all these years.

Shaking his head as though he could cast away these feelings, he kicked his gray gelding into a trot. Joe's bay followed, and they soon approached the outskirts of Rush Springs.

* *

A tall auburn haired woman emerged from the small frame house. She wore a simple gray mourning dress which only accentuated her handsome looks. As the morning mist swirled around her, she took on an ethereal appearance.

"Joe!" Annie cried in her husky voice. A mixture of emotions played across her delicate features, joy at seeing her brother mingled with grief.

Joe dismounted and ran into the open arms of his sister's embrace. At last the emotions he had hidden within the depths of his soul burst forth, and he wept openly against her shoulder. Annie held her brother, stroking his hair, rocking him gently, while gazing beyond him into the face of Luke Josey. Luke reached down and picked up the reins of Joe's mare, acutely aware of the woman standing before him. Giving Annie a brief nod, he turned to find the livery.

✶✶✶✶✶✶✶✶✶✶✶✶✶✶✶✶✶✶✶✶✶✶✶✶✶✶✶✶✶✶✶

The pervasive morning fog was melting under the warm golden rays now shining through from the eastern sky. The horses were snug in their stalls eating a well deserved ration of oats and hay. With a final glance at the animals, Luke paid the smith for a week's board, and headed back to Annie's house.

Standing before the neat frame home, he noticed the quiet elegance of wild roses beginning to bud along the trellis, two wooden chairs set neatly on the porch with a small table between. These details of simple domesticity were so evocative of his own family home in Kansas, that he felt a stirring in his heart at the memory. As if to complete the compelling vision, Annie appeared in the doorway framed by a glowing light from the fire within.

"It's good to see you again, Luke."

"How's Joe doing?"

"All right. He's resting some. I've breakfast and coffee ready, if you'd like."

Luke wondered for a moment if he should accept the offer. He searched her eyes, but could find no hint of emotion beyond simple hospitality. Had their last meeting been a dream? The reality of it was still so raw in his own heart, had she simply dismissed it as being of no consequence?

"Sure, sounds good." He said at last. As Luke stepped forward to enter the small house, Annie remained squarely in the doorway for a tense moment before moving to one side allowing him to pass. He could feel her nearness, smell the spicy aroma of her. His pulse quickened as he hurried to the table.

As they ate, Joe and Annie spoke quietly together of Zora, and reveled in sweet memories of Sam. The tears were mixed occasionally with laughter, for which Luke was thankful. The first step towards healing was the ability to remember the past, and not fear it. Their conversation was interrupted by a knock.

Annie smiled at her brother, "That must be Luther."

Joe leapt to his feet. Crossing the floor in two great strides, he flung open the door and was immediately swept into a huge embrace by a large man. "Luther, what are you doing here?" Joe cried.

"Just passin' through. Annie wrote me about Zora."

"I'm going to miss them, Luther."

The two men, as different as night and day, yet somehow cut from the same cloth, entered the room. "Luke, I'd like you to meet my brother, the Marshal!" Joe said proudly.

"I've certainly heard a lot about you," Luke said extending his hand.

"Any friend of Joe's....." Luther replied, grasping Luke's hand. "Well, almost any friend," he amended looking pointedly at his smaller brother. Joe gave an almost imperceptible shake of his head, and Luther's grasp tightened. "Very glad to meet you!" he finished.

A plate was heaped with food for Luther, and the family fell to talking, almost forgetting about Luke. Staring out the front window, Luke was glad that Joe would have these people to support and encourage him. He sometimes missed his own sister, but that life was lost to him now.

He was startled by a soft touch on his arm. Turning, he was met by Annie's direct gaze. She had draped a lavender shawl about her shoulders, accenting the deep green of her eyes.

"Won't you walk to the garden with me?" Annie asked. "The boys won't miss us," she added, indicating the table where the brothers were lost in deep discussion.

"I'd like that." Luke held the door for her as she swept passed him.

They walked awhile in silence, listening to birds calling in the distance. The sounds of a city awakening to a new day were growing audible around them.

"I've missed you, Annie." Luke stopped, waiting.

Annie continued on to the garden gate before pausing, her back to Luke. "Michael has asked me to marry him. I told him yes."

Luke felt the cold statement like a gut punch.

She stood for a moment seeming to contemplate the freshly plowed earth that was beckoning to be harrowed and planted, to grow new life. "I'm with child."

A dull roar began in his head, "Annie…."

"This child will have a father! A father who's home to watch him grow, to teach him! You will be forever off chasing cows or searching for…" She paused, choking back her anger and her tears. "I will not live like Zora did, alone, always wondering where her husband is, when he'll be home next. Dying alone…." She turned, tears streaming down her face.

The roar grew to deafening proportions. "Annie…"

"No!"

The cold simplicity of that one word cut through the haze of anger clouding his brain. He felt drained and empty. Looking at the proud, cold woman before him, he knew that arguing was useless. "I would marry you."

"Yes, but you wouldn't love me," she replied, her voice bitter. "Would you stay here? Would you be happy?" The tears continued to flow, but little else was reflected in her face. "What happened between us was wrong, Luke. You don't love me. I gave in to my own passion, so did you."

"I care for you."

"It's not enough. Michael loves me. He knows the circumstances, and still he wants to marry me, now more than ever. He has forgiven me. Would you?"

Luke swallowed hard, choking back a thousand protests, a thousand lies. Annie was right. What happened between them was a brief, flaming passion. It was wrong. He knew it then, and he knew it now. Michael was a solid, hard-working Christian man who owned a mercantile in Kingfisher. Annie and the child would be cared for and adored. What could he offer? He didn't even have a home to call his own.

God, why have you turned so far from me as to take my child?

The bitter pain tore at his heart. Without another word, he turned and walked to the livery where Rio waited for his master's return.

✳ ✳

Hooves pounding over the dry ground, sides heaving, sweat dripping from his flanks, the tired horse stumbled, falling to his knees. Luke was pitched forward, lost his seat and lay where he fell, winded, not caring what might happen next as the horse struggled to regain his footing. The blue sky above, the unyielding earth below, Annie's words, all melded together, burning through Luke's mind in a tormenting crescendo until a primal scream was torn from his very soul.

Rio started at the sound. Snorting softly, he drifted a few paces away from the mad man writhing on the ground before him. At last Luke lay utterly still and drained. A prayer tried to form itself in the depths of his mind, but the words would not come. A demanding voice echoing from the shadowy recesses of the past began somewhere in his heart.

Likewise the Spirit also helpeth our infirmities: for we know not what we should pray for as we ought: but the Spirit itself maketh intercession for us with groanings which cannot be uttered.
A coldness came over him in that instant. He sat up, shutting out the voice and the thoughts that came with it. *No, that's not the way it is for me! I don't* need *you.* Throwing himself down, he lay prone in the dust of the road, his body wracked with sobs until there were no more.

✶✶✶✶✶✶✶✶✶✶✶✶✶✶✶✶✶✶✶✶✶✶✶✶✶✶✶✶✶✶✶✶✶✶

A gentle rain washed his weary body. Luke woke with a start. It was dark. Head pounding, he sat up, unable to focus his thoughts. How long have I been laying here he wondered. Wiping his face on a sleeve, he winced as his body ached from the fall, his nerves raw. Hunger gnawed at his stomach, swallowing through his parched throat was agony. Despair overwhelmed him as his mind tried to turn to Annie.

Shutting out all thoughts and feelings, he raised himself to look for Rio. Whistling, he called the horse, and heard a rustling and creaking of saddle leather. He could just make out the bulk rising before him. Rio had bedded down a short distance away. Standing and giving himself a good shake, he trotted over to Luke, nudging him on the shoulder as he approached.

"Looks like it's just you and me again, boy," Luke shivered in the cold rain. Unstrapping the buckles on his saddlebags, he reached in past farrier tools, a spare shirt, and a couple of books, groping blindly for his jacket. It was only then he realized the mistake. He had left the jacket in Annie's front room. It had contained a few personal belongings and his pay from Addington. Leaning his head against the horse's warm wet flank, he shook his head. "So now we're alone *and* penniless." His mouth twisted in a wry grin. "God, you must really have something against me."

Trembling from cold and anger, he swung into the saddle. Clouds obscured the moon, and thunder rolled ominously in the distance. He should stop, make camp until morning, but he had an unrelenting

desire to keep moving, putting distance between himself and the pain
he had suffered in Rush Springs. Picking up the reins they headed off in
a northeasterly direction. He realized ironically that his father's home
lay in that direction, as distant in time as it was in miles.

The rain stopped sometime after midnight, and Rio plodded
along. Luke dozed intermittently in the saddle, falling prey to the bitter cold. A faint light glowed on the eastern horizon as the sun began
its journey above the land once more. The sky lightened, and the
birds began their songs of joy that were as old as time itself. Luke
rode on, his fingers frozen in their grip on the reins. As the sun rose,
the warm rays dissipating the chill that clung to the earth, he began to
feel his toes and his fingers again.

"Whoa, there, Rio," Luke said, reining in the big horse. "Maybe we
ought to take stock of our true situation, here. What do you think?"

Rio snorted and tossed his head, stopping as though in full agreement.
Luke dismounted, and made a quick check of the saddlebags. There was
enough dried jerky and hardtack to last a few days, that is if he didn't mind
some hunger pangs. His canteen was full, though in this part of the country ponds and creeks of fresh flowing water were plentiful.

"Looks like we're either going to have to find us a job or turn to a life
of crime. Don't believe either one of us would really relish the latter,
huh?" Luke pulled a set of hobbles from the bottom of the bags.

"You look like you could use a bit of time off there, old friend."
Unsaddling the horse, he placed the hobbles on his front feet and
turned him loose to graze upon the rich prairie. Standing the saddle
upright so as to protect the tree, he stretched himself out on the soft
green grass and soon fell into a fitful sleep.

CHAPTER V

"Jolene, sit still! It's hard enough to get these shoes buttoned without you squirming all over the place." Exasperated with her daughter and the chaotic preparations for the trip to Fallis, Kate finally managed to finish the buttons on Jo's high black shoes. Laying the buttonhook aside, she stood and looked at Jo critically. "Okay, you'll do. Now scoot."

Jo jumped up, wiggling her toes in her dress-up shoes, "These shoes feel too tight!" she complained. "Oh, Mama, you look so pretty! And won't Jonathan like my dress? Where's Candy? Candy, Candy, here girl."

Kate smiled as she watched Jo run off in search of the pup. She was indeed a vision in her deep blue calico jumper and white lawn blouse, her dancing red curls tamed into a matching blue ribbon. She sighed at the darned black stockings and too-tight shoes, but they would have to do until she knew what the future held.

Kate took a last look at herself in the small dressing table mirror. The image reflected there was at least fresh and clean. The dark green dress she had chosen seemed utterly feminine after spending so long in men's clothes. Her skin, normally pale and creamy had tanned to a deep bronze accented by naturally pink cheeks and lips. Deep amber colored eyes fringed by dark lashes gazed at her from the mirror, and her thick brown hair, now shimmering with golden highlights from the sun, was pulled back softly from her heart shaped face.

She shifted her attention from the mirror to a small tin type in an ornate frame. She and Will had looked so young on their wedding day. Even in the severe mourning dress she had chosen to wear, Will had made her feel special and pretty. He was smiling at her from the image, just as he always had in life, with a look that told her she was the most beautiful creature in the world to him. Her eyes misted as she lightly caressed the picture, "I miss you, Will."

✳ ✳

Jake had the team hitched to the wagon. Nana, Jonathan and Jo were already tucked securely in their places. Kate carried out the basket that contained the roast chicken, fresh bread, pies and relishes that she and Nana had spent the better part of Saturday preparing. Handing the basket to Jake, Kate couldn't help smiling as she noticed the gleaming golden coats and brushed white manes and tails of the mares. The harness shined from its recent oiling, and Jonathan had obviously spent a lot of elbow grease on getting the buckboard in top condition. Jake secured the basket into the wagon, then handed Kate up to the front seat. She thought they must make a pretty picture as they headed off down the road to Fallis for the Sunday meeting.

Though the trip to Fallis was only a little over four miles, it would take them more than an hour to make the trip by wagon as the road was a rough one, where it even existed, but the sun was up and beginning to warm the air around them. Even Jolene was silent for a moment as they drank in the beauty around them.

"Are you going to see Mr. Johnson there, mama?" came the innocent question.

Kate paused a moment, "He said he would be there today, so I expect we'll probably see him."

"Well, I'm not sitting by him. I don't like him!"

"Jo, why would you say such a thing?"

"Because he's mean. He tried to cheat you. And I saw our horse, I think he hurt him."

"Jo, you mustn't talk like that. You should respect your elders!" Kate admonished sternly, "even if I happen to agree with you," she added under her breath too quietly for her daughter to hear. Jake glanced in her direction. He was the only one close enough to hear her last comment.

The conversation between Nana and the children in the bed of the wagon turned to the prospect of the meeting and the picnic to follow. They gleefully discussed who would be there, and what the preacher might be like. Kate smiled listening for a moment before Jake's question took her attention. "How was the colt? You saw him, didn't you?"

"I did," she sighed.

"And?"

"I don't know, Jake. I didn't see any cuts or obvious wounds on him. He was thin, and maybe a little rough looking—I don't know—it was like the spirit had just left him."

"Um-hmmm."

"That colt doesn't belong to me anymore!"

"I know."

For a long moment there was nothing but the sounds of clopping hooves, harness jingling and the carefree conversation drifting from the back of the buckboard.

Kate sighed. "When Matt Johnson rode through our place the other day, Jake, it was as if he were appraising something he already owned!" A cold fear grabbed the pit of her stomach. "What if I can't do this, Jake? What if I can't make a go of this? I can't bear to see someone like Johnson just walk in and take over our dream!"

Jake gave a slight flick of his wrists, and the team picked up their pace as they came to the main road. He was silent for a few moments before he looked at her pointedly and said, "of course *you* can't do it."

"Oh, I know I have you and Jonathan, but…."

"That's not what I meant."

Kate stared straight ahead. Jake was getting older. He knew it, and so did she. As strong as he was, he tired easily, and last winter he had a mild heart attack. She worried about him every time he was out. Jonathan was a boy. He was a hard and diligent worker, but he was shy and slow mentally. He simply didn't have the mind or the aptitude to run a full ranch operation. "So you think I should marry again?" She asked quietly, not daring to meet his eyes.

"For someone who spends so much time reading that little Bible there, you sure seem to miss the point sometimes!" Jake sounded both amused and exasperated. "Isn't there a place in there somewhere that says sumthin about, 'I can do all things through Jesus who strengthens me?' Well, why wouldn't that apply to runnin' a ranch as much as it would to anything else? Have you tried asking Him for a little help?"

"Oh, Jake," Kate laughed, "every day! And you know, I think I'll just keep on asking!"

✶ ✶

The rest of the trip passed uneventfully. As they approached the growing town of Fallis, the sense of anticipation grew. Kate felt a gnawing angst that she didn't understand. Was it the prospect of seeing Matt Johnson again, or was there something else? Whatever it was, she tried to put it from her mind as Jake pulled up before the General Mercantile. A small, plain woman with dark hair was sweeping the boardwalk in front of the store. As the wagon approached, her face was transformed by a radiant smile and sparkling eyes. Placing the broom against the wall, she wiped her hands on her crisp white apron as Kate stepped down from the buckboard.

"Kate!"

"Martha!"

"It is so good to see you. I've missed you these last months." Kate was enveloped in a perfumed hug from her friend. "Jo, come up here. I have some horehound in the jar, go get yourself a piece."

"Oh, thank you, Mrs. Jansen. Can I get one for Jon, too?"

"Certainly, dear." Martha took Kate by the hand and led her into the cool, dark store as Jo scampered ahead. Finding the candy as promised, she grabbed the treasure and fairly flew down the steps to find Jonathan. "She hasn't changed any, has she?" laughed Martha.

"Not a whit!" agreed Kate. Standing in the dim interior of the large mercantile, Kate felt a sense of calm steal over her as she and Martha renewed their friendship. "I didn't think you would be open today. Where's that new husband of yours?"

"Oh, Lars is helping the other men get the tables ready for the big picnic." Martha blushed and smiled, showing a charming dimple. "I'm not really open today. I was just getting ready to go to meeting when I saw your wagon coming, and I just knew Jo would want that horehound."

"I know you, Martha, you didn't open the store just for that! What is it?"

Martha paused for a moment, her gaze shifting from her friend's sun bronzed complexion to her calloused hands. "Kate, you've been doing all that ranch work yourself, haven't you?"

Casting her eyes down and hiding her hands within the folds of her skirt, Kate replied softy, "We had two hands working there when….when it happened. They stayed on for a bit, but eventually they drifted off, said there were 'other opportunities,'" she shrugged, "but I know they just couldn't take working for a woman."

"Humph! Typical. So, have you tried to hire help?"

"Oh, I tried at first, but it was always the same thing. They'd stay on a week or two, until taking orders from me got to be too much for them, then off they'd go."

"You sure that's what it was?" Martha asked, brows raised.

"What do you mean?"

"I overheard a conversation a few weeks ago that I did not like!"

"What about?" Kate prompted when Martha paused, seeming to ponder whether to continue.

Eyeing her friend speculatively, she took deep breath before continuing, "A couple of punchers were in the store, one says how he'd been working for 'that woman what lost her husband'—that got my attention, mind you—and he let on how old Mr. Johnson offered him half again as much pay if he'd quit her ranch and tell all the other boys to do the same."

Kate gasped, "But he can't...."

"Now, Kate, I know how you feel! Hear me out."

"Martha, I can't believe that Matt...." the bell above the door jangled startling the women into silence.

Martha glanced at the man who had entered the store, shook her head slightly and drew Kate further back. Looking over her shoulder, Kate saw a tall, lean man with thick brown hair, and a hard, worn look about him. She gave her friend a questioning look.

"Kate, you need help out there." Martha continued, ignoring the quizzical look.

"I know, but I'm not even sure I can afford it right now."

"You can still offer room and board, can't you?"

"Well, yes, there's the bunkhouse still, and Nana does cook enough to feed a veritable army!" Kate laughed in spite of herself. Something about Martha's simmering exuberance piqued Kate's curiosity. "Why?"

"Well, a drifter came in a few days ago. He seems a nice enough fellow, and he really needs a job. I gave him a few odds and ends to do around here to keep him in town. Once I decided he was all right, well, I explained about you, and the situation out at your place."

"Martha Louise Jansen! You had no right..."

"Oh, Hush! You sound just like a spoiled child!" Martha's eye flashed, but she continued to smile. "Here I go trying to help, and this is the thanks I get?"

Kate maintained her defenses, but she listened as Martha continued. "Like I said, he seems all right, and I've warned him about Matt Johnson, so unlike some of the local hands, he'll be more likely to stay around. What do you say? At least meet him, talk to him?"

Kate sighed, weighing out the options. Her gaze drifted to the man waiting by the counter. Once again she felt the cold fear snaking its icy tendrils into the pit of her stomach. "We're going to be late for church meeting. I really don't—oh, all right, I'll talk to him at least. After church? You need to go take care of your customer."

"Good!" Martha's eyes gleamed. "I'll see you at the meeting."

Kate hugged her friend and turned to leave, brushing by the waiting man. As she passed she could feel him watching her. Looking up she encountered clear green eyes that held a quiet sadness, and a grim resolution. The intensity in his face caused a stirring within her that she didn't quite understand. Dropping her gaze, she quickly left the dim atmosphere of the quiet store for the bright warm sunshine and bustling activity of the streets of Fallis.

Following the crowds, she found her way to the schoolhouse where the Sunday meeting was to be held. It was a charming white building with a wide portico, adorned with window boxes bursting with the colors of early blooming flowers and trailing green ivy. Kate smiled at the simple beauty and was filled with a sense of respect for a teacher that would find the time to create such an inviting place for her students. She knew it would soon be time for Jo to start attending a regular school. At only six years old, Jo was already learning to read and write under the tutelage from Nana and Kate, but with her sharp little mind, she needed to be in a real school. Maybe she would see about sending her to school here in the fall. Four miles would be awfully far, but maybe somehow they could find a way.

As Kate stood lost in thoughts of school years and Martha's proposal, she was startled by a hand upon her sleeve. Flinching at the touch, she instinctively reached to protect her arm.

"I'm sorry. I certainly didn't intend to frighten you," Matt breathed into her ear. "You look absolutely beautiful, far too pretty for church!"

"Thank you, Mr. Johnson," she said coldly, her heart pounding.

"Shall we?" Matt asked, taking her by the elbow. Without waiting for an answer, he steered her into the small room, and found them seats side by side on the hard wooden benches. The schoolhouse was already filled. Jo and the Insleys were seated a few rows ahead.

"Mama, here we are," Jo called waving madly.

"My daughter…." Kate began.

"She's with your help, she'll be fine. Besides, there's really no room left up there." Matt protested. "Your mother is going to keep me company, sweetheart. Now be a good girl, turn around and listen to the preacher."

Jo scowled at the man. As Kate prayed that her daughter wouldn't stick her tongue out, Jo turned a baleful glance on her mother; Kate shrugged. Jo turned back around, plopping into the seat and crossing her arms. Kate felt the cold settle permanently in the depths of her very being as Matt leaned back, his shoulder crushed against hers.

Oh, Lord, is this what you would have for me? Have you sent a husband in the form of this man? I don't even like him, much less love him. Lord, you are the great provider, and I know that I don't always understand your ways, but I trust you. Could you just maybe make it a little easier to see Your hand here?

The congregation rose and began singing "Rock of ages cleft for me, let me hide myself in thee." The words which normally filled her soul with peace and hope, seemed hard and shrill as she stood next to this cattleman. So many emotions flooded her. Martha's words haunted her memory. She stole a glance at his face as he sang in a rich baritone. His eyes were hard, as though hiding something within.

The singing over, they sat, and the circuit preacher began a sermon on God's redeeming love. She found it hard to concentrate. Her mind wandered as she heard those words, *redeeming love*, taking her back to a time when she had been sure that there was no love left in the world, from God or anyone. In that horrible time after the fire had swept through their home, killing her mother and father in a raging inferno that had threatened to take her own life as well, she knew that a loving God could not exist. She would never forget the screams of agony coming from her mother's room as the flames engulfed her parents. Beating upon their door her sleeves caught fire and she suffered severe burns over her arms and chest, before being overcome by the smoke and losing all consciousness.

She awoke three days later in pain and confusion, Mrs. Insley ministering to her burns as tenderly as she ministered to her aching heart. Her parents had already been buried and the few items salvaged from the smoldering remains of their home were safely packed away in a trunk standing in a corner of the room where Kate lay. The Insleys had taken her in. They had always loved the little golden haired girl that had played down the street. She would pick wild flowers and bring them to Nana to set upon the table on the porch where they would sip lemonade on sweltering summer afternoons. They watched her grow into a charming young woman. The Insleys had been as surprised as her own parents when she announced her intentions to attend university and study for a law degree. Now Kate needed them, and they were prepared to give all they had to make sure she survived.

As the days passed, and Kate grew stronger, she longed to know how she had survived that awful fire. Nana could not have saved her, that she knew. She was not strong enough to have pulled her from the flames, and Jake had been away on one of his freight hauling trips.

One Sunday afternoon while Nana and Jonathan were attending church, Kate sat quietly in bed reading her Bible. A gift from her parents on the day she was born, she never went anywhere without it. It was tucked safely in her pocket that fateful night as she returned from another late evening studying at the library to find the flames engulfing their home. Now that Bible was one of the few remnants of her vanished life.

"Lord, I don't understand," she prayed. "How could you let this happen? I should have been there! What did my parents do to deserve this? What did I do, Lord? Are you there? Can you hear me?" she screamed her frustrations.

Knowing in her heart that the Lord had not deserted her, still she railed at Him, not understanding how He could stand by and let the agony continue. She looked with disgust at the weeping flesh that covered her arms, the physical scars would be horrific, but what about the scars on her soul, she wondered. Tears streamed from her eyes and she buried her head in the pillow.

A rich quiet voice filled her ears. "May I come in, please?"

She looked up into the compassionate blue eyes of Will Shaughnessey.

"Will, what are you doing here?" she asked wiping at her eyes and blowing her nose on the hanky he held out. Will and Kate had grown up together. Their families had lived next door to each other since they were both in diapers.

"Just thought it was about time I came to see if it was worth my time pulling you out of there."

"You…" she gasped.

"Well, I thought twice about it, you know, seeing as how you put that frog down my shirt once. And you were awful confound heavy—but I decided if I still planned on marrying you I better get you out of there," he joked.

"Marrying me? What are you talking about?"

"Aw, c'mon, Kate, you know I've been in love with you since we were ten or twelve. What do you say, will you marry me?"

"Will, look at me! I'll never be the same, I'm scarred, and burned, and…."

"That doesn't matter."

"It does to me! Besides, I—I don't love you," she finished weakly, looking away.

"You like me, don't you?"

"Of course I do!"

"Good. Then you can learn to love me. My love will be enough for both of us until God's redeeming love brings you around!"

"But…"

"I've always thought a winter wedding would be nice. How about December? You ought to be pretty well healed up by then."

And so they had married, and God's redeeming love had saved her. She had grown to love Will in a strong and faithful way.

"…through God's redeeming love!" The preacher closed, and the congregation began stirring around her. She shook her head as Matt reached his hand down to her. This hard, cold man was not Will, she would never grow to care for him as she had Will. Standing, she stepped away from him and looked for her family. Jake appeared at her elbow. Almost shaking with relief, she made her excuses to Matt and allowed Jake to escort her out toward the large oak tree beneath which the tables were laid for the afternoon picnic.

✶✶✶✶✶✶✶✶✶✶✶✶✶✶✶✶✶✶✶✶✶✶✶✶✶✶✶✶✶✶✶

Nana had spread the cloth in a secluded area just away from the main tables. The baskets were already open and Jo and Jonathan were arguing about who could eat the most pie. Sinking slowly to the ground, she closed her eyes and breathed in the rich earthy aroma of sun-warmed grass, new spring flowers, and the mouth-watering scents of fried chicken, fruit pies, and fresh baked breads. She smiled at the petty bickering between the children, and soaked in the love of these people she called family.

"You all right, Kate?" Jake asked.

"I am now."

"Well, good. Then perhaps you could see to giving me a hand with setting out this food!" Nana said. "Jon, you go draw water from the pump there, and Jo, I want those napkins folded proper. Just because this here's a picnic, don't give us no reason to behave like heathens."

"Yes, Ma'am," all three chimed in at once. Bursting into gales of laughter, they each set about their appointed tasks, while Nana supervised with an exacting eye.

✶✶✶✶✶✶✶✶✶✶✶✶✶✶✶✶✶✶✶✶✶✶✶✶✶✶✶✶✶✶✶✶✶✶✶

As the afternoon wore on, Kate sat in the shade beneath the old oak, watching the children run and play. Jake dozed contentedly nearby while Nana busied herself with knitting. The lazy drone of bees working a nearby patch of pink and white clover had all but lulled Kate to sleep, when she was startled awake by a familiar voice.

"Kate, there you are. I've been looking everywhere for you," Martha called. "Come and walk with me a while."

"I'll be back soon," she called to Nana. Rising and brushing the grass from her full skirts, she joined her friend, already anticipating the coming meeting.

"He's waiting for us at the livery. Lars is there with him, so there's no need to worry. Just talk to him. You need the help, and I know you'll like him." Martha fairly bubbled with enthusiasm. Kate was as nervous and reticent as Martha was gay and excited.

"Let's get this over with then."

"Kathleen Rose Shaughnessey!" Martha mocked her, "You straighten up that attitude, young lady," she smiled.

Kate gave her a withering look as they approached the large gray barn that served as both Livery and blacksmith shop. Two men stood in front, along with a large grey gelding, saddled and tied to the rail. They were examining the horse's front feet as the women drew near.

"Hello, Lars," Kate smiled. She truly liked Martha's tall, lanky husband. He was as large and fair and quiet as she was small and dark and talkative. They were a unique and special couple.

"Miss Kate," he nodded.

"Kate, I'd like you to meet Luke Josey. Luke, this is Mrs. Shaughnessey." The other man set down the hoof he had been inspecting. Straightening and turning to face the women, Kate was met by the same green eyes she had seen in the mercantile. A muscle twitched near his jaw as he held out his hand, "Pleased to meet you, ma'am." His voice was rich and warm.

"Mr. Josey." She reached out to shake his hand, and found hers completely engulfed in his firm grasp. A long moment of silence ensued as each studied the other. Finally retrieving her hand, she took a step back.

"Well, somebody say something!" Martha's sharp command seemed to break a spell.

"I understand you could use some help on your ranch."

"I can't offer you much."

"I don't need a lot."

"I have a small bunkhouse, meals, and when I can I'll pay twenty dollars for a month's work. It's hard work." Glancing at his horse, she added, "If you'd like, I can provide a horse in place of one month's pay."

He chewed on one corner of his lower lip as if chewing over her offer. Looking at Rio, he seemed to make up his mind. "That old cow pony of mine isn't getting any younger, you're right. I reckon he could use a break now and again. Tell you what, I'll stay on through the fall, you give me a good horse, and hundred dollars. If you want, you can pay me only half of each month's wages at the end of a month, then the balance at the end of the fall."

Closing her eyes, she prayed, *Dear, Lord, what do I do? I need the help he's offering, but I'm afraid. What am I afraid of?* As she opened her eyes, Matt Johnson appeared from around the corner of the building.

"There you are, Kate. Will you come? There are some matters I'd like to discuss with you."

"I'm rather busy right now. Can it wait?"

Taking her arm in a possessive grasp, Matt continued, "Oh, but I really think…."

"The lady said she's busy." Luke's voice was low pitched, just shy of threatening.

Wresting her arm from his grip, Kate turned to face him. "Mr. Johnson, when I've finished my business here, I'll gladly meet you at the Mercantile in twenty minutes." Her voice was steady, belying the fear within.

Casting a dark glance in Luke's direction, Matt paused for an instant before replying curtly, "Twenty minutes. Don't keep me waiting, Kate."

Shaken and distraught, Kate sank onto the bench near the front of the livery. Martha grasped her hand, and held her friend. Regaining her composure, she raised her eyes toward heaven, then with a wry grin, she turned to Luke, "If you still want the job, you're hired."

CHAPTER VI

While Martha took Luke to meet the Insleys, Kate and Lars headed to the Mercantile. The cold fear returned to plague her. As they approached the boardwalk in front of the store, Matt Johnson rose from where he was seated on one of the benches against the front of the building. Lars placed a comforting hand on the small of her back, giving her strength in the knowledge of his presence.

"Mr. Jansen, I believe I can take it from here," Matt drawled, clearly dismissing the man.

Lars looked at Kate as though seeking her will in the matter.

She nodded slightly. "But don't go far, please," she whispered.

Tipping his hat, Lars entered the mercantile taking up a post just inside the door.

"What can I do for you, Mr. Johnson?"

"Please, Kate, won't you call me Matt?"

She remained silent, waiting for him to continue.

"Let's sit down, shall we."

Hesitating for a moment, Kate sighed, then took the offered seat.

Sitting beside her, Matt began, "Kate, I'm a businessman. You know that. I work hard, and when I see something I want, I go after it. I've even been accused of not playing 'fair' sometimes." He smiled at her. His deep hazel eyes softening for the first time. "You've been alone now for—what?—nearly a year?"

"Nine months," Kate whispered, fighting back tears.

"Nine months. You've done a remarkable job out there, keeping everything running, but aren't you growing tired?"

His concern was beginning to disarm her. The fear abated slowly to be replaced by a growing wonder about this man she thought was the enemy. Did he really care? Were her fears unfounded? As he reached out to take her hand, gently encasing it in both of his, she did not pull away.

"I've made no secret over the years about how much I'd like to have your place—Providence, isn't that what you call it? A beautiful name for a very special piece of land."

Kate nodded, but it was more than a piece of land, it was her *home*.

Still holding her hand between his, he spoke more passionately, "Kate, there's more than that. I'm a man. I have feelings. There are times that I have found myself growing lonely. You're an incredible woman, Kate Shaughnessey, but you need someone in your life. Will you consider marrying me?"

A rush of conflicting emotions collided in a burst so intense that it felt like an explosion going off in her very soul. She could do no more than stare at the man before her. Her throat constricted, so that no words could escape as she fought to regain control.

Taking her silence as encouragement, he continued, "You have three more months of mourning before you can respectably marry again. So for now, please, think about my offer."

"Matt, I…" her voice was hollow; she felt like she was drowning. *Lord, help me*, she pleaded silently.

"In the meantime, I can pay you court, and I'll have time to prepare our home in Guthrie to suit a woman and her daughter." He pressed her hand to his lips. "Now if you'll excuse me, I have some other business to attend, my dear Kate. I'm sure Lars will see you safely back to your wagon." He rose, settling his hat squarely over his black hair, and strode off down the street.

Kate sat in stunned silence on the bench outside the store. She felt as though a cannonball had just landed on her chest, and she was dying, unable to breathe beneath the weight of it.

✳✳✳✳✳✳✳✳✳✳✳✳✳✳✳✳✳✳✳✳✳✳✳✳✳✳✳✳✳✳✳✳

Matt smiled to himself as he walked away from the woman sitting on the bench. He wanted that land, and if marrying her was the only way to get it, well, so be it. There were worse things he could think of than a pretty wife. Besides, once they were married and the land was safely transferred to his name, he could leave her and her brat at the house in Guthrie and continue on with his life just the way it was.

As he passed by the Livery, two of his men joined him.

"Any news, boys?" he asked.

"Maybe sumthin you ain't gonna like," one of them said darkly.

Matt stopped, waiting.

"New man drifted in, went to work for that Shaughnessey woman."

"Did he now?" Matt's face darkened. "We'll have to see what we can do about that."

✳✳✳✳✳✳✳✳✳✳✳✳✳✳✳✳✳✳✳✳✳✳✳✳✳✳✳✳✳✳✳✳

"There she is! Mama's here. Mama's here!" Jo shrieked excitedly, bouncing in the saddle as the grey horse stood patiently, never flinching at the little girl's energetic flailing.

"Hello, baby. I see you've met Mr. Josey." Kate said. Luke and the Insleys were standing with Martha, Luke holding the reins, while they chatted amiably.

"Oh, yes, Mama. He's ever so nice. He even let me ride his horse. His name is Rio de Esperanza, that means River of Hope. Isn't that a funny name for a horse?" She sat straight in the saddle, patting the gelding's neck. "And isn't he *handsome*?" she added in a conspiratorial whisper.

"Rio or Mr. Josey?" Kate asked with a smile.

"Oh, Mama! Of course I meant Mr. Josey." Jo giggled.

Kate reached up for her laughing daughter. Lifting her down, she held her close, taking comfort in the small warm body. She breathed deeply of Jo's fresh scent, burying her face in the soft red curls. As though knowing instinctively what her mother needed, Jo relaxed against her, laying her head on Kate's shoulder, and patting her back reassuringly.

"So? What did our *friend* want?" Martha asked.

Kate swallowed, unable to speak.

"Well, don't worry about him. That will take care of itself. You have Luke now." Martha stated with confidence.

"Oh, Martha." *If you only knew*, Kate thought. She wanted to confide in her dear friend, but glancing around at the others, she couldn't expose her feelings and fears here, it was still too raw. Her emotions flooded, threatening to spill over in a rush of tears. She bit her lip. Setting Jo down in the bed of the wagon, she hugged Martha. When Lars walked over and took Martha's hand, Kate felt a fleeting stab of jealousy, wishing that Will was standing beside her, holding her hand that way.

"The wagon's loaded. We're 'bout ready to move out." Jake said. "Hand up?"

"Thank you, Jake," Kate said taking his hand and stepping up to the high front seat.

"Good bye! When will you be back to town?"

"I don't know, Martha, soon though, I have some shopping to do."

Luke swung into the saddle, and turned Rio to follow the buckboard. Jake climbed up beside Kate, took the reins and the wagon lurched forward, heading home to Providence.

✳ ✳

The first mile passed in silence. Nana and the children slept soundly on a pile of blankets in the bed of the wagon, rocked by the gentle swaying. Luke Josey rode beside them, sometimes talking to Jake about the land, the crops, or the cattle. Kate sat stiffly, staring straight ahead, trying not to think.

As Luke and Rio drifted off to ride alone for awhile, Jake looked at Kate from the corner of his eye. "Wanna talk?"

"Not really."

"Can't keep it bottled up inside forever."

"Why not?"

"Ain't good for ya. You might bust."

Throwing her head back and laughing, she let the tears stream down the sides of her face. "Jake Insley, whatever am I going to do with you? Can't even let a girl brood in peace."

"Never did much good."

Wiping away the tears with the back of her hand, Kate sighed and fell silent again.

"Matt Johnson asked me to marry him," she stated after a moment.

She could see a muscle tighten at his jaw line, but Jake remained silent. The horses plodded along; birds sang in the distance. Kate looked down and toyed with a fold in her skirt. "Well, aren't you going to say anything?"

Jake turned slowly until he was facing her. His face was sorrowful, the lines more deeply etched than Kate could ever recall. "That's a decision that only you can make." His voice was low and steady but tightly controlled. It pierced her heart. This man had been like a father to her, and now he seemed to be drawing away, leaving her. She felt so alone, so utterly alone.

✳✳✳✳✳✳✳✳✳✳✳✳✳✳✳✳✳✳✳✳✳✳✳✳✳✳✳✳✳✳

Luke studied the man and woman riding side by side on the high front seat of the buckboard. He liked Jake. The older man was open and honest. Kate Shaughnessey was another story. She was beautiful, but distant. Something was eating at her, that much was obvious, and Luke had the feeling that she wasn't too happy about his presence in their lives right now. Well he needed a job, and this one would be as good as any. He'd do his best by them for the next five or six months, then he could be on his way.

Thinking of the future inevitably brought thoughts of Annie. She would be about to deliver his child in six months. No, he wouldn't think of that. Annie was safe in another world. She and the child deserved a better life. He needed to simply shut that part of his life out for good. He would never be the right man for any decent woman. The shame he felt created an empty void inside. Better to stop feeling all together, than to live with that kind of loneliness and pain.

The buckboard slowed and was turning on to a smaller road. Glancing about, Luke liked the looks of the land. Grass was deep, nearly belly high on his horse, a mixture of native bluestem, bermuda and buffalo grasses that were rich and nourishing. Red Indian paintbrush, purple phlox and pink clover dotted the hillsides, adding vivid splashes of color among the verdant greens. Trees grew along the creeks and shaded the ponds. In the distance, he saw a small herd of predominantly black cows with calves cavorting in the fading golden sunshine. Riding alongside Jake, he asked, "Some of yours?"

"Those're some of Mrs. Shaughnessey's Angus, yep," he replied, a hint of pride creeping into his voice. "You can see the fence line just comin' up."

As Luke looked in the direction indicated, he saw the road narrow until it was no more than a cart track, where it passed between two rough pillars, spanned by a graceful carved sign. Luke saw Kate's mouth curve in a wistful smile, her eyes deepening pools of liquid amber, as she watched the entrance come into view.

She must really love this place. What must it feel like to be a part of something so real, he wondered.

Another quarter of a mile down the rough track and around the side of a rise brought them in sight of the homestead. His heart constricted at the simple beauty of it. The setting sun cast purple shadows across the land. The last golden rays gilding the plain white home, and casting a golden glow around the trees, fences and barns gave an ethereal presence to the place. He felt a peace settle over his heart that he hadn't known in years. Was there some magic here? Was this an enchanted haven?

✻ ✻

They pulled up at the kitchen porch of the house, and three sleepy passengers piled out from the back of the wagon. Jonathan scrambled up to the front seat as Kate jumped down.

"Jake, will you show Mr. Josey to the bunkhouse? I'll get some fresh bedding out there as soon as I get Jo in bed."

"Yes." The answer was curt and withdrawn. Kate withered inside.

Nana looked from Kate to Jake and back again, clearly puzzled. Jake said nothing more, clucked to the team, and drove to the barn.

"Mrs. Insley, can you help me get these things in, and Jo to bed, please."

"I can. And we'll get breakfast set for tomorrow as well."

"Oh, I don't think so, you're tired, and so am I. We'll get it in the morning."

"Humph!"

Kate shook her head, picked up her sleepy daughter and followed Nana in the house.

The two women worked quickly putting away the odds and ends. Kate tucked Jo in with kisses and prayers and promises of tomorrow. When she went back to the kitchen, Nana already had a fire glowing in the fireplace, and a stack of linens and towels on the table. "There's a good mattress ticking there that just needs to be stuffed with straw, couple of sheets, one wool blanket, a towel and some spare wash rags." Nana ticked off the items as though it were an inventory.

Kate smiled, "Why don't you go home and get some rest? It's been a long day."

"I'll be going when I've finished here."

"All right," Kate acquiesced. "I'm going to take these things to the bunkhouse."

She gathered up the pile of goods and stepped out into the cool evening air. Walking toward the barn she tried not to think of the events of the day, but the nagging fear would not go away. She knew she needed to pray, turn it over to God. She vowed to spend time in the Bible tonight no matter how tired she was. It was the only thing that helped in these trying times.

The men were still in the barn, the wagon was set back in it's place and the team of mares had been turned out in the paddock. A fresh mound of hay had been pitched into the manger, and they stood contentedly munching away. Kate smiled.

Horses were such a blessing in her life. Working with them, breeding, gentling, and riding, was the one thing she knew she could do well. When they had arrived in the Oklahoma Territory, she knew how to ride, but had never done anything more than pleasure riding on one of her father's horses. Her family had grooms and stable hands to tend to the horses then.

Once established on their ranch, she had taken an active interest in the role of the cow ponies in daily ranch work. Through observation and personal use she began to see which ones had the stamina and conformation to excel at their jobs. When Will had brought home a small, smoothly muscled black colt, she had seen the potential he possessed and convinced Will not to geld him. She named him Raven. The decision proved a fruitful one. They used him as a three year old to work cattle, a job he relished. He was catty and quick. He could cut a cow from the herd, and hold it for as long as you asked him. When a calf was roped from his back, he would stand firm and keep the rope as taught as a wire until told to release it. As a four year old they began crossing him on the best mares they could afford. The foals they produced were some of the most sought after horses in the territory.

As Kate entered the barn, Raven nickered softly to her from his stall. She reached out to rub his velvety nose, breathing in the rich scent of horse.

The men had lit a few lanterns to cast a light over the dim barn, and were gathered near the tack room, talking and laughing together. They stopped as she entered. "I've brought a mattress and linens for the bunk. Jon, will you stuff the ticking for Mr. Josey?"

"Yes, ma'am." He grabbed the ticking and dashed off to the straw pile.

"Make sure it's good sweet straw, Jon, I don't want any dusty stuff!" Luke laughed.

"Oh, yes, sir, I'll get the best," Jon replied earnestly. The two men laughed as the boy ran off. Jon was clearly in awe of Luke.

"Have you seen the bunk house yet, Mr. Josey?"

"Nope, but I expect it's time to mosey that way." he said with a twinkle in his eye.

"It's right through that door." Kate said, shifting the linens to pick up a lantern. Armed with a light against the dark, she started past them.

As she reached for the handle, a large hand fell on hers. "Allow me, ma'am." Luke opened the door and stood aside for her to enter. Kate paused an instant, a tentative smile acknowledging the manners so often lacking in many of the cow hands.

Jake watched the interaction, then turned to finish the evening chores.

Entering the large room, she wrinkled her nose at the dust, realizing for the first time how long it had been since the bunkhouse had been used. "I'll come out in the morning and give the room a good cleaning, Mr. Josey. I apologize for the state it's in, but then I didn't know you'd be here tonight."

"I think I'll survive the dirt. It's better than most I've seen," he grinned. "And by the way, my name is Luke."

"Luke, then." She looked around the room. There were three frame and rope bedsteads, a small trunk at the foot of each. A washstand stood beneath a cracked mirror, with a white pitcher and basin. The one window was large, surrounded by sack cloth curtains, and an old black iron stove stood in the corner. It was frugal but serviceable. Luke should be comfortable enough here.

"Jake is usually here just after first light for morning chores, and breakfast is generally at seven. You can come up to the house through the kitchen door. It's the one we use most often." She paused, "and most everyone calls me Kate."

He smiled a shy engaging smile. "It suits you. Kate."

She found herself smiling back at this man in spite of all that happened that day. Swallowing hard, she excused herself, and hurried back to the house.

✶✶✶✶✶✶✶✶✶✶✶✶✶✶✶✶✶✶✶✶✶✶✶✶✶✶✶✶✶✶✶✶✶✶✶

Nana was still working in the kitchen when Kate came through the back door. They worked together in companionable silence for a few minutes before Nana took a good long look at Kate. "That man Johnson ask you to marry him?"

Kate flushed, "How did you know?"

"A woman's been around as long as me knows these things. What'd you tell him?"

"I didn't tell him anything," she cried, "I couldn't! I was in shock, and now he thinks he can court me." Once again the tears she had fought all day began to trickle down her cheeks. "Now Jake is mad at me, I feel so lost. Oh, Nana, what am I going to do?" Kate didn't often call her Nana, it was always Mrs. Insley, until she needed her mother, only then did she break down and call the woman by the childhood endearment.

The older woman sighed and sat down near the fire. Patting the bench beside her, she whispered, "Come here, dear."

Kate walked over and sank to her knees, putting her head in Nana's lap. The feeling was safe and warm. She thought of her own mother, and the comfort she always sought in her wisdom. *I miss you, mama. I need you so much* she thought.

Nana stroked the girl's soft hair for a moment, letting her find the solace she needed before continuing. "Jake's not mad, you know. He's just gonna let you find your way in this."

Kate sniffed, staring into the flickering flames, as the sun set and the shadows lengthened in the quiet room.

"Search your heart, girl, God will place the answers there. Listen for His voice, you'll hear it." Saying no more, she bent and placed a tender kiss on Kate's cheek. Taking the girl's face in both of her small worn hands she searched her eyes. Seemingly satisfied, she nodded. Rising, she packed her few things away in her basket and headed toward the front door.

"What in the world?" came the exclamation as Nana opened the living room door to the front porch. Jake, heading over from the barn heard her cry and hurried around to the front, while Kate came from the kitchen.

There on the front steps was a haunch of venison, smoked and cured, laying on a length of clean muslin. Nearby Kate noticed a small colorful bunch of wild flowers tied with a leather thong and a hawk's feather. She smiled, picking up the bouquet. "Tochoway," she whispered, searching the gathering darkness for any trace of the tall dark man.

"Tochoway? You mean that savage was back here?" Nana sounded mortified. "I don't like the idea of savages sneakin' around here when we're not home!"

Jake looked at his dear little wife, "Would you rather they were sneakin' around here while we *were* home?" he asked, eyes twinkling.

Nana gave him baleful look.

✶✶✶✶✶✶✶✶✶✶✶✶✶✶✶✶✶✶✶✶✶✶✶✶✶✶✶✶✶✶✶✶✶

Tochoway sat on his pony watching the family return from Fallis. He saw the stranger on the gray horse. A strong man, that was good. He watched as the women entered the house, and the men went to the

barn. Still he waited. His eyes riveted on Kate as she carried a large bundle from the house. He smiled as she paused to watch the horses.
Tochoway believed the horse was a special spirit for Kate. The Great
Father's creation was not limited to man. Did not the very rocks and
trees echo His existence? How much more so, then the living, breathing
animals to whom He gave life? The Great Father made all creatures, and
to some He gave the gift of communion; Kate's special gift was the
horse, just as his was the hawk.

The evening stretched on, it was nearly dark and he was growing
weary when his token was finally discovered. He saw Kate pick up the
flowers. Would she know the healing properties of each? He hoped the
significance would not be lost on her. As her fingers toyed with the
hawk's feather and her eyes scanned the horizon searching for him, he
was satisfied. Raising his hand in peace, he turned his pony and rode
into the night.

* *

Kate sat on the edge of her bed, her Bible clutched tightly in her
hands. Emotions raged through her heart. So many changes had
occurred in just one day, she couldn't grasp the significance of any of
them fully. Closing her eyes she tried to pray, but the voices in her head
would not be stilled. Standing, she drifted to the window, and looked
out over the land. She opened the curtains and raised the pane letting
the cool night air rush in. The sheer cotton nightgown she wore bil-
lowed about her as the wind filled it like the sails of a great ship.
Breathing deeply of the cleansing breeze, she willed her mind to peaceful repose. Turning her eyes upon the Lord, she finally managed to still
the fears within her.

Returning to the bed she sat upon it and let her Bible fall open. She
smiled. It had been years since she had chosen to read at random like
this. She had tried to order her reading like she managed the rest of her

life. Strictly reading passages that she knew, or finding the ones she believed applied to a certain situation. She remembered how her mother had once shown her to open the Book, and blindly point to scripture at random. So many times those verses held more meaning than those she would laboriously track down.

Closing her eyes she placed her hand upon a page, stopping midway down. She opened her eyes and began reading from the Book of Psalms, *Trust in the Lord, and do good; so shalt thou dwell in the land, and verily thou shalt be fed. Delight thyself also in the Lord; and he shall give thee the desires of thine heart.* What a beautiful promise. The Bible was filled with God's promises.

Trust in the Lord. She stared out the open window, the land stretched as far as she could see. She did trust in the Lord, and the land was provided. Could she be the kind of steward the Lord would have her to be? They continued to be fed and provided for. Trust.

Delight thyself in the Lord. But what *were* the desires of her heart? Jo's smiling face danced before her mind's eye. She smiled. Suddenly, an image of Luke appeared in her mind, but behind him were dark and soulful eyes shimmering in the distance as though seen through a fog. She frowned. What about Luke?

A hawk screeched in the night, breaking the spell. The air flowing through the window was turning colder. She rose and closed the window, turned out the lamp, and went to bed secure and peaceful in God's loving promises.

✳ ✳

Luke unpacked his few belongings from the saddlebags. He put the farriers tools in the chest at the foot of the bunk he had chosen. There were hooks on the wall above the bed to hang his clothes and his chaps. The straw filled tick already lay soft and inviting on the rough frame, and he covered it with a muslin sheet and dark blanket. He threw a couple of books on the bed The other cowboys he had worked with weren't much for reading, but he still enjoyed good literature, and he continued to carry a book or two, trading them for new ones whenever he could. Not everything his father had tried to instill in him had gone to waste, he thought ruefully.

Picking up his razor and a few other personal items, he carried them to the washstand. Jonathan had filled the pitcher with fresh water before leaving for the night. Opening the door on the front of the cabinet he reached in to stash his belongings. As he dropped the things, his hand bumped an object already there. Curious, he pulled out a book. He turned it over and realized that it was a Bible. The word was intricately scrolled across the front in fading gold leaf. The leather cover was worn, and the pages fragile from use.

In his mind's eye he saw his father standing in the pulpit reading from just such a Bible every Sunday. The stern commands and fiery words casting fear through Luke's young mind. Later, when Pa had sent him to seminary, the Bible had taken on different proportions and meanings. He had dutifully studied the Word, finding in it an interesting history, and useful narratives, but he never seemed to find the deep, abiding love that others found there.

Rising, he glanced out the window into the quiet moonlit night. Something caught his eye, looking again, he realized that a light was on in the main house, and a figure stood silhouetted at the window. He watched as she opened the pane and the breeze caught her white gown, blowing it against her. Loose brown hair blew softly across her face obscuring her features. He watched in stunned silence for a moment before averting his eyes and closing the curtains.

Who was this woman he now worked for? He knew only what Martha had told him. Kate Shaughnessey was widowed a few months back, running the small ranch by herself, she needed steady help, and hadn't been able to find any. Martha said that Kate was too proud to ask for much, and she had alluded to some trouble brewing with one of the other ranchers in the area.

The woman he met in Fallis today was obviously strong and independent, not something he generally preferred in women, but it seemed to suit her. He sensed an undercurrent of emotion that was just below the surface, something she kept a tight rein on. After she had returned from her meeting with Johnson, she had grown hard and cold. Was Matt Johnson the man causing trouble?

Tossing the Bible onto the bed with his other books, he vowed to see this woman and her family safely through the fall market before he would leave Providence. He heard a hawk calling in the night, a haunting sound as though its heart were breaking.

CHAPTER VII

The sun was already peeking through the lace curtains when Kate's eyes opened. "Oh no!" she cried jumping out of bed. She could hear Nana banging pots around in the kitchen. "How did it get so late?" She must have slept half way through morning chores. Pulling on a pair of trousers and a clean cotton shirt, she tucked it in quickly and cinched up the leather belt. She stuffed her feet into wool socks and a pair of old leather boots that had seen far better days, but were oh so comfortable, and dashed out to the kitchen.

"Oh, Mrs. Insley, I'm so sorry. I didn't have the fire going or anything," she apologized.

"No mind. I've done it myself. Hurry off and get those horses tended to before the men have to do it all themselves."

"I'll hurry!" Kate replied slapping the old felt hat down over her loose curls and grabbing her jacket from the peg by the door.

She reached the barn in time to see Jake beginning to pitch the hay into Raven's manger. A stab of guilt shot through her. "Jake, I'm sorry I'm late. Give me that. I'll finish the horses."

"You're taking to sleeping in as late as my Jon!" he grinned. "No need to worry. Between Luke and I we got 'bout all the chores done already."

Luke! In her rush this morning, she had nearly forgotten about the new hand. Looking around the dim barn, she saw him watching one of her mares in the foaling stall. Pitching the hay to Raven and giving him a quick pat, she walked over to join him.

Jake was busy hitching his mares to the plow, while Jonathan milked the jersey cows they kept for milk and butter. The rest of the morning's chores had already been finished, leaving Kate feeling quite guilty and almost useless for a moment.

✷✷✷✷✷✷✷✷✷✷✷✷✷✷✷✷✷✷✷✷✷✷✷✷✷✷✷✷✷✷✷✷✷

Luke did a double take as Kate entered the barn. It was the first time he had ever seen a woman dressed in men's clothing. He had to admit, with those curls floating around her face beneath that old dusty hat, she was actually quite charming, but it would sure take some getting used to.

"She's due next week, but since she started bagging early, I brought her up last Friday." Kate offered quietly coming to stand next to him.

"Has she waxed?"

"Haven't checked yet today, but she hadn't yesterday morning." Kate answered, opening the stall gate. She ran a hand down the dun mare's golden side. Feeling the life within moving lazily, she smiled a radiant smile. Luke realized that it was the first time he had seen her smile. It lit up her entire face, giving her a simple childlike glow that was hard to resist. He found himself wondering if she would ever smile at him in just that way.

Reaching lower, she felt the mare's udder. It was full and swollen, dripping a creamy looking milk. "No wax, but she's milking, should be soon."

"Do you want me to keep an eye on her tonight?"

Kate looked up as though she had forgotten that he was standing there. "You don't mind?"

"Naw, I'm right next door," he laughed.

"You've foaled out a mare?"

"A few."

"Well, it would set my mind to ease some," she agreed. "I've been a little worried about how big she is this time. I can't afford to lose one."

"Has she had any problems in the past?"

"No, and this is her third foal, but I still worry. Next to Gypsy, this is my favorite mare." She stroked the horse's nose as she spoke, and the mare placed her head on Kate's shoulder. Sighing, she opened the stall door and stepped out, closing it behind her.

Luke watched her with appreciation. She definitely had a way with horses, and spoke as naturally about them as any man. She didn't blush or use euphemisms when discussing the intimate details of foaling, as most women would.

"I thought we could saddle up and I'll take you on a tour of the ranch after breakfast. That way we can discuss your duties, and you'll have a chance to see some of the operation here." Kate said as she walked to the tack room.

"Sounds good."

Grabbing a leather halter and lead, Kate headed out to the pasture that served the remuda. Luke noticed about a dozen horses here, bays, duns, sorrels and even a couple of buckskins and one palomino. All were sleek, well muscled horses. He watched as Kate whistled and a sorrel mare lifted her head from the grass. Seeing her mistress, she trotted over to the pasture fence. Kate slipped through the fence, haltered the mare and led her through the gate into the barn.

"This is Gypsy, the one I use most. She's a good old girl." Grabbing a saddle and blanket from the tack room, Kate swung them up over the horse's back in a fluid motion, settling the blanket first and cinching the saddle up quickly. "Most of the older horses in the remuda are broke to ride. We use the mares as well as the geldings. A mare has to prove their worth around here before we use them as breeding stock. Mares with foals or about to foal are out in the far pasture. The two year olds in there aren't broke yet, but you can ride any of the older ones that you want."

"Think I'll stick with Rio for now until I've had a chance to look them over."

"Suit yourself," she said busy with her own horse. Finding a pick from the wooden box hung on the wall, she bent to lift the mare's front hoof.

"Here, let me do that for you."

"Thank you, no! I'm perfectly capable of doing this for myself," Kate snapped.

"Sorry." Luke scowled at the rebuff and strode off to find Rio and ready him for the day's work.

✴✴✴✴✴✴✴✴✴✴✴✴✴✴✴✴✴✴✴✴✴✴✴✴✴✴✴✴✴✴✴✴✴

Kate set the mare's hoof down. Why had she been so rude? He was only offering to help. She watched him leave the barn. Sighing, she finished her chores, and joined the men on the way to the house for breakfast.

Jo and Mrs. Insley had a grand breakfast laid out for the hungry men and Kate. The plank table groaned beneath the weight of platters heaped with scrambled eggs, sausage links, biscuits, butter, jams and even pancakes. Jake let out a low whistle, and Jon's lower jaw dropped in surprise. Nana didn't usually set out such a fare every morning. Jo was dressed and sitting at the table waiting when they entered.

"Good morning, Mr. Josey, look what we made for you!" Jo glowed.

"My, my, it does look delicious!" Luke's eyes twinkled merrily at the little girl.

"Yes, doesn't it?" Kate asked raising her eyebrows at Nana.

"Man should have a good start here, and he looks a might thin to me," was the acerbic response.

"Well, what are we waiting for?" asked Jon as he took his seat.

"You sit here by me, Mr. Josey," Jo bubbled indicating the seat next to her on the bench.

They all took their places, and joined hands for the blessing. Jo reached for Luke's hand, and he took it, reaching for Kate's across the table. She placed her small hand in his tentatively, and gave him a quick smile as she began the blessing. "Dear Lord, we thank you for what we are about to receive, and Lord we offer our thanks for Your bringing this good man into our lives. We ask that You bless and protect each and every one of us as we face the day ahead, and ask that You will bring us together again safely this evening. Lord, forgive us of our sins, and keep us in the center of Your will. Lead us to do those things that you would have us to do. It is in the name of Jesus we pray, Amen."

"Amen," was murmured around the table, though Kate noticed that Luke did not join in.

Plates were passed and piled with food, steaming mugs of coffee were poured. Smokey and Candy dashed in the open door looking for any scraps that may have fallen, and the conversation was lively. Kate surveyed the scene with a sense of calm assurance that she hadn't felt in months.

"How many head are you running out here?" Luke asked amid the commotion, startling Kate from her reverie.

"I'm sorry?"

"How many head are you running? I figure now's as good a time as any to figure out where I'm going to be needed."

"Well, It's a pretty small operation. I've got about eighty-five head of cows and about seventy of those have calves at their side now. Another eight or so should calve here any time." She creased her brow, for a moment with a distant look on her face. "I think there's about fifty head of three year old steers coming ready for market this fall, and another eighty yearlings and two year olds."

"Have you branded the calves yet?"

"No," Kate sighed. Branding was a time she was dreading. "I'm waiting for the rest to calve, and I'm just not sure that I'm up to it alone. Will and the hands always saw to the largest part of that. I suppose I've just been putting off the inevitable."

"Well, I can see one of the first things will be an accurate count, branding and castrating the calves." Luke said in a matter of fact tone.

"That takes an entire crew!" Kate cried.

"It has to be done. You know that as well as I do." Luke took a sip of the coffee, and thought for a minute. "What about Lars Jansen and some of the men from Fallis?"

"What about them?"

"What if we planned a day, asked them all to come help out. You and Mrs. Insley could cook up a meal, their wives could come, make a day of it. I'll bet even Jon here could mount up and help out."

"Oh, you bet I could!" Jon agreed.

"And I don't see no reason we couldn't butcher one of them steers and have us a real shindig," Nana supplied.

"Even have us a mess of calf fries!" Jake threw in.

"Oh, yes, mama, lets! It would be such fun!" Jo clapped her hands bouncing up and down.

"I don't know…"

"You were planning on doing it all yourself?" Luke asked, raising a brow.

"It's such an awful lot to ask of folks."

"Would you do it for one of your neighbors?"

"Well, yes, of course, but…"

"Then it's settled. You must let them do the same for you."

Kate looked at each of the expectant faces around her table. They waited in hushed anticipation. Even Nana seemed to be in favor of his plan.

"Well, I suppose…"

"Oh, yes!" Jo jumped up and threw her arms around Luke's neck in an unexpected hug, taking him off guard. He tensed for a moment before relaxing and giving her a quick squeeze in return. Jo ran around the table to her mother and gave her in an equally enthusiastic embrace. Letting go she grabbed her puppy, "We're going to have a party, Candy!"

Kate smiled and shook her head. There was more life in her family this morning than there had been in a long time.

✴✴✴✴✴✴✴✴✴✴✴✴✴✴✴✴✴✴✴✴✴✴✴✴✴✴✴✴✴✴

The horses ambled along in the crisp morning air. Kate was glad she had thought to bring a warm coat. She would have no need of it soon, but for now the warmth was comforting as a chill breeze blew across the plain. "The Angus herd is just to the east of that fence line. I think you saw some of them on our way in yesterday."

"Yes, big black cattle, no horns, kind of ugly, aren't they?"

Kate Laughed a little at the description. It was exactly what she had thought when Will brought the first ones home. "Yes, I suppose they are, but they sure fatten quick, they're strong enough, but they don't hold up as well over long drives. Since the rail line came into Guthrie, though, we don't have the long haul anymore, and I can get more pounds to market in a shorter period of time."

Kate paused a moment remembering the herds coming through the first years that they had settled here. She still remembered one of the Texas drives coming up over their place that first fall. It had looked like a sea of cattle, brown waves undulating across the prairie. The waddies had stopped for an evening with them, recounting tales of stampedes and how this was really a small drive compared to days gone by. Kate had wondered exactly how many more cattle could be moved, thinking of the vastness of the herd around them. The trail boss told her that they were driving about a thousand head all the way to Montana Territory, but just a few years before they had moved three times that many.

Now the settlers, farmers and smaller ranchers had strung their fences across that great land, the herds no longer moved freely from one range to the next. This part of the country was lush with grass, and managed properly, one could run a small herd profitably on a section or two.

"The herd on the west side is more typical of the area. There's a mix of longhorn, some free range cows, and those have been bred back to the Angus to give us a nice mixed breed that matures well and is surprisingly hardy in the bad years." Bringing her mare to a stop, Kate looked back at Luke. He sat hunched in the saddle not saying much. It was only then she realized that he wore no jacket, and was fighting the bitter cold wind.

"Forget your coat?"

"Sort of mislaid it, I guess."

"You'll need something."

"It'll warm up quick. Should be down right hot by this afternoon."

"Maybe, but this is springtime in Oklahoma Territory. It may be blazing hot today and bring on a blizzard tomorrow!"

"Don't I know it," he responded miserably.

Her eyes narrowed and she shook her head as they continued on to inspect the cattle.

The herd was just visible as they topped the last rise. The vista spread before them was awash in the early light of a fresh spring morning. Dew sparkled over the grass, and cows grazed contentedly along the banks of a small stream. The trees along the creek fluttered new green leaves in the breeze while the water rushed along its course.

"Look over there," Kate pointed toward a large black cow, apart from the rest of the herd. A small wet calf struggled mightily in its first valiant efforts to stand.

"Now isn't that a sight," Luke smiled.

They rode on toward the herd of cows and gamboling calves. One bold little heifer, danced up to Rio who snorted sending the calf into a spinning turn, bawling frantically to find its mama. Kate laughed, delighted to be alive on such a beautiful morning. She could even feel some of the burdens being lifted away by having help here at last. *Thank you, Lord, for this life, this beauty, this land,* she prayed silently watching the herd and soaking in the sheer exhilaration of the day.

"I count forty-seven cows, forty calves here, looks like another fifty head of steers," Luke said, breaking into her thoughts.

"That sounds about right. I know I should have better records, but it has been so hard keeping an accurate log of them all without being able to ride the herd every day," Kate sighed.

"You have catch pens set up down near the ranch, don't you?" Luke asked.

"Yes, for branding and sorting. They need some work, but they'll do."

"Can we get Jake and Jonathan to help us round up the herds and drive them in?"

"Jonathan will jump at the opportunity, but it's been a while since Jake has been in the saddle, I don't know."

"Well, I'd like to have at least four, but I'm sure that the three of us can get them in for the branding." He paused watching the herd, and calculating the distance and the gates between here and the main ranch. "You say the other herd is about the same size?"

"Maybe just a bit larger, and they're the mixed breeds. They'll be a bit rangier than this lot," she smiled looking over the docile cows.

"It'd be nice if we could get them all in and done at one time, make for a long day, but we could probably do it if we had two or three good ropers."

"A *very* long day," she agreed. "Come on, I'll show you the fence lines between here and the east side of the section. I haven't had a chance to ride them in a while. It'll be a good time to check them over." Kate turned the mare and headed down toward the creek, wading across at a wide shallow spot. The icy water splashed up over her boots chilling her legs, and reminding her just how early in the year it still was. Luke followed closely, and she hoped he wasn't too cold without a jacket.

As they approached the fence line, Kate noticed a broken spot near a small grove of pecan trees. The fertile bottom lands in this area were rife with pecans, and Kate loved the rich nutty flavor they imparted to Nana's fall baking. Frowning, she rode to the spot where the barbed wire hung limply between two wooden posts.

"What in the world…" Kate stopped. For one strand to be broken was one thing, but all four were neatly cut and lay apart here. Rage built in her chest as she realized that this was a deliberate cutting of her fence.

"Rustlers?" Luke asked, riding up beside her.

"I don't know. Looks like it," she answered between clenched teeth. Dismounting, she walked over and picked up the ends of the wire. They were neatly cut, and she assumed it had been done recently as there was no evidence of any cattle having passed through the break. "There's a bundle of wire and fencing pliers in my pack," she called back to Luke. "We can get this fixed, but I want to have a look around."

Tying the horses to a nearby tree, Luke retrieved the tools and they set to work splicing, stretching and tightening the broken wires. It took them the better part of the next hour, and by the time they finished the last strand, Kate had removed her heavy jacket and was beginning to feel the heat of the day coming on. She replaced the pliers and what was left of the wire in her saddle bags, tied her coat on behind the cantle, and took out her canteen, taking a long swallow of the refreshing cool water. She wiped off the mouth of the jug and handed it to Luke.

"Thanks," he said drinking his fill, and handing it back.

"I'm going out beyond that hill there, take a look, see if there's anything unusual." Kate said indicating a small rise some distance away.

Luke nodded. They left on foot leaving the horses tied in the shade of a pecan tree. Stooping to ease herself between the strands of barbed wire, Kate realized that they were being held apart. Looking up, she was met by smiling green eyes as Luke lifted the fence wires for her. The open pasture was easy to walk over, and they covered the distance quickly. On the far side of the rise, the remains of a small campfire still smoldered. The grass was trampled and grazed short in a small area where one or two horses had obviously been staked out. Luke nodded to the east. Following his gaze, Kate could see the indications of a trail still faintly visible in the tall grass.

"We must have surprised them before they had the opportunity to get any cows out through the fence," Kate said.

"Problem is, they'll be back." Luke observed, squatting by the cooling embers.

"What's that?" Kate asked seeing him pick up a small slip of paper from the dust near the fire.

"Looks like a receipt of some kind. It's been burned, there's not much left of it. Here."

Kate studied the charred remains. There was a partial amount visible, and part of a name on the pay to line, Richard We…The detail that caught her attention, though, was a short horizontal bar over the letter J. Bar J. Matt Johnson's brand. Had one of his men left and turned to rustling? It was easy to imagine. He would hire just about any hand that wandered in looking for work. More than one of his men had been in scrapes with the law.

"What is it?" Luke asked as she creased her brow in thought.

"The brand on here, it belongs to Johnson," she mused.

"Do you think he has something to do with this?" His tone was sharp.

"Oh, no, surely not. I would think one of his men took off, turned to rustling, probably. Either way, I don't like the feel of it."

"Me neither. Let's go."

Slipping the bit of paper into a pocket she followed him back to the horses.

✳ ✳

The sun was high and beginning to slip toward the west when they came into sight of the western herd. The cows here were leaner and hardier than the Angus. This was a breed that Luke was familiar with, cattle that could withstand the droughts of Texas, long droves across barren plains and bitter weather, yet still calve easily in the spring and be fit and better than ever. The horns of these beasts swept out in graceful curves, some more than five feet across. Their hides were every color of nature, reds and browns, black, mottled here and there with white. Calves played and butted one another in mock battle while the cows and steers grazed, though ever alert, ready to bolt at the merest suggestion of trouble. The mixed blood cattle among this herd were beefier and easy to spot, mostly black and some without horns. Kate had called it polled. She said that they were born that way naturally.

This was an interesting ranch run by a brilliant but inscrutable woman. Luke was finding it more of an adventure than he had ever imagined. When Martha Jansen had first approached him about Kate Shaughnessey, he was unsure of taking on a job with a woman. Too many trials, too much trouble. He was through with women in his life for now, he needed time to get away. He had ridden into Fallis hoping to find work with one of the larger ranches. He gravitated naturally to the livery and then the general mercantile avoiding the saloons. He was not a drinking man, and had no use for those who were, just muddled your head and led to strife. He'd seen enough of that with some of the Texas outfits he'd been with.

Martha offered him odd jobs in exchange for meals for a few days, and it had seemed to be a good way to get a feel for the area and find a regular job for a while. Some cowboys had drifted in and out during those few days, and Luke had not liked the men he'd seen. About the time he had decided to ride on, Martha approached him about Kate. Something in him wanted to deny her and simply leave, but when he heard about the death of her husband, a small daughter, the aging couple and trouble with a neighboring rancher, the part of him that just couldn't stand injustice had overwhelmed him and he agreed to at least meet her.

Shaking his head, he wondered again what providence was at work here, bringing him to a land that he had never seen, but felt more like home than any place he had ever been, and to a family that welcomed him with open hearts, treating him more like a long-lost brother than a hired hand.

"These are probably more what you're used to!" Kate laughed pulling him back to the present. "As fat and docile as the Angus are, these will always be my favorites."

"These critters own their own destiny, don't they?" Luke agreed.

She looked at him then, "I never thought about it just that way before, but yes, in a sense, I guess they do." They watched the herd in silence for a moment, enjoying the beauty of the mighty beasts. "For every beast of the forest is mine, and the cattle upon a thousand hills." Kate whispered.

"What was that?"

"Oh, just remembering a Psalm Will used to quote whenever he got to thinking too much about 'his' cattle," Kate smiled. "Are you hungry? Mrs. Insley packed us some lunch."

"Starved, especially if it's some more of her good cooking."

"I won't tell her you said that, she'd cook everything I have on the place and try to force feed you!" Kate said stepping down from her saddle.

Luke laughed openly, and joined her in the shade of a lone oak tree, where they enjoyed a lunch of bread, sausage, dried fruit and pickles. They spoke easily of the ranch, the cattle and what work needed to be accomplished first. It was decided that Kate would make a trip to Fallis later in the month for supplies and to enlist the help of the Jansens and a few others for the spring branding while Luke would take on the bulk of the responsibility for the herds, fences and repairs at the ranch itself. The issue of the cut fence and rustlers was gone over and over with no workable solution forthcoming. Kate worried that they would be back, but who was there to watch over four miles of fences? For now there was no resolution and Luke knew it left Kate with a feeling of unease as they packed up and headed back to the ranch.

✶✶✶✶✶✶✶✶✶✶✶✶✶✶✶✶✶✶✶✶✶✶✶✶✶✶✶✶✶✶

Kate sat once again before her ranch journal, recording the events of the last few days by the flickering light of her oil lamp. The charred scrap of paper lay on the desk. She slipped it into the journal for safekeeping.

Jo was tucked in bed, and the Insleys had long since retired to their own home. Dinner had been a boisterous affair, alive with plans for the upcoming branding. Jake reported that the spring planting would be finished the next day and Jon would then be free to help Luke with the herds. Jon was ecstatic at the prospect, and Kate planned to surprise him with a new pony in honor of the occasion.

Glancing out the window, Kate could see a light moving within the distant barn. Luke must be checking the mare in the foaling stall. She smiled thinking of the little dun mare and the colt that would soon be joining her.

It was cold again this evening, and Kate was thankful for the glowing fire that warmed the small house. She remembered the chill morning air and Luke without a jacket. Laying aside her pen, she walked over to the trunk in the corner. Opening the heavy lid, she rummaged down past the extra quilts and wool blankets, until she found what she was searching for. She lifted out an oiled canvas coat with a warm woolen lining. Running her fingers over the rough surface of the material she felt tears begin to trickle down her cheeks. She held the coat to her face and breathed deeply. Yes, Will's musky scent still permeated the fabric. She held it close, letting the tears flow freely as she enveloped herself in the memories that his smell aroused.

"Oh, Will, I miss you so much. You always did the right thing, didn't you? Even when it was the hardest thing in the world for you to do." The raw wound on her soul was starting to heal. She could feel the salve being applied to that spiritual hurt just as surely as she had felt the healing ointments that Nana had applied to the burned flesh of her arms. Kate sighed deeply. Taking the coat and shaking it out, she laid it over her arm and started to the barn.

The large door was open slightly, and Kate could see Luke standing relaxed before the stall, his arms resting lightly on the top of the gate. The mare was quiet, dozing in the warmth of the barn. Holding the jacket against her breast and catching a hint of Will's familiar scent one last time, she steeled herself for the task ahead, and entered the barn.

✳ ✳

"How is she doing?"

Luke looked up, startled by her silent approach. "Fine. She was a bit restless earlier, but she's quiet now."

"Good." She hesitated, then started in a rush, "Look, I found an old coat I had laying around. I want you to take it. If there's one thing I don't need, it's for you to catch your death of cold. I hired you to work, not lay around here sick."

He began to protest, until he saw the look in her eyes. This was some sort of sacrifice she was making, and he needed to honor it. "Thank you," he said taking the coat.

"It's nothing really. I just can't afford to have you out of commission," she replied brusquely, as she turned to the mare in the stall.

There was a gulf of silence between them. Kate continued to study the mare, though Luke could see that her thoughts were far from the impending birth.

"What was he like, Kate?" Luke asked softly.

For a long moment there was no answer. He saw her shoulders tense, and a single tear slip silently down her cheek, glittering in the lantern's glow. Just as he was turning to go, sure that he made a terrible mistake, she spoke.

"He was my friend." She spoke quietly and with great reverence. "And I miss him."

Luke said nothing, though his heart ached for her loss, and for himself, who had never known that kind of love.

✳ ✳

The mare grew restless and began pawing the floor in agitation. Luke opened the gate, stepping into the large stall, while Kate went to the tack room for gunny sacks. By the time she returned, the mare was laying down, and two small feet were just visible emerging from the birth canal. The birth was an easy one and soon a dark wet foal lay in the straw beside his mother. Kate rubbed the rough burlap over his small body to help dry him and keep him from catching a chill while Luke tended to the mare.

Within moments the large healthy colt began the first efforts to stand. Kate laughed at his antics and was filled with joy as he found a wobbly footing. His dam stood and sniffed him, encouraging him to nurse. It wasn't long before he found the full udder and began noisily suckling the warm rich milk.

Luke and Kate stood together outside the stall watching the content-ted pair within. "I believe he is going to be a grullo, if I'm not mis-taken." Luke commented.

Grullos were highly sought after horses. Many believed that they were stronger or carried some special power, possibly because it was such a rare color. The little colt was a dark, smokey gray with a prominent black stripe running down the length of his spine; another dark stripe ran across his shoulders and there was black barring on his legs. The coat was fuzzy and soft, and Kate knew that the color could change as the colt grew, but she hoped Luke was right and that this was truly a grullo.

"I hope so. I had heard of them before, but I've never actually seen one. Isn't it beautiful?" She asked with wonder in her voice.

"Yes," Luke replied softly, though his eyes weren't on the colt.

Chapter VIII

The days of spring slipped by in a flurry of activity at Providence. Luke and Jon rode out each morning to tend the cattle, checking as they went for any further signs of rustlers. No more fences had been found cut and all the cattle remained accounted for, to Kate's great relief. Their afternoons were spent on repairs and building. Slowly the fences of the corrals and catch pens began to look like new.

Jake watched over his fields like a mother hen, as the new sprouts emerged from the warming soil, growing and flourishing in the sun and the abundant spring rains that finally came. He plowed up the larger garden patch close to the house for the women to begin the spring vegetables.

Kate and Jo planted row after row of snap beans, carrots, peas, tomatoes, peppers, onions, and many other favorites. The strawberries in beds along the front of the house had already shed their pretty white blossoms and the green berries that appeared in their place were growing plump and shading to red. Wild plum and choke cherry trees were laden with new buds, promising a fruitful harvest later in the summer. Kate watched with thanksgiving in her heart as her family blossomed into life in imitation of the world around them. It was as if a shroud had been lifted, and the darkness surrounding them in the months since Will's death was pierced by the brilliant light of life.

Kate rose early on the morning of the trip to Fallis. She dressed in a blue cotton skirt and fitted white shirtwaist. Taking a warm shawl from the peg near the fireplace she hurried out into the early morning mist before anyone else awoke. Walking along a seldom used path from the house, she came at last to a willow tree growing alone in a secluded area. Beneath the tree was a small picket fence surrounding two graves, each covered in new grass and adorned by a simple cross. Kneeling in quiet solitude, she prayed, lifting her face to the heavens, a prayer of thanks and praise. Turning her eyes back to the graves, she still felt the burden of grief, but it had changed. It was no longer a bitter gall, but now a sweet aching memory of her husband and their baby son, who had died in infancy two years earlier.

"Oh, Will, there's so much I want to tell you, to share with you. Jo is growing so big, and more beautiful every day. She still looks just like you. How I wish you could see her grow and change. Are you there with our son? How is he? I'll bet he's big and strong and handsome. I'm so glad he has his daddy now. I never thought of it that way before, but Caleb isn't alone anymore, is he? I miss you both so much, but I'm glad you have each other." Her tears flowed freely now, but they were tears that brought with them healing and peace.

She rose from the peaceful garden and felt the burgeoning of joy beginning anew in her soul as she headed down the path toward home. The early morning sun was playing hide and seek behind a bank of large grey and white clouds that held the promise of rains to come. Kate hoped that the rain would hold off until after they returned tonight. The air was already tinged with warmth, and it promised to be a very hot day.

Jake had her buggy hitched up to one of his mares by the time she returned. Only she and Jo would be making the trip today, and the buggy made better time, while still having enough room for the supplies she would purchase. Jo had climbed the garden fence and was swinging on the gate. Her brilliant white apron covered a worn calico dress, and she wore a simple sunbonnet tied tightly over her red curls.

She was altogether charming. Kate scooped her up off the gate and covered her face with kisses while tickling her ribs.

Jo squealed with delight, squirming to get away from her mother's tickles, and they both ended up in heap on the grass. Kate lay on her back laughing and gasping for breath. Seizing the opportunity, Jo pounced and began tickling her mother until they were both exhausted and lay together quietly, eyes closed, giggling sporadically.

Opening her eyes at last, Kate found herself staring up into Luke's handsome, smiling face, his green eyes alight with suppressed mirth as he stood watching them. She could feel the heat rise in her cheeks as she sat up, pulling her shawl around her and straightening her disarrayed skirts.

"Oh, hello, Mr. Josey!" Jo piped up beside her. "Have you come for breakfast? Nana made oatmeal, and I got the milk from the spring house all by myself. I found enough red strawberries for us each to have two on our cereal. Do you like strawberries? Momma says they taste like sunshine melting in your mouth."

"Does she now?" Luke asked, offering his hand to Kate. "I don't believe I've ever tasted sunshine before, but I am partial to fresh sweet strawberries."

She took his hand and he lifted her to her feet as though she weighed nothing. His hand was large and strong, sending sweet warmth coursing through her. Instead of releasing her, his eyes held hers as he tucked her arm beneath his and escorted both mother and daughter to breakfast.

✶ ✶

Luke watched as Kate and Jo settled themselves into the buggy for the drive to town. Kate picked up the reins, clucked once, and the mare trotted off. Jo waved goodbye, clutching her only doll tightly in one hand. They would be gone most of the day, and Luke felt an unexpected sadness at their leaving. Shaking his head, he realized that he was becoming far too attached to these people. Jo had his heart wrapped around her little finger. He found himself looking for her in the mornings, smiling at her fresh innocence as she gathered eggs in her basket, or rolled on the dew wet grass with her pup. He thought about the small unfinished doll cradle hidden beneath his bunk. It was slowly taking shape as he carved a little more each evening on it. He couldn't wait to see the look on her face when he surprised her with it. Perhaps he could enlist Mrs. Insley's help to fashion a small blanket and pillow for the cradle.

How will I ever be able to leave Providence? Luke thought with a stabbing pain of regret. He had only been hired through the fall, and was planning to leave then, head on to a larger ranch down south somewhere, hire on as an outrider. It would be better, then, if he could remove himself from these growing feelings for Jo, the Insleys, and Kate. At the thought of her name, an image of Kate rose in his mind so intense it made him shudder. He could see her face, calm and strong, but always with that undercurrent of emotion held so tightly in check, yet every so often breaking the surface of her features like ripples on a pond, sometimes bringing tears, at other times that radiant, glowing smile. Will had been a lucky man, a very fortunate man.

Jon appeared from the barn leading two horses already saddled and a third pack animal loaded with tools and other supplies. "Luke, are you ready?" he called.

"Just coming, Jon." Luke replied, striding toward the boy. They mounted up and started off.

"Where are we riding today? And why so many tools and such like on old Maude?"

"First, I want to check the west herd, then I have a bit of a surprise for you."

"Oh, what is it?"

"Patience, Jon!" Luke laughed.

They rode to the west, Jon's dog Smokey bounding ahead, until the herd was sighted grazing in a meadow far beyond their normal range.

Something must have spooked them in the night, Luke thought, *for them to have moved this far.*

"Why do you s'pose they're way over here?" Jon asked, echoing Luke's thoughts aloud.

"Hard to say. Something moved them, though, that's certain."

"Look, over there!"

Luke peered in the direction Jon indicated, at first seeing nothing out of the ordinary. Riding on a short distance, he could see Smokey worrying over something. Then he saw it, the carcass of a small calf, bloody and mangled.

Luke searched the ground in vain for any traces or signs of what attacked the poor calf. The thick grass and hard ground yielded no testimony to what had transpired.

"Wolves?" Jon asked.

"It would appear that way."

"Miss Kate sure ain't gonna like this."

"No, I don't expect she will." Luke paused, "Have you had problems with wolves before?"

"I can't rightly recall. I believe Mr. Will shot a few when they first come here. That was a long time ago, and I was jest little then, but I remember my Pa sayin' something about a big hunt. All the neighbors got together and killed 'bout forty of 'em at one time. Don't recall any trouble in recent times."

"I didn't think there were any around. Guess I better start carrying my Winchester, just in case." Luke sighed. "We'd best bury the rest of the carcass so as not to attract any other vermin."

They worked silently, digging a pit, and hauling the remains into it. When they had filled the hole, they found as many large rocks as they could to cover it further, thereby discouraging other scavengers from digging it back up.

"Nothing else we can do here for now. Let's go." Luke said dryly.

They rode back in the direction of the ranch, until Luke spotted the tree he was looking for.

"Jon, do you see that, about halfway up the trunk?"

"What is it?"

"Bee tree!"

"Honey! Let's cut it."

"No, I've got a better idea." Luke rode ahead into a small clearing he had scouted out previously. There he found an old deadfall. The tree had obviously been down for several months. "Do you know what this is?"

"No."

"It's a black gum tree. If we cut through, you'll see it's hollow."

"So what?"

"We can set up a bee gum."

"What's that?"

Luke though for a minute. "Kind of like farming your own honey, you might say."

"Really? You mean have honey anytime we want it?" Jon's sweet tooth fairly ached at this idea.

"Pretty much. If we do it right, you can rob it a couple times a year and get near fifteen pounds of honey at a time." Luke unloaded a cross-cut saw from the pack on Maude, and he and Jon set to work on the trunk. They soon had a section of hollow trunk about thirty inches long. "Now we need a couple of sticks, nice and straight, about as big around as my finger, and maybe two feet long. You find those while I smooth the inside out."

"Yes, sir."

By the time Jon returned with the sticks, Luke had finished smoothing the inside of their new beegum and had bored four holes opposite one another about half way down. Taking the sticks, he fitted them into the holes, through the trunk at right angles to each other. "This is where the bees will hang the brood combs. They'll keep the honey comb up top where we'll be able to get it out, nice and clean. See, we'll take this, fix it over the top, " Luke pulled a plank from the pack and fit it over the top of the gum, "and they'll hang the honeycomb right from here."

"You knew we was going to do this today?" Jon said with awe as Luke seemed to have everything they needed packed in those bags.

"I spotted that tree a few days ago, been thinking on it." Luke grinned.

"How're we gonna get the bees in there?"

"That's the tricky part," Luke agreed. "See, I've cut a notch here at the bottom. That's their door, you might say."

Jonathan nodded, "But what's gonna make 'em come in here?"

"We're going to put them in there."

Jon's eyes grew very round.

They set to work, first building a smokey fire, then felling the bee tree. Using some old rags, they began smoking the hive to pacify the bees, though they both suffered a few stings. As they cut into the trunk near the opening, they found the brood combs. Luke stood, victoriously holding the queen carefully in his hand. Other bees began to swarm and light on his hand, and he carried them reverently to the new bee gum, shaking them off on the base in front of the notch. The queen and several attendant bees immediately entered their new home. Luke and Jon wore identical smiles of triumph as they placed a covering over the gum to keep off rain and other predators, and carefully lifted it up onto a platform resting in the remains of the fallen black gum.

"We'll check it once a week or so, and in a couple of months we ought to have our first batch of honey. For now, go find that tin in the pack. We'll take Nana a heap of comb and honey from the old hive."

"I brung the biscuits from our lunch, too," Jon said returning to the fallen tree where Luke was busy widening the opening to find the clean honeycomb.

"Well now, biscuits and honey sound mighty fine right about now, don't they?"

They scooped the golden liquid and bits of broken comb into the clean tin until it was nearly overflowing. Licking their fingers of the sticky treat they dipped their biscuits right into the hive and bit into the sweet satisfying flavor.

✶✶✶✶✶✶✶✶✶✶✶✶✶✶✶✶✶✶✶✶✶✶✶✶✶✶✶✶✶✶✶✶

The buggy bounced along the rutted paths on the way to Fallis. The birds were chirruping in the trees, but the gray, lowering clouds obscured the sun. Jo chatted incessantly commenting on everything she could see.

"Jo, what do you think of Mr. Josey?" Kate asked taking advantage of one of Jo's infrequent lulls in her nonstop dialog.

"What do you mean? He's wonderful, of course!"

"Well, I mean—I don't know what I mean. Forget I asked!" Kate laughed.

Jo shrugged. Adults could be very strange sometimes. "Are we going to eat lunch with Mrs. Jansen today?"

"I would think so. I have some shopping to do there, and she usually invites us, doesn't she?"

"Yes, and she always has candy for me. Do you think she's ever going to have a baby? I think she really wants one. Mrs. Hall is going to have another baby. Kathy told me so." Jo paused to take a breath and clutched her little doll close to her breast. "I miss our baby sometimes."

Kate's heart skipped a beat. Jo seldom spoke of Caleb. Sometimes she wondered if her daughter had any memories of his short life with them. "He's with God now, sweetheart."

"I know, and daddy, too," Jo spoke slowly, but she did not cry.

"Do you think about them often?"

"Um-hmm. Do you think God has a big rocking chair, like the one you used to rock the baby in?"

"I don't know, but I'll bet he does." Kate looked over at Jo, who was staring straight ahead. "Did you know that Caleb would have been three years old today?"

"Really? Then today would have been daddy's birthday, too!"

"That's right," Kate said. Will had been proud to share his birthday with his son, and he had been so brokenhearted when the baby died mysteriously only a month later. They had cried and clung to one another, until they were able to lay their son and their grief to rest in God's peace. The following year's birthday had been a day of quiet celebration, not only of birth, but of the peace God had given them, and the sure knowledge that their son was in His care.

Her early morning visit to the small graveyard had been her only plans to celebrate this year, the first one since Will's death, but now that it was out in the open, her grief given over to her Heavenly Father, she felt like sharing her joy, "What do you say we have cake and ice cream at the Hotel today, kind of our own little birthday party?"

"Oh, yes, Mama!" Jo clapped her hands together in delight. "Daddy would have liked that. I'm going to have chocolate cake, that was his favorite. Do you think they would put a candle on it if I asked them?"

"I'm sure they will."

"Look, I can see the town, we're almost there!"

A few minutes later, they were pulling up in front of the mercantile. Jo jumped down, and dashed inside while Kate made sure the mare was tied securely to the hitching rail. Reaching into the back of the buggy, she pulled out the baskets of eggs and jars of preserves that Nana had sent. Entering the store, she found Jo sitting on the counter engrossed in conversation with Martha while Lars was busy stocking shelves behind them.

"Well, don't you two look mighty cozy!"

"Kate, it's so good to see you," Martha said, coming around the end of the counter to embrace her friend.

"You, too." Kate smiled. "Business first!"

"All right, whatever you say."

"First, I have four dozen large brown eggs, I hope you can use them, and there are six pints of blackberry jam, and six of strawberry." She unpacked the glass canning jars from one basket, and opened the lid on the basket of eggs for Martha to inspect them.

"Hmmm, Nana's preserves always sell quickly. I can give you fifteen cents apiece for the jams, and fifty cents for the eggs."

"Great. Put it to my account," Kate agreed, closing the basket. Turning to her daughter, she said, "Jo, come over here. I want you to try on these shoes."

"New shoes?"

"Yes, it's about time you had some that fit for a change."

Jo tried on shoes until they found a pair that suited them both, shiny tan leather, high button shoes that were just large enough to offer growing room, but still comfortable for now. Jo preferred the white ones, but Kate adamantly refused, choosing practical black ones instead, until they finally compromised on the tan. Placing the shoes on the front counter, they turned next to the numerous bolts of calicos and ginghams, flannels and woolens that lined the far side of the store. Kate fingered a beautiful deep blue satin, imagining the way it would feel and drape if she were to make it up into a dress. Sighing, she selected four bolts of practical calicos in shades of blues, yellows and greens and a bolt of white muslin.

Looking around for Jo, she found her near a small display featuring a china doll and tea party dishes. Her heart ached for the little girl, but there was just no way that she could afford something like that right now. If everything went well, perhaps she could have enough set aside to get something special for Jo's birthday in October.

"Jo, are you ready?"

"Yes, momma. Aren't they pretty?"

"They're beautiful."

Jo placed her small hand in her mother's and they walked to the counter to pay for their purchases, but Kate couldn't help noticing Jo's gaze returning to the display.

"I need two dress lengths of the yellow and one each of the others, Martha."

"Are you going to be doing some sewing?"

"Between Nana and I, we manage to get it done," Kate laughed. Her sewing skills were not her strong suit, and Martha knew it. "How much will I owe you after you take off for the things I brought?"

"Let's see, four dollars and seventy-five cents."

Kate quickly calculated what she had brought, saving out enough to give Jo the promised treat at the hotel. "In that case, give me three mens shirts, and a small shirtwaist, Nana's size." Jo had wandered over to the candy display. "And how much is that tea set and doll?" Kate asked in a hushed whisper.

"That would be five dollars and fifty cents."

Kate's heart sank. It was far too much, with everything they needed, that little luxury would have to wait. "Maybe this fall."

"Okay." Martha nodded.

Their purchases wrapped and stowed safely in the buggy, the two women and Jo went to Martha's house for an early lunch, leaving Lars in charge of the store.

✳ ✳

Martha's kitchen was light and airy. Delicate lace curtains hung in the many windows. The table was polished white ash, as were the chairs. Lunch was served on beautiful fine china, hand painted with a blue willow pattern, matching pieces lined the shelves along the wall. The women savored small cucumber sandwiches on thinly sliced bread spread with fresh butter, and sipped honey sweetened sassafras tea. After lunch, Jo found the trunk filled with picture books and toys that Martha kept in her living room, and busied herself with those, while the women sat at the table enjoying another cup of tea and generous slices of rhubarb pie.

Martha's dark eyes danced with anticipation as she and Kate sat together. "So how is he working out?"

"You mean Luke?" Kate asked.

"No, I mean the man in the moon!" Martha bristled. "Of course I mean Luke."

Kate laughed. "Better than I had hoped," she relented. "I had my doubts, but I think he's going to be fine. He certainly has the rest of my family under his spell!"

"So he and Jake are getting along?" Martha inquired. "I admit I was a bit worried about Jake feeling usurped."

"Jake thinks the world of him. I actually believe that Jake is relieved to have someone there to share the burden, and Luke does it in such a way that no one feels like they're being overlooked or edged out." Kate paused a moment, pondering, "Some how Luke manages to set things in motion, get things done, and he involves everyone, yet it never seems like he takes charge. I just can't explain it."

"Well, it's about time you had some competent help out there!" Martha smiled.

"As though *I'm* not competent?"

"Oh, that's not what I meant at all! But you cannot do everything all by yourself, and you know it, Kate!"

Kate's face softened, "I know, and having Luke there these last few days has really made me realize that, in ways you can't even begin to imagine.

"Speaking of not being able to do it all myself, there's something I need to talk to you about." Kate added quietly with downcast eyes.

"Whatever is it?"

"Well, spring branding needs to be done, and soon! Even with Luke there, we can't do it all by ourselves," Kate spoke quickly now before her courage could fail her. "Luke thought—that is, we decided—Oh, bother! Do you think that you and Lars and some of the other men from town could come out a week from Saturday and help with the calves? I wouldn't ask, but…"

"Of course we will! Now you just stop fretting. That's what friends are for." Martha's tone was comforting, and she grabbed Kate's hand in a gentle squeeze. "You just leave it all to me. We'll come, and I know Bert at the livery would do it for you, and Mike Hall—his oldest boys could help out, too—then there's Jim Kelly, and…"

"Stop! You're going too fast for me." Kate laughed, her head spinnning. "Oh, Martha, do you really think this will work?"

"Yes! Now, are you and Nana going to cook? I can get the women-folk to bring pies and cakes, preserves and such like, if you'll supply the main course."

"We thought we'd dig a pit and roast a steer, what do you think?"

"Can you afford it?"

"It's well worth it to me if we can get this branding done!" Kate exclaimed.

"Then it's settled. You get the calves in and leave the details here in town to me," Martha bubbled with enthusiasm and plans. "So, I see Luke has things pretty well in hand out there! Is he taking charge of any-thing else?" Martha asked with a deliciously wicked smile and a twinkle in her eye.

"Martha!"

"Well, c'mon, Kate, he *is* very handsome, he seems intelligent and well educated for all his rough appearance, and he'd sure beat old Matt Johnson hands down, if you ask me!"

"How did you know?" Kate gasped.

"Oh, honey, he's been going all over town letting it be known that you are now 'his property.' Please tell me that it isn't so?" she pleaded.

"He asked me to marry him."

"And?"

"And what? I didn't tell him anything. Obviously, I'm going to have to talk to him, tell him something, aren't I?"

"Yes, the sooner the better!"

"Is he really so very bad?"

"Worse than you think! Why I even heard that he has Little Dick West working for him!"

"You mean the man that rode with Bill Doolin?" Kate asked, incredulous.

"The very one!"

"But I thought they were all killed or taken in after the big jail break in Guthrie last year!"

"No, Dick West and one other man escaped. The other one was killed later, but they never got Little Dick, and I heard he was working for Matt. In fact, I saw him here in town with Matt just last week!"

An image of the charred receipt she and Luke had found flashed through her mind. *Richard We…*was all she had been able to make out, Richard West? Little Dick West? But if Martha had seen him with Matt just last week, then he was still working for Matt when the fence had been cut. A feeling of fear and anxiety rose within her, constricting her chest, threatening to cut off her very breath.

"Martha, are you absolutely certain?" she managed to say at last.

"Yes, of course I am. You remember the pictures of him that were printed in the Guthrie papers after the jail break. I know it was the same man."

Kate nodded, unable to speak.

✶✶✶✶✶✶✶✶✶✶✶✶✶✶✶✶✶✶✶✶✶✶✶✶✶✶✶✶✶✶✶

As Jo and Kate prepared to leave, Martha presented Kate with a parcel. "Here, I want you to have this. It's just a little something for each of you."

"Martha, I can't…"

"Yes, you can, or you'll really hurt my feelings!"

"Thank you." Kate said hugging the small woman fervently. True friends were so hard to find. Martha had been through so much with Kate, and still stood by her, a true friend. "I love you, Martha."

"And I you!"

"Bye, Mrs. Jansen, thank you for lunch. I had a very nice time," waved Jo, as they turned the corner of the main street and headed for the hotel.

"Are we still going to have our party, momma?"

"Of course we are. I promised, didn't I?"

"You just seem kind of worried about something. I thought maybe you were too sad after all," Jo said with an insight and wisdom beyond her tender years.

"Oh, baby, I'm sorry, of course I want to have our party. Why, it will be just the thing to make all these worries go right away!" Kate said cheerfully.

"Good!"

They entered the large hotel dining room. Kate carried the package Martha had given her. She decided it would be just the thing to add presents to their small birthday celebration. They were seated at a table near the large front window. It was adorned by a white table cloth and large linen napkins. Jo had never seen such finery before and was suitably impressed. Kate smiled at her daughter. She had taken these things for granted at Jo's age, but living the way they did now, she realized that Jo was far more comfortable with the simpler pleasures of life.

She ordered two slices of chocolate cake, a cup of coffee for herself and a glass of milk for Jo. As they waited for their cake to arrive, Kate produced the package.

"What's this?" Jo's eyes grew round in anticipation.

"Presents from Martha, shall we open them?"

"Oh, yes!"

Untying the string and opening the brown wrapping paper, revealed several smaller parcels, each carefully wrapped in shiny colored papers and marked with their names. Finding the gifts for Jo and Kate, they set them aside and carefully re-wrapped the others.

"You go first, Jo."

"Can we say our blessing first, momma?"

"Why that's a wonderful idea. Would you like to do it?"

"Yes, please."

They bowed their heads, joined hands, and Jo began, "Dear, God, I just wanted to thank you for all the wonderful things you do. Thank you for Nana and Papa and Jon and Mr. Josey. God, take especial good care of my daddy and my baby brother, and if You can, will you give them some chocolate cake today so they can eat with us? And please take away all of momma's worries. I know You can take care of her, 'cause she always tells me so. Amen."

"Amen," Kate echoed with tears in her eyes. "Now, how about opening these presents?"

Jo took the one with her name on it, and quickly tore into the wrappings revealing a beautiful picture book, a slate and several pieces of chalk to practice writing. Her face glowed. "Look, momma, my very own book, isn't it wonderful? And a brand new slate to draw and write! What did you get? Oh, look, here comes our cake."

The waitress carried over two china plates, each with a rim of gold, and a slice of the richest looking chocolate cake that Kate had ever seen. Setting the plates before them, she placed a candle in each slice and lit them.

Smiling at Jo, she said, "Happy birthday, honey."

"Oh, it's not my birthday," Jo said in a solemn voice, "it's my daddy and my brother's, they're having their cake in Heaven!"

"Oh, my!" The poor waitress looked so stricken, that Kate quickly stepped in.

"It's all right, we're celebrating here today!"

"Oh, I see," she replied, though she obviously did not. After placing the coffee, milk and silverware on the table, she quickly retreated.

Jo and Kate watched the glow of the candles for a few moments, each lost in their own memories of Will and Caleb. Finally they blew out the candles together and dug into the luscious cake.

"You haven't opened your present yet, momma!" Jo observed after a few bites, chocolate frosting decorating the corners of her mouth.

"You're right. Let's see what it is." Kate carefully opened the paper, removed the cover from the box, and exclaimed over the delicate handkerchief within. Dainty cutwork embroidered flowers adorned the white lawn, and tatted lace ran gracefully around the edges. Below the beautiful hankie was a layer of perfumed soaps, oils and lotions. Picking up one of the small vials, she carefully removed the stopper and breathed deeply of the musky aroma of sandalwood. Handing it gently to Jo, she shared the exotic treat. There were jars of lavender and lemon verbena as well. She couldn't remember the last time she felt so pampered. Oh, bless you, Martha, she thought. They each dabbed a small amount of the oil behind their ears. Giggling, they shared an afternoon of girl talk and memories.

✳✳✳✳✳✳✳✳✳✳✳✳✳✳✳✳✳✳✳✳✳✳✳✳✳✳✳✳✳✳✳

The buggy swayed and bumped along the rode home. Jo sat snuggled next to Kate, and they rode in companionable silence. A few moments later, Kate noticed that Jo had drifted off into a light sleep. Sighing, she flicked the reins and the mare extended her trot. Kate wanted to make it home before the threatening clouds finally let loose the torrents of rain they seemed to promise.

Alone with her thoughts at last, Kate's mind turned back to Martha's news and the bit of charred paper she had found. Was it coincidence? After all, that could have been anyone's name. Would Matt really stoop to such nefarious schemes to drive her from her ranch? If he really thought that she would consider marrying him, then what reason could he have? No, she decided, it must have been rustlers, and the receipt was simple coincidence and nothing more. But her mind was restless and her heart beat heavily in her chest as they drove along beneath rain laden clouds.

"Momma, stop, she's gone, she's gone!" Jo shrieked.

Frightened, Kate pulled on the reins bringing the startled mare to an abrupt stop. "Jo, what is it?" Kate asked in a panic stricken voice.

"My dolly, I can't find her, she's lost!" wailed the grieving girl.

"Are you sure? Perhaps she fell on the floor here, or next to the seat."

"No, she's gone, I know she is."

"Jo, calm down. When was the last time you had her?" The doll had been a part of Jo's life from the time she was an infant. Losing it would be a shock.

"She was in my hand when I fell asleep, and when I woke up she was gone." Tears flowed down her cheeks.

"Are you sure you've looked under the seat and everywhere?" Kate asked. They both searched the floor boards, under the seat and all around to no avail.

Glancing at the darkening sky, then at her daughter's tear-stained face, Kate made the decision. "We'll go back down the road a little ways and see if we can see her, but Jo, honey, listen to me, we can't take too long, there's a storm coming, we've got to get home soon. Do you understand?"

Drawing in a long shuddering breath, Jo nodded mutely, her sorrowful eyes breaking Kate's heart.

"All right. Now, I'll drive slowly, you watch the ground, and so will I."

They traveled back over their trail for several minutes in fruitless searching, Jo crying and Kate torn between her daughter's plight and the growing threat of rain.

"Momma, look, in there!"

Kate looked where Jo was pointing into the dense growth along the side of the road, but saw nothing. "What is it?"

"I saw someone."

"Who?"

"I don't know."

"It was probably a deer or something, Jo. I don't see your doll anywhere."

Jo sniffed, "Me neither, what am I going to do?"

"Kate." A deep male voice spoke from behind them, sending tendrils of fear through Kate's stomach.

Turning, she was met by black eyes set in a dark, familiar face.

"Tochoway." Kate said, relief flooding her.

"This is Jo's baby?"

"My doll," Jo cried reaching out for the precious possession.

"Thank you, how did…" Kate began.

"I was coming to meet you." Tochoway cut her off. "I have a message from the father of Nocona. He says to tell you his son lives, and he is grateful."

"Oh, I'm so glad. Is he healing well? Does he have use of his arm?"

"Nocona will be a fine hunter and horseman. His arm is healed, and he is well, thanks to you."

A flash of lightning split the air followed by a crash of thunder that shook the trees around them, large drops of rain began to fall.

"Come." Tochoway said, melting into the foliage beside the road.

Kate stepped down from the buggy, securing the brake. Tying the mare to a nearby tree, she grabbed her shawl for protection and held it over Jo as they followed the path Tochoway made. After a few moments they came to a clearing where a simple hide tent was erected and two ponies were tethered. Holding back the flap covering the entrance, Tochoway beckoned them to enter. Kate took Jo's hand and led her in without hesitation. As Tochoway entered, the sky was split asunder and torrents of rain began to fall. The sound of the rain drumming upon the hides was deafening, but they were safe and dry within the cozy shelter.

"This will pass," Tochoway reassured them. "The storm is moving quickly, and will soon be gone."

"I hope so. I'm worried about the mare and the buggy." Kate replied.

"They will be fine."

"I hope you're right," she said, not convinced.

Lightning flashed and the thunder rolled, but it grew more distant with every flash. Within minutes the rain began to lessen until it was no more than a gentle patter against the sides of their tent. The spring storms would sometimes do that here in Oklahoma Territory. They would brew all day, the heat and humidity building with every passing hour, until it seemed the air could no longer contain the storms that it was holding and they would be unleashed with a violent intensity, and be gone, the energy entirely spent. As they emerged from the small shelter, the air was fresh and clean and the rich scents of rain washed leaves and damp humus clung to their skin.

"Thank you. You came along just when we needed you." Kate said.

Tochoway flashed a brief smile and watched the woman before him intently.

"I guess we'd better be getting home before they worry too much and start looking for us." Kate said, watching Jo, and stooping to pick up the shawl she had dropped. As she reached for it, Tochoway picked it up and held it for a moment, fingering the soft material, before handing it to her. "Thank you," she said. His dark eyes held hers, and she felt a stirring response within her at his intense gaze. At last, she dropped her eyes to the ground, and turned to leave.

"Wait." Tochoway said quietly, placing a hand lightly upon her arm.

Kate turned, her heart racing.

He paused for a moment before taking her gently by the arm, and leading her toward the ponies that were tethered near the shelter.

"Nocona's father sends you this horse in exchange for his son's life."

Kate gasped at the sight of a beautiful white mare, heavily muscled, her coat glistening from the rains. Upon a closer inspection, she realized that the horse was not completely white, but had chestnut over the ears and poll and a patch of the same color over one eye. Her eyes were blue, something Kate had never seen before. She had heard this type of horse described as a medicine hat, and she knew that they were held in the highest esteem by the native people. Two hawk feathers braided together on a narrow leather thong were intertwined in the mane just behind her ears, and draped gracefully down her neck, the deep red shading on their ends matching perfectly the red accents of the horse.

"Oh, but I couldn't…" she gasped.

"Yes, she is yours."

Kate stared at the mare, speechless. She tentatively reached a hand out to the magnificent animal. The horse quivered beneath her touch, turning her head, and nudging the woman in return. Kate ran her hand firmly down the horse's neck and up over the withers, feeling the power within the taut muscles.

Tochoway placed a hand-tied rope halter over the mare's head, untethered her leg and handed the lead to Kate. She still couldn't believe this was happening. How had Tochoway found them that day?

Returning to the buggy, Kate let out a sigh of relief to see the mare standing calmly where she had been tied. Their packages had survived safely packed away beneath the seat in the storage box. Tochoway tied the white horse behind the buggy, and lifted Jo up to the bench.

Turning to Kate, he held out a hand to assist her into the buggy. She paused for a moment, searching his face.

"Why?" she asked finally.

He said nothing, but helped her up to the high seat. Picking up the reins, she looked at him one last time, before clucking to the mare and giving a flick of her wrist to start her down the road to Providence.

"What you have done for the least of these…." he spoke quietly.

Kate's heart soared as she heard the parting words, and her mind finished the phrase, "….*you have done to me.*"

CHAPTER IX

Kate could see Nana peering anxiously through the kitchen window as they approached the house. Bringing the horse to a stop near the porch, Kate and Jo jumped down, happy to be home. Jake came from the barn as Nana appeared from the back door.

"Where have you been?" they both asked at once.

Kate laughed, "To town of course, but it's good to be home."

"We expected you back near an hour ago!" Nana scolded.

"What's this?" Jake asked, seeing the white mare tied behind the buggy.

"It's a horse." Kate answered mischievously, unpacking the buggy as she spoke, and handing the parcels to Jon, who had appeared from the bunkhouse with Luke.

"Well, I can see that. Where did it come from?" Jake asked, annoyed.

"She was a gift."

Luke let out a low whistle, Jake's eyes narrowed, and Jon nearly dropped his burden at her declaration.

"Get those things in the house, Jon, and we can have supper if it's ready." Kate said looking at Nana.

"It's ready," came the terse reply. "Has been for a while now." Nana turned and entered the kitchen without another comment.

"Luke, will you unhitch the buggy and see to Rosie. I want to settle this new mare in before we eat."

"Sure," he replied, shooting a questioning glance at Jake.

Jake shrugged, watching Kate lead the mare to the barn.

Kate turned the mare into an empty paddock, removed the halter and leaned on the rail to watch as she ran the fence line for a moment before dropping her head to graze on the sparse grass. Watching the graceful beauty of the mare, her mind turned to the man who had given her the horse. She wanted to tell Jake about Tochoway, but she didn't know how. Her feelings for him were confused. She was very attracted to him, but he was from such a different world, though his actions and words showed him to be a Godly man, more so than many "Christian men" she could think of.

Lord, protect him and keep him. Let your spirit fill his soul, and let his feet continue to walk in Your ways. She prayed silently.

"Beautiful animal." Luke said walking up behind her.

"Isn't she?"

They watched the mare trot toward the fence adjacent to the pasture where the remuda grazed quietly in the gathering dusk. Her flowing tail flagged over her back, neck proudly arched, she cantered along the fence, neighing to the others. Several mares and geldings from the herd lifted their heads, nostrils flaring, as they eyed the newcomer.

"How soon before you turn her out?"

"I'll give them a few days to get acquainted over the fence first. And I want to see if we can get her in foal to Raven. I think they'd make an outstanding cross." Kate replied, voicing her thoughts aloud.

"Good idea."

"I think Nana's probably going to be livid if we don't get in to dinner soon." Kate sighed, not wanting to leave the peaceful sight.

"I believe you're right. Shall we?" He asked holding out his arm for her.

She hesitated a moment before reaching up and tucking her hand into his secure grasp.

✦✦✦✦✦✦✦✦✦✦✦✦✦✦✦✦✦✦✦✦✦✦✦✦✦✦✦✦✦✦✦✦✦

After the dinner dishes were cleared away, Jo was given the task of distributing the gifts from Martha. As each was opened and exclaimed over, the air of tension that had been present since their return began to ease. There was a new wild rag for Jon, a beautiful blue silk neckerchief just like all good cowboys wore. He put it on with pride, and Luke helped him to tie it just so. For Jake there was a new Farmer's Almanac, and for Nana, a crisp new apron with bib and pockets. Lastly, Jo pulled out a small wrapped package for Luke.

"Me?" Luke exclaimed taking the package.

"Why not?" Jo asked ingenuously, "You're a part of the family now, aren't you?"

The innocent remark struck him like a blow. *A part of the family?* No, anything but that.

"Well, Jo, don't forget, I'm just the hired hand around here. I'll be moving on once the steers are sent to market." Luke said stiffly, the weight of the gift heavy in his hands.

The stricken look on Jo's face tore at his heart. Better that she realize now, though, than become too attached. Silence filled the room. The tick of the old grandfather clock in the corner loud in his ears.

"What did Martha send for you?" Kate asked, breaking the awkward moment.

Opening the colorful paper revealed a leather-bound volume. The Tragedy of Pudd'n Head Wilson by Mark Twain, was emblazoned across the spine. "Well, I haven't read this one, though I do like Twain." he said attempting a cheerful tone, sorry for the grief he had caused.

"Do you like to read?" Kate inquired.

"It passes the time," Luke shrugged.

"Well, I have a small collection in the living room you're more than welcome to browse through."

"Thanks."

The atmosphere was still grim despite their best efforts to lighten the mood. Jo approached her mother and climbed up into her lap, tired after the long day and saddened by Luke's outburst.

"Come on, punkin, I think it's time you were in bed." Kate placed a kiss on the sleepy girl's soft hair as the others prepared to leave. "Jake, would you mind waiting? I want to talk to you."

"Sure. Jon, you walk Nana home."

"Yes, sir." Jon said, helping Nana with her shawl and opening the door for her.

Luke watched Kate accompany Jo to her loft, and listened to the quiet murmurings of prayers. He stared blankly into the dying embers of the fireplace.

"You really planning to move on this fall?" Jake asked.

"Well, that was the agreement."

"I don't expect Kate would mind an extension of that agreement, seeing as how you seem to be working out all right."

"I don't know."

"Think about it."

"I'll see you in the morning, Jake." Luke grabbed his hat from the peg by the door, and strode out into the clear night air. The clouds had departed with the passing of the storm and the stars shone against the deep black of the heavens. His heart raged within him. Why had he done that? It was one thing to separate himself from his growing feelings for this family, but it was something else entirely to crush the spirit of a child.

Of course Kate wouldn't want him to stay on, not after that little episode tonight. He'd be surprised if she didn't ask him to leave in the morning. He reached the bunkhouse, slamming the door as he entered. Seeing the Bible laying among the other books on the small shelf, he grabbed it and threw it against the wall. Just another example of God's work in his life. Give him a taste of something tangible and sweet, then yank it away again. Anger coursed through his body. Unable to quell the storm within, he burst through the door into the night. The house glowed from within with the warm inviting light of a spirit filled home. Tearing his eyes away from the sight, he strode off into the dark, breathing heavily, tight bands of pain constricting his chest, not knowing or caring where his path would lead.

✶✶✶✶✶✶✶✶✶✶✶✶✶✶✶✶✶✶✶✶✶✶✶✶✶✶✶✶✶✶✶✶✶✶

Jake sat staring into the dying fire as Kate returned from tucking Jo in for the night. The glow illuminated his tired features, and Kate was struck by how much he had aged in the months since Will's death. Had she been so caught up in her own grief and anxieties that she had failed to notice the effect on others?

"Would you like another cup of coffee, Jake?" Kate asked, startling him from his thoughts.

"Sure, sounds like just the thing," he replied, joining her at the kitchen table.

"You look tired, is everything all right?"

"Oh, yeah, just the spring planting and all, keeps me pretty busy, probably not getting as much sleep as I should, you know."

Kate took a long sip of the black coffee, mulling over what it was she wanted to say.

"You didn't ask me to stay to tell me I look tired. What's eating at you, Kate?" Jake asked laying a hand on hers.

Sighing, she stood and walked over to her desk. Withdrawing her journal from the bottom drawer, she opened it to the last entry, and took out a small scrap of paper with charred edges. Silently she handed it to him.

"What's this?" Jake asked studying the paper.

"We found it a while back, where the fence had been cut."

"Yeah, you said y'all had scared off some rustlers."

"That's just it, I'm not sure now that it was rustlers."

Jake peered at her, "You want to tell me what this is all about?"

In a rush of words, Kate told him Martha's story. "So I don't know what to think! If Little Dick West is working for Matt Johnson, then is that receipt his? And if so, is Matt trying to run me off this place? But why would he have asked me to marry him, if he's going to try to strong arm me off of here?"

"Whoa there, slow down a minute." Jake said, grabbing her hand and steadying her. "First, you don't even know if this paper has anything to do with that man. It's a very common name, and could be pure coincidence."

"Don't you think I've told myself that a thousand times?"

Jake nodded. "You know how I feel about Johnson. If anyone's gonna think the worst, it'd be me."

"I know." Kate whispered.

"But I can't convict a man based on this alone." Jake paused head bent in thought. "How seriously are you entertaining his proposal?" he finally asked in a low voice.

"Oh, Jake, I'm not, not at all!" she cried.

Kate could see relief flood Jake's features. In a matter of moments, it seemed as though he had shed ten years of grief. "Oh, Jake, I'm so sorry to have caused you so much pain. I just didn't know what to do. For an instant that day in Fallis, it all seemed so easy, just marry the man, and have done with it, but you know I could never do that! I realize now that I could never let this place fall into his hands."

"You don't know how glad I am to hear you say that."

"I think I have some idea!" She laughed.

The tension between them melted as they talked far into the night about plans for the branding. Jake related the news of the calf lost to predation, and the fact that Luke planned to carry his rifle from now on.

"Do you think it was wolves, Jake? We haven't had any sign of them for so long now."

"Can't rightly say, could be wolves, could be stray dogs gone feral. Smoke was worryin' at the door t'other night, and I thought I heard something prowling."

"What about a cougar?"

"Possible, but they're pretty scarce 'round these parts, too."

"Well, whatever it is, we'd better get it soon, before it gets to liking the meals around here," Kate said grimly.

"We'll put a stop to it," Jake agreed. "Do you want to tell me about that new mare you dragged home?" he asked with a familiar twinkle back in his eye.

Kate smiled, "A gift from Nocona's father. Seems the boy is going to be just fine, and his father is well pleased."

"Delivered by Tochoway?"

"Yes."

"You know, I used to trade throughout the Territory. The natives here have very funny ideas when it comes to paying a debt of honor, especially to a white, and a woman at that." He paused a moment searching for the right words. "I like Tochoway, he seems a decent man, but be careful, Kate, you just never know with a Comanche."

Kate's eyes sparked with an indignant rage. "Jake Insley! I cannot believe that you, of all people, would speak like that! Tochoway is no different than you or Luke or….or…" she sputtered with anger.

"I didn't mean it like that, it's just that…"

"To think that a Christian would condemn his fellow man just on the basis of his birth, why it absolutely makes me ill!" Kate continued her tirade. "Maybe one of the problems with this whole Territory is that us good, upstanding Christian settlers keep an entire race of people locked on reservations and quell any spirit they have with our prejudices. Did you know that he could be shot on sight and the killer would be upheld by the law? Do you realize that he risks his very life every time he sets foot off of the reservation? And you dare to say that they have a funny idea of how to pay a debt? He owes me no debt and yet he risks his very life to show me the kind of Christian love that no white man has ever shown him!"

Jake hung his head feeling the sting of her chastisement.

Kate's features softened as she approached the man she thought of as a father. Kneeling before him, she took his rough work worn hand in hers. "Jake, I know what Nana went through, the horror of seeing her parents killed by Indians. But the men that attacked her family were acting as individuals. They do not represent Indians as a whole anymore than the white men who have perpetrated such atrocities on the Indian tribes represent you and me." She paused for a moment searching his face, wanting desperately for him to see Tochoway as a man, not some representative of a people. "God's love extends to all of His creation, not just certain select groups. Should we do any less?"

Jake lifted his head to meet her steady gaze. "Kate, you might as well be my own daughter, the way I feel about you. I know in my heart you're right, but I can't help remembering the past, and thinking they're different. They have beliefs and customs that...." He shook his head wearily, at a loss for words. "I worry about you, is that so wrong?"

"No, Jake, of course it's not wrong," Kate sighed.

✸✸✸✸✸✸✸✸✸✸✸✸✸✸✸✸✸✸✸✸✸✸✸✸✸✸✸✸✸✸

Luke sat on a small outcrop of rock nearly half a mile from the main house. The dark night enveloped him like a shroud. He had stumbled several times, and hit his knee against a fallen trunk hard enough to make him cry out in pain. The throbbing sensation coursing through his knee began to move inexorably down his leg, and he knew that he would be in agony by morning.

Sitting quietly, he began to hear the myriad sounds that make up the songs of night. Crickets chirruped in chorus, joined by the rasping of cicadas among the trees. Frogs boomed and croaked near the pond in the pasture below. A cow lowed softly in the distance. Night birds sang their gentle melodies, lulling him into a state of watchful rest.

The tension within him eased, and he started thinking over his actions that evening. He felt miserable over the hurt he had inflicted on Jo, and yet Kate hadn't seemed angry at all. In fact, she had tried to come to his rescue and lighten the mood now that he looked back on it. His heart tightened thinking of Kate. His growing feelings were beginning to cloud his judgement.

His scalp prickled as he heard a soft step from somewhere behind him, every sense heightened. He moved his hand instinctively toward his hip, but he had not carried a gun nor any other weapon with him.

Straining his ears, he listened, but there was no warning until the low thrumming snarl of a large cat pierced his ears as it leapt from the brush behind him, muscles rippling beneath a golden coat, amber eyes slitted intently upon the prey. Luke's heart froze; his instincts took over as he flung himself to the ground and rolled beneath the fallen tree that had claimed his knee earlier. Shaking with fear he braced for the blow, seeing the heavy body falling towards him. Landing with a thud, the animal lay motionless only inches from his face.

Luke stared at the cougar, his mind racing, uncomprehending. After nearly a minute had passed, he rose slowly from his position below the log and approached the still form. Reaching out a tentative hand, he nudged the warm body. Nothing. With a great effort he finally rolled it over to discover the shaft of an arrow buried deep within the chest of the tawny cat.

Fear welled again as he spun to search the night in the direction from which the arrow must have come. He saw nothing but the endlessly shifting shadows; he heard nothing but the night sounds, suddenly stilled, beginning to stir again.

Luke took a tentative step in the direction of the ranch, watchful and wary, knowing that at any moment the unseen assailant would attack. Cursing himself for leaving without a weapon, he cautiously made his way down the trail, every rustle in the undergrowth demanding his full attention, every creaking branch a sure threat.

He reached the bunkhouse door, his nerves raw, and his heart pounding. Glancing at the house, he could see Kate dimly through the front window seated at her desk, her form silhouetted against the glow from the dying embers in the fireplace. Relieved that all was well within, he opened the door and stumbled into the dark room.

Fumbling for matches, he managed to light the lantern and turn the wick up to illuminate the darkness. He turned to peer out the window into the deep black of the night, straining to see any movement within the bushes. Finally, exhausted, he turned haunted eyes toward heaven, *God, are you out there? Are you listening? What would you have me do? I should be dead now, but have You delivered me? Is there something I'm supposed to see?*

Anguish filled his soul. Why couldn't he find God's love and have His peace when so many others found such comfort there? What was wrong with him? Even Kate—who should have more reason to hate God than he—even she had a sense of peace about her. *How, Lord, how do I find that peace?*

Turning from the window, Luke noticed the Bible laying open upon the floor where he had thrown it in anger. He reached to pick it up and glanced at the yellowed page revealed before him. His eyes instinctively began scanning the words:

For I know the thoughts that I think toward you, saith the Lord, thoughts of peace, and not of evil, to give you an expected end. Then shall ye call upon me, and ye shall go and pray unto me, and I will hearken unto you. And ye shall seek me, and find me, when ye shall search for me with all your heart. And I will be found of you, saith the Lord: and I will turn away your captivity, and I will gather you from all the nations, and from all the places whither I have driven you, saith the Lord; and I will bring you again into the place whence I caused you to be carried away captive.

As he read the words his heart began to beat in a steady rhythm, while his mind struggled to comprehend the meaning. Was this his answer? *Is it really that easy, God? Just ask?*

Luke closed his eyes, not knowing what it was he prayed for, nor why, he fell upon his knees and prayed.

CHAPTER X

The day dawned bright, the cloudless blue expanse shimmering with a promise of the heat to come. Kate prayed again for the weather to hold at least through the branding on Saturday as she walked along the path to the barn.

Luke already had the stalls cleaned and the horses fed by the time Kate appeared.

"Gee, and I thought I was early this morning!" Kate exclaimed.

"Didn't sleep much last night. Figured I might at least make myself useful." Luke replied.

He looked tired, and she noticed a pronounced limp as he approached her. "Something bothering you?" she asked.

"Kate, look, I'm really sorry for what happened last night with Jo. I wouldn't hurt her for the world," Luke offered apologetically.

"I know that."

Luke paused, watching the new medicine hat mare canter the fence line through the open doors. Dust motes danced in the golden shafts of sunlight. He looked back to Kate, "There's something else."

"What is it?" she asked with a furrowed brow.

"I have to show you. I'm not sure I believe it myself."

"Well?"

"Come on," Luke said, picking up a Winchester '73 propped near the tack room door.

They walked along a path leading away from the barn that meandered up a small hillside until they were out of sight of the main ranch
buildings. Morning glories grew along here, beginning to unfurl delicate purple tinged white blooms in all their splendor. Kate watched as
Luke scouted for signs along the low bushes lining the edges of the
faintly worn track. Spotting some broken branches he veered off the
worn path into the dense growth. Kate followed, wondering where he
could be leading her. Soon they came to a small clearing dominated by
an outcropping of native stone in shades of grey and red streaked here
and there with tan striations.

Kate gasped at the sight of the lifeless cougar still laying where it had
fallen. The sun gleamed across the tawny coat, and a light breeze ruffled
the fur as though the large creature might spring to life at any moment.
Taking a step back in alarm, she turned questioning eyes on Luke.

"What happened?" she whispered.

Luke took a deep breath, letting it out slowly as he tried to form an
answer that he wasn't sure of himself. "I came out last night, walked for
a while. I was angry at myself, or at God, I'm not even sure now." He
paused a moment, studying the dead animal as though trying to convince himself that it was real. "I sat down, over there. I heard it before—
before it attacked. I barely had time to think, and when I realized that it
was going to leap, I somehow ended up over there, under that log."

Kate looked at the spot he indicated, and could see the imprint of his
hands and knees still visible in the damp ground. "But..." her voice
trailed off, fear and confusion marring her delicate features.

"Instead of landing on me in a death grip, it fell dead at my feet."

"How?"

Luke rolled the big cat over with his boot. Kate's eyes widened, fixing
on the arrow shaft embedded deeply in the cat's chest.

"Tochoway." it was a mere whisper.

"What?" Luke asked sharply.

"Tochoway," she repeated, shifting her gaze to Luke's ashen face.

"You know who did this?"

She nodded mutely, finding a seat on the outcrop as her legs threatened to collapse beneath her.

✶✶✶✶✶✶✶✶✶✶✶✶✶✶✶✶✶✶✶✶✶✶✶✶✶✶✶✶✶✶✶✶✶

She related the story of the Comanche boy who had been shot, and the man who now seemed to be protecting her at every turn. Luke felt a growing sense of amazement turning gradually to anger tinged with jealousy.

"Why haven't you told me about this before?" he demanded.

"Why should I?" Kate asked defensively.

"Don't you think I have a right to know who may be coming and going from here?"

"Excuse me, but you said yourself, you're just the hired help! Who may or may not come on this property is *my* business." Kate's eyes flashed angrily.

Gazing into the amber depths of her eyes, he could see the golden sparks flash as she glared at him, challenging his right to protect this family. Closing his eyes he fought to regain control of his own raging emotions. He longed to reach out, take her in his arms, erase the anger and the fear written so clearly in her eyes. *No!* He told himself, *don't even think that. She's your employer; she has no interest in you, and you have no right to her!*

Opening his eyes again, he searched her face, "I'm sorry, you're right," he said, offering his hand to help her to her feet.

As Kate reached up, a shot rang out, the bullet ricocheting from the rocks behind her. An involuntary scream escaped her lips as Luke pushed her roughly to the ground. Covering her with his body, he groped for the Winchester laying a short distance away.

"Stay here, keep low and don't move." Luke spoke quietly, hardly glancing at Kate at she lay against the base of the rock outcrop.

"Where are you going?" she hissed.

"I just want to see if I can get a look where that shot came from." He rose cautiously, leveling his rifle before him. Another shot rang out, this time going far to the west of their location. Luke made his way to the trees along the perimeter of the clearing, staying as low to the ground as he could. Peering through the leaves and dense growth, he could just make out a roan horse standing ground tied some distance away.

A movement just beyond the horse caught his eye in time to see the sun glinting off the barrel of a rifle leveled in his direction. He dodged and rolled to the right wincing as a jolt of pain shot through his knee, just as the third shot rang out. Recovering quickly, he levered the Winchester into action. With little time to think or aim, he fired off a shot off in the general direction of the attacker. The report loud in his ears, he saw a puff of dust as the bullet landed below the horse's rear hooves, sending it into a frenzied buck.

Luke could just make out a small figure in a dark coat. Taking closer aim this time, he levered the gun and carefully squeezed off another round. The distant man jumped back, dropping his gun and grabbing his left shoulder.

He found cover within a stand of trees, just out of sight of Luke's searching eyes. The large roan horse had finally come to a rest nearly fifty yards away from the injured man. At a low whistle, the nervous animal pricked its ears and trotted toward its master. Retrieving his gun, the wounded man maneuvered himself into the saddle, and kicked the horse into a run. Luke tried a final parting shot that went wide of the fleeing man.

Seeing no others join him, Luke assumed that the man had been acting alone. Still he searched for signs of an accomplice. After several moments of silence, he rose cautiously and returned to where Kate lay trembling.

Kneeling, he helped her to sit. She trembled violently, taking deep ragged breaths. He held her hands for a moment, finally he put his arms around her and cradled her head against his shoulder, rocking her gently, whispering calming endearments against her ear. He could feel her heart beating rapidly against his chest, and smell the warm rich scent of her hair. His senses, already on edge, were nearly overwhelmed by her nearness.

Little by little her heartbeat slowed, the trembling stopped, and with a weary sigh, she pushed away from him as she regained her composure.

"Are you hurt?" Luke asked finally.

Shaking her head slowly, she looked at him with frightened eyes, "You?"

"No, but I think our 'friend' may be a little worse for the wear."

"You hit him?"

"Not sure how bad, but I at least winged him."

"Rustlers?"

"No, at least I don't think so. They don't usually work alone, and any experience I've had with them, they'd rather run than fight. That felt a whole lot more like an intentional ambush."

Kate gasped. "Ambush? Why? Luke what's going on?"

"I was about to ask you the same question." Luke replied scathingly. "Any chance this is Johnson's work?"

Kate dropped her eyes, "I don't know." It was no more than a whisper.

"We'd better get back to the ranch." He offered his hand again, and lifted her easily to her feet.

✶ ✶

Kate's mind raced as they made their way to the ranch. Could Johnson be that vindictive? Was he so serious about acquiring her land that he would kill her to get it? Stealing a glance at the tall man beside her, she began to wonder—who was he really? She knew almost nothing of him. Was there something in *his* past catching up to him? Fear began to snake its icy tendrils throughout her body. Who was Luke Josey?

"Luke, Kate!" Jake's troubled voice interrupted her thoughts. "What's going on out there? We heard shots fired."

Kate and Luke exchanged a wary look before Kate answered, "It seems we were ambushed. Luke thinks he may have hit the man in the shoulder. Whoever it was is gone for now."

"Ambushed? By who? What for?" Jake's face was a mask of concern. "And what in blazes were you two doing out there anyway?"

"Calm down, Jake," Luke spoke calmly to the frightened man. "I think the predator has been taken care of. I was showing Kate the remains of a cougar. At least that's one worry off our minds for now." He took a deep breath before continuing, "Let's go in for breakfast and discuss this, shall we?"

"I think that's the best thing," Kate agreed quickly, before Jake could protest further.

Nana appeared from the house, wiping her hands on her apron as the trio approached. Kate saw her cornflower blue eyes shadowed by dark rings and realized for the first time how old Nana and Jake were growing. The thought sent waves of sorrow through her, how would she manage when they were gone? They had been a source of strength for her through so many years now. She smiled tenderly at Nana and placed an arm around the small woman's stooped shoulders. "We're fine, Nana," she whispered against her ear, *and I love you*, she added silently as they went in to breakfast.

"Mama, Mr. Josey, what happened? Did you shoot the wolf that ate our baby cow? Jon says most likely you was out shooting. Did you kill him dead?" Jo bounded into the room full of enthusiasm and questions, fiery curls glinting in the morning sun that streamed through the open windows.

"Not exactly, sweetheart," Luke replied catching her up in his arms, and carrying her to the table. "It was a cougar, and he is dead now," he continued, depositing her on the bench.

"A cougar?" Blue eyes, round with delight, regarded him intently. "Did you shoot him?"

Luke gazed at the little girl seeing a fare amount of hero worship shining from her innocent face. "Not, me, honey. It would seem that your mama's Comanche friend may have saved my life last night, shooting that cat clean through the heart!"

"Really?" Jo gasped. "Tochoway was here? He is so wonderful. Did I tell you he found my dolly? I was so very worried, but then there he was, holding her for me, and he kept us dry from that storm. He's such a nice man, and now he saved your life, too!" Jo chattered on, then suddenly grew very still, a perplexed look on her small face. "If that happened last night, then what was all that shooting a little while ago?" she asked.

The room became gravely quiet as expectant eyes were turned on Luke and Kate. An uneasy look passed between the two of them. "Let's all sit down, shall we? I think we have some important things to talk about." Kate said, taking charge of the situation.

"Luke is right about the cougar, but that is far from our worries right now." She related the events of the morning quietly and succinctly, as her family listened. "So the question now is who and why," she concluded, casting a pointed look in Luke's direction.

"Well, until we know more, or find out what exactly is going on, I don't think any one of us should go out alone." Luke began, "We need to always ride out with at least one other person for now, and everyone needs to carry a weapon."

Jake nodded his agreement. "I have an old Winchester '73, and Jon has a '90 model. We both know how to use them."

"Good, what about you, Kate?" Luke turned to her.

"Will taught me to shoot before we ever moved here. I have his Colt 45 and Winchester '73. I'll put the holster back on my saddle. I think there's three boxes of .44–40 cartridges on the shelf in the pantry."

"Smart man, your husband." Luke said.

"Yes, he was." Kate replied evenly.

"Either Jon or I will escort Nana and Jo wherever they go. Surely they'll be all right here at the house, don't you think? Otherwise how are

we ever going to get the cattle rounded up and down here for the branding?" Jake asked.

After a moment's thought, Luke said, "No, I don't think it's a good
idea to leave them here alone. I think it would be best if you stayed with
them while Jon, Kate and I bring the herds in. We'll manage."

As the plans were made, Kate couldn't stop the gnawing thoughts
that Luke might not be what he seemed. Yet at the same time, she could-
n't help but notice the tenderness and concern evident as he made certain her family would be protected.

"We'll take two days to bring the herds in, the east one the first day,
then the west herd." Luke continued. "If we get started Thursday morning, we should have them in and ready for Saturday."

"Well, I'll be baking and such like, so you best just stay out from under
my feet, Jake Insley!" Nana stated. "Can't figure having a man underfoot
at a time like this." she muttered shaking her head. "Best set you to digging the pit and laying the fire to roast that steer. That's what you'll be
good for," she said with a firm nod of her head. This set everyone to
laughing, easing the tension, and bringing them together once again.

✶✶✶✶✶✶✶✶✶✶✶✶✶✶✶✶✶✶✶✶✶✶✶✶✶✶✶✶✶✶

Luke leaned against the rough wood of the corral fence, watching the
young colts and fillies of the remuda playing and bucking in the late
afternoon sunlight that filtered through the emerald canopy above.
Shadows danced and wavered over the gleaming coats as they ran at one
another in mock battle, kicking out, turning and racing the wind
toward an unseen goal. A three-year-old buckskin gelding caught his
eye. He watched young horse show exceptional athletic ability, solid
muscles rippling beneath his golden hide as he came to a sliding stop,
rolled back in a perfect pivot and took off again without hesitation.

This was the one he wanted. Kate had offered him any horse from the
herd in exchange for one month's pay, and this was the one he had

decided on. Catching, gentling and riding him was another thing, but Luke knew that he could do it. It was about time he got started on it, and since they had agreed to stay at the ranch until the round up Thursday morning, he had time to start now.

Glancing in the direction of the garden, he could see Kate and Jo talking quietly together, pulling weeds. Jo was no doubt exclaiming over the tender new shoots emerging green from the dark brown earth, and planning what she would wear for the "branding party" as she called it, while Kate worked earnestly in the heat, nodding her head now and then and adding a quiet comment in between Jo's monologues.

Luke wondered again why the two- and three-year-old colts were left to run without being saddle broke. He knew she planned to sell as many as she could to the men coming on Saturday, but he also knew that she could get a far better price for them if they were broke to ride. For such a sensible woman in most areas, this just didn't make any sense. Sighing and shaking his head, he went to the barn for a halter.

A few minutes later he had the buckskin colt haltered and was leading him to the small round working pen near the corrals. The colt had obviously been worked with some, as he was quiet and easy to catch and lead. He had soft liquid brown eyes, a small star just off center on his forehead, and a pleasant expression about him. Luke turned the horse into the round pen, following behind with a stiff lariat in his right hand.

Removing the halter, he shooed the colt away from him and sent him out to the fence. He watched closely from the center of the pen, staying well back, but moving always toward the horse's hip just enough to keep him moving. Soon the buckskin broke into a slow easy trot around the perimeter of the pen as Luke slapped the hard rope against his own leg and made a slight kissing sound to the horse.

"What do you think you're doing?" Came a cold hard voice from behind him.

He turned to see Kate standing at the corral gate, hands on her hips, amber eyes flashing in anger. Luke turned his attention back to the colt, urging him forward into a faster trot. "I'm working with my horse," he replied calmly.

"Your horse?"

"You said to pick the one I wanted. Well, there he is." He nodded toward the trotting horse.

"I said you could pick any of the older mares or geldings. Those colts aren't broke."

"He will be soon enough, if you let me get back to work."

"No."

The tone of her voice sent a shiver through his spine. He stepped quietly toward the colt's shoulder and said, "Whoa, boy." The horse stopped and stood looking warily at the man, nostrils flaring, trying to fathom what would happen next.

Luke turned his attention away from the colt and walked to the gate where Kate stood motionless. An indefinable air about her made him pause. Anger flashed from her eyes, laced with fear, and—and what? He couldn't quite grasp the emotion that emanated from her, filling her very being. His own anger dissolved as he studied her face. Reaching out, he ran his thumb down the side of her face, smoothing back a stray lock of silky brown hair with work-hardened fingers. She remained motionless, breathing rapidly, a slight quiver within her jaw, the only sign that she felt his touch.

"Kate...." he began.

She turned and fled, lifting her skirts as she ran. He watched as she disappeared into the house. Standing in the hot sun, he focused his eyes on the door, willing her to return, to come to him and lay her troubles at his feet. He wanted to be her comfort. When she did not reappear, he sighed, and returned to the pen where the buckskin colt stood patiently waiting for him.

✶✶✶✶✶✶✶✶✶✶✶✶✶✶✶✶✶✶✶✶✶✶✶✶✶✶✶✶✶✶✶

Luke was breathing heavily as he watched the colt's sides heaving in imitation of his own from the exertion. They had both worked hard over the last hour. Luke urging the young horse around the pen at a trot, then a lope, always driving from the hip, as he watched the colt intently for certain signs. When he saw the horse lower his head or lick his lips, he would step toward the buckskin's shoulder, cutting into the animal's path. The horse would turn on his haunches, away from the man, and reverse his direction.

As man and beast worked together, a rapport began to develop. Luke was able to control the flight with more precision. A step toward the shoulder and back, elicited a turn, but this time the turn was toward the man in a dance as old as time, movement following movement, in a complex sinuous motion, predator and prey evolving into master and willing servant. The horse began to pay closer attention to his driver. Soon Luke had the colt stopping as he moved forward and said "whoa," in a calm steady voice.

Jon stood watching from near the corral gate. Luke had seen him take up the vantage point some time earlier, but the lad was quiet and respectful, and Luke let him watch, glad for the company.

Beast and man stood facing one another, breathing heavily in the late afternoon heat. Luke took a step towards the gate and the buckskin turned his head to follow the man with his eyes.

"Good, boy!" Luke encouraged. Another step to the gate, again the colt followed with his gaze. One more step, this time the horse swung his head back to a more comfortable position, his focus leaving the man. Luke kissed sharply slapping the riata against his leg. The colt returned his gaze to the man. Again Luke stepped toward the gate. This time the colt moved his front feet around and repositioned himself to face the man. A broad grin broke across Luke's tired features, and he knew that he was gaining the horse's trust and attention.

Relaxing, he motioned to Jon. "What do you think?" Luke asked

"That's pretty amazing. What exactly are you trying to do with him?"

"Well, first, let him know that I'm the boss, but not in the way a lot of wranglers will try to do it. Some, they just get on and let 'er rip, try to wear the bronc out of 'em. I guess it works for some folks."

"Yeah, so how are you telling him that you're the boss?"

"I tell him when he can move, where he can move, and when he can stop. If you've ever watched a herd of horses—I mean really watched—then you'll start to see that there's always one ole boss mare. She tells every single member of that herd just where they can eat, when they'll move, and so forth."

"How?" Jon asked, puzzled.

"She does it with her body. Lay her ears back, bare her teeth, come at the horse from the hip if they don't move fast enough. Plant a good kick on 'em, if they dare to invade her area." Luke laughed.

"Hmmm, now that you mention it, I guess I have seen that kind of thing. Never thought much of it, 'cept maybe that was one mean hoss!" Jon exclaimed with a grin.

"Mean doesn't have much to do with it. It just shows that she's the leader, the boss. So I figure if you want to gain control of a horse, you've got to be just like that ole boss mare." Luke stopped for a minute, watching the buckskin colt, whose focus was beginning to drift away. A loud kissing sound and a slap of the hard rope against his leg, and the colt's head snapped back to attention. "A few more sessions like this, and I'll be ready to put him under saddle."

Jon's eyes widened in alarm. "You ain't really gonna ride him, are you? Does Kate know?"

"Why wouldn't I ride him?" Luke's exasperation broke through. "Someone's got to break these colts. They're all just going to waste out there, and Kate won't get a decent price for them the way they are!" He stormed. Seeing the look on Jon's face, he stopped. "Jon, what is it? Why won't she do anything with them?"

"You don't know, do you?" Jon asked quietly, his face somber.

"Know what?"

"Mr. Will was killed ridin' the colts. Miss Kate don't want no one doin' that no more."

"Oh God," Luke exclaimed as the realization washed over him, leaving him feeling cold and empty. "Oh, God have mercy. I had no idea. No wonder...." He looked toward the house, the anguish in his soul a bitter gall, as understanding dawned within him. Looking back at Jon, he searched the fresh young face, "Jon, this is a better way. I have yet to have one even offer to buck doing it this way. Sure it takes more time, but they're more willing, and far better trained when I do it like this."

"It ain't me you've got to convince, sir."

* *

Kate sat on the soft feather bed, praying, seeking desperately to quell the tumultuous emotions raging within her. The sight of Luke in the breaking pen with a young horse had caused her heart to stop for a split second. She had sent Jo in to help Nana prepare the supper before approaching the pen to confront Luke.

Trembling from the fear that welled within her at the memory of Will's final ride, and angry that Luke would defy her wishes, she spoke harshly. His response had disarmed her. His green eyes filled with concern as he drew near. At his touch, the realization struck her. She was falling in love with him. Overcome by the emotion, she fled.

"God, oh, God, I need you now. How can I love this man?" she prayed. "I don't even know who he is."

Confused and heavy hearted, she rose from the bed. At her dressing table, she picked up the tin type photograph of Will and herself on their wedding day. Running her fingers over the image, she caressed his familiar features. Their love had grown slowly, gaining its strength from their mutual faith in God and their trust in one another. Will had accepted her just the way she was. He found her scars a beautiful part of her.

"They are your badge of courage and honor," he had told her one night when he found her crying over her disfigured arms. "Wear those scars proudly. They are beautiful because they show your true heart." His words echoed through the shadows of her memory, clearing away the cobwebs of doubt, and a sense of peace descended upon her heart.

She moved to the window where delicate lace curtains hung limply in the afternoon heat. No breeze stirred, even the birds were stilled. Kate could hear the banging of pots, and slamming of cupboard doors from the kitchen. The low pitched murmur of voices and occasional giggle told her that Nana and Jo were diligently working on the preparations for the branding.

From the window, she could see Jake planning the roasting pit. The steer was to be slaughtered tomorrow. Jon already had the wood chopped and stacked neatly waiting for the pit to be dug. She smiled weakly at the everyday sights and sounds. This was her family, her life was here. What part in that did Luke play?

At the thought of his name, she looked toward the breaking pen, just visible from her window. She watched intently for several minutes. Luke worked the colt slowly and steadily. What exactly was he trying to accomplish, she wondered. She had never seen anything like the intricate maneuvers being performed by man and horse.

Kate believed in working with the foals from the day they were born, touching them, talking to them, gentling them when they were small. Then they were turned out until they were ready to break. The time she spent with the babies showed in their easy going natures, but at breaking time, it was always the same, catch them, snub them up to the post, throw a saddle on, climb aboard and ride the buck out of them. Some had more than others, and she always watched to see which of the colts and fillies were the easy ones, keeping those as potential breeding stock, and selling the rest.

Will had always taken great delight in breaking the young stock himself. Kate's heart had paused a beat every time he climbed on one of them, but she never voiced her fears to him, sure that they were unfounded. The moment it happened, she knew that she would never allow another colt to be ridden on her place. She'd sell them unbroke, even if it meant losing money on them. She knew the breeding and cow sense on her colts was enough to build a reputation, let someone else take the risk on their backs.

Her anger subsided as she watched Luke and the buckskin from her bedroom window. Interest in his methods intrigued her in spite of her fears. She could see the tension leaving the horse as trust began to replace the fear evident in the animal's bearing. She remained at the window until Luke took the colt out of the pen and led him into the barn.

Curiosity overcame her. She let herself out through the front door so as not to disturb Nana and Jo, and walked to the barn her heart pounding in rhythm to her quick strides.

Through the open door, she could see Luke standing at the horse's shoulder. His back was turned toward her, but she could hear the soothing sound of his low-pitched voice as he spoke to the buckskin. He brushed the gleaming coat with long sweeping strokes, working in a steady rhythm. The horse stood in docile repose, head low and relaxed, his eyes half closed listening to the man murmuring beside him, calmed by the gentle stroking.

Kate leaned against the rough wooden frame of the barn. The western sun cast its rays through the window in the loft. The dapple of golden light and purple shadow across the man and colt blended them into a picture of perfect harmony.

She watched as Luke continued his gentling process. He ran one hand firmly down the length of the colt's front leg, then went back to the grooming. The horse picked up his head, and flinched slightly at the unfamiliar touch. After Luke repeated the action several times, the buckskin accepted it as natural and returned to a relaxed state. He began the same motion on a rear leg, but the colt hardly seemed to notice it this time.

Pausing for a moment, Luke rested his forehead against the colt's flank. The rough muslin shirt he wore clung damply to his back following the curves of muscles built and strengthened by years of hard labor. His skin was bronzed by the sun, and his dark hair gleamed in the evening light showing golden glints throughout. Kate watched silently, drinking in the sight of him, her senses filled to overflowing. The scent of sweat and sweet hay mingled together, tickling her nose, as the sun warmed her back and a gentle breeze stirred her hair. A dove cooed softly from the rafters, and Raven nickered to her from his stall.

"Luke?" Though little more than a whisper, the word rang loud in her ears as anticipation knotted her stomach.

The buckskin raised his head and twitched his ears in her direction, and she could see Luke's shoulders tighten as she spoke.

"Luke, I wanted to—to apologize." Kate waited. There was no response, though she sensed a change in him. "We need to talk."

When he turned to face her, his green eyes were filled with compassion and wet with unshed tears. "You don't owe me an apology, Kate. I had no idea. Jon told me." His voice thick with emotion.

Kate's heart pounded. Her eyes riveted on his as she struggled to gain control of her emotions. In two quick strides he was standing before her, clasping both of her small hands in one of his. She caught her breath and her nostrils filled with his earthy scent. He traced the line of her jaw with one finger, cupping her cheek gently in the palm of his hand he drew her to him, kissing her tenderly on the forehead. She closed her eyes and drew in a shuddering breath as she laid her head on his shoulder and felt his arms go around her in a warm, protective embrace.

****

"Mama? Mama, where are you? Nana says to come to supper." Jo's voice called from the garden moments later.

Loosening his embrace, Luke stepped back. Kate's head remained bowed, her eyes closed. Reaching out, he lifted her chin with his finger. As their eyes met, she smiled a beautiful, radiant smile that cast all doubt from his mind. Swallowing hard, he reached out and took her arm to escort her to dinner.

"What about your horse?" she asked, indicating the buckskin still standing quietly tied to the rail.

The words 'your horse' struck home and he smiled. "He'll be fine for now. We'll come out later and see to him."

CHAPTER XI

Kate watched Jonathan lead his old sorrel mare into the barn in the dim light of dawn. Smokey padded silently behind, faithful to his young master. Rio and Gypsy, saddled for the day's work, waited at the fence, ears twitching at the sounds of morning, swishing their tails at the ever present flies.

Jon prepared to heave his ancient leather saddle on the mare's back, when Kate stepped out of the shadows and laid a hand on his arm. "Why don't you turn old Sally out. She deserves a rest after all the years she's put in." Kate could see the crestfallen look on Jon's face. "I think today would be the perfect opportunity to try out your new horse," she added quickly, as Luke entered the barn leading a small bay gelding and handed the lead to Jon.

The boy's eyes shone as he struggled for words. "You mean, he's mine, Miss Kate? All mine? Really mine?"

"I thought it was about time you had a good cow pony of your own. After all, Sally has been hauling you around most of your life, and she wasn't young when she started doing that. I think it's time she earned her retirement, don't you?"

Jon spoke not a word as he ran his hand over the gelding's coppery coat, fingering the silky ebony mane.

"He's about ten or eleven, we've used him before on the ranch here, maybe you remember Will riding him for a couple of years?" Kate continued.

"Yes, ma'am, I do. He's a fine horse. Does he have a name?"

"Funny thing, we always just called him Jesse's bay colt, because we bought him from Jesse McDonald, do you remember him?"

"I think so. Isn't he the man that 'steaded the quarter section down south, then sold out to Mr. Will the year after?" Jon asked.

"That's right. What do you think you'll call him?"

"Well, maybe I'll jest call him Jesse since he probably already knows that."

"Jesse it is then." Kate said.

Leaving the boy to saddle his horse, she took Sally and turned her out to the tall grass pasture. Luke joined her at the gate where they stood together watching the old mare trot out and flag her tail like a filly with the scent of new grass filling her nostrils for the first time.

"She deserves this. That old mare has hauled him around faithfully for the last ten years. Why, I'll bet she's twenty-five years old or better." From the corner of her eye, Kate could see Luke watching her and shaking his head. "What?"

"I still can't get used to the sight of you in mens' clothes," he said with a grin.

"Well, it may not be feminine, but it's a lot more practical for what we have to do today." She wore Levis, a pale blue cotton shirt, a brown vest with large roomy pockets, and worn leather boots. Her hat hung down her back by the stampede string, and a pair of deerskin gloves were tucked into her belt. Thick brown hair was caught up in a ribbon at the nape of her neck, but unruly curls insisted on escaping, framing her face in a wreath of soft tresses.

"Oh, I'd say on you the effect was utterly feminine." Luke reached out and caught one of the wayward curls, tucking it behind her ear. His touch sent a thrill through her, and she closed her eyes and stepped away, not yet ready to face the flood of emotions that were still so new.

She sighed softly. "We'd better get moving if we're going to get them all in today."

They returned to the barn to find Jon tightening the girth on the saddle of his new pony, eager to start the day's trip. Kate and Luke went over their own tack one last time, checking bridles, bits and tightening girths. Stiff lariats were tied near the pommels and each saddle had a holster carrying a Winchester '73 carbine. Luke wore a gunbelt with Will's Colt .45 in it. The sight of the armament worried Kate, but she knew it was necessary. There had been no further incidents in the last few days, but the threat was real and they couldn't be too careful.

They rode through the morning mist over emerald fields, Jon loping far ahead, then trotting back to where Luke and Kate rode together in companionable silence. Smokey followed along, tongue lolling, chasing the occasional rabbit, and returning with a doggy grin on his face to ride again by Jonathan's side.

"He's going to wear that poor pony to a nubbin before the morning is over," Kate observed with an indulgent smile.

"That horse will still be going strong when Jon is home abed tonight."

"You're probably right."

"He reminds me of myself when I was a boy," Luke remarked watching the lad whooping and hollering in sheer youthful exuberance.

"Where did you grow up?" Kate asked.

"We were originally from Indiana, but my father moved us to Coffeyville, Kansas, when I was just a babe. He pastored a church there." Luke spoke evenly, but there was a hard set to his eyes.

"I didn't know your father was a man of God," Kate exclaimed. "Do you have any brothers or sisters?"

"One sister. She's five years older than me, already married and a baby of her own, when…" Luke stopped, a distant look settled on his face.

"When what?"

"Kate, you believe in God, don't you?"

"Well, of course."

"But you don't *just* believe, you know Him—I mean, He's real to you, isn't He?"

"Luke, He's my friend, my confidant and comforter. He's my savior. He's there when no one else is, I can trust in Him and He never fails me." She felt at a loss for words to tell him what Jesus meant in her life. Did he not know? How could he be the son of a preacher and not know God?

"How, Kate? How do you know that it's God directing all this?" he asked with a vague wave of his hand indicating the vastness surrounding them. "And if He is there, then where was He when your husband was killed? Where was he when my mother lay dying? And why is my father so full of hate?" The anguish in his voice ran deep, but his face remained impassive. Kate's heart ached for the pain she sensed there.

She sat deep in the saddle and checked the reins, bringing the big sorrel mare to a stop. Luke's gelding walked on a few more steps, before he swung around to face her.

"Oh, Luke," she began not knowing how to voice the passion in her soul. "I could quote you scripture after scripture. God is not the author of confusion, but of peace. All things work together for good to them that love God, to them who are the called according to his purpose. God's will is a mystery to us, your faith should not stand in the wisdom of men, but in the power of God." Seeing the grim set of his jaw, she sighed, her eyes straying to the meadow beyond where a few cows were peacefully grazing.

"Even if we didn't have the scriptures, Luke, look around you. God is evident in every aspect of His creation. You can see him in every leaf on a tree, in the clouds, the beasts of the field, the birds of the air. Look at the perfection in the face of newborn babe. How could you look at all of this and not see God?"

Luke shook his head slowly. "Kate, I know the Bible. I studied it for over a year in the seminary. I listened to my father preach it every day for eighteen years. And, yes, I can even see a divine hand in the creation around us. But why can't I *feel* Him, Kate? What is it I'm missing?"

She looked at Luke's strong hands gripping the leather reins, and reflected back over the past weeks, seeing him in her mind's eye, taking control of every situation, planning, preparing, protecting. Kate realized that never once had she seen him in prayer over any of these circumstances, never seeking God's will or His direction.

"When was the last time you sat down and talked to Him?" she asked.

His stony face remained unchanged, but a flicker in his eyes encouraged her to continue.

"He wants a relationship with you, Luke, but on His terms, not yours. You're going to have to let go of your pride, give Him control before you'll ever know that sense of peace you're looking for." She sighed, rubbing her scars absently through the thin cotton shirt. "It doesn't happen overnight, trust me, I know," she added quietly.

The bay appeared from around a bend. "Luke, the main herd is just over that rise, c'mon, we're almost there!" Jon called out, brimming with anticipation.

Their eyes held for a moment longer and Kate could see the battle raging within before he shifted his gaze and they headed the horses out to meet the challenge of the herd.

They rode past a few cows and calves in the near meadow.

"We'll pick these up on the way back through." Luke commented.

"I want to check that pond south of here and the few gullies beyond that for any other strays." Kate said.

"Good idea. We'll regroup on the other side of the herd, plan our search and drive the stragglers up to the main herd, then push them this way to pick up these, and on back to the ranch."

Kate nodded and pushed her mare into a long, ground covering trot.

The three came together in the shade of a large oak on the far side of the herd. Smokey flopped down in the welcome coolness of dewy grass while Kate, Luke and Jon surveyed the cattle. Sleek black cows grazed in the morning sun, taking little notice of the riders in their midst.

"Between these and the eleven I counted in the first meadow, I'd say we're probably only missing twenty-five or so." Kate was glad that so many were here together.

"Jon, you take Smoke and head to the east, pay special attention to large shady areas, and any water sources. Work 'em slow and drive them this way. Stay well back, and move 'em real easy," Luke instructed. "Kate, you work the south pond and any ravines out that way. I'll cut back and forth in the gullies and creeks behind you both."

"Yes, sir, I know how, and so does Smoke. We're old hands at this."

"Yes, they sure are. He's been helping us move the cattle around for a good five years now," Kate added with a smile and a note of encouragement to the boy. "But this is the first time on your own, Jon, be careful! If anything were to happen to you, your grandpa would skin me alive."

"More like Nana would!" Jon laughed and waved as he turned his pony to the east and rode off at a lope.

Luke shook his head. "You really think he can handle this?"

"If there's one thing that boy can do, it's work the cattle. He'll be fine, and once he starts working them, he'll settle down and move them right. Besides, Smokey is one of the best cow dogs I've ever seen. They're quite a team those two."

"Well, we better get after our own, then, don't want them showing us up, do we?"

Kate laughed and headed her horse out to the south. She rode in silence until the screech of a hawk shattered the stillness. Kate looked up to see the great bird drifting in lazy circles, riding the warm currents effortlessly. Red feathers glinting in golden shafts of sunlight reminded her of Tochoway, and her heart grew troubled.

✯ ✯

Luke rode alone along the top of a rise, watching for cattle among the trees or near the creek. Kate's words played relentlessly through his mind, "…let go of your pride, give Him control." If there was one thing Luke was sure of, it was his ability to take control. His self assurance was the strength he relied on. Surely that was a gift from God, not something to be cast aside?

As he rode, a verse of scripture learned many years before rose in his mind, *Ask, and it shall be given you; seek, and ye shall find; knock, and it shall be opened unto you.*

"Lord, I haven't been very good at asking or seeking Your face, Your will. God, I want so much what I see in others, how they trust You. Show me, Lord, show me how to subserve myself and seek Your will."

Come unto me, all ye that labor and are heavy laden, and I will give you rest. Take my yoke upon you, and learn of me; for I am meek and lowly in heart: and ye shall find rest unto your souls. For my yoke is easy, and my burden is light.

Luke felt his heart constrict at the familiar words. Heavy laden? Weary? Oh, yes, that he had in plenty. Would he ever learn to lay his cares at the feet of the Father? He shook his head to clear away the troubling thoughts and focus on the work at hand.

A movement in the shadows of the tree line caught his attention. Peering into the verdant foliage, he could just make out the shapes of cattle milling in the restful shade. Urging Rio along, they approached the beasts cautiously. Luke began a slow side to side sweep as they neared the location of the cows, reining the horse right for several steps then steering back to the left, moving slowly but consistently forward.

A large cow bellowed a protest heaving her bulk up from a soft grassy nest. As she walked away from Luke's inexorable advance, others turned to follow. Soon he had a small group of cows and calves moving along before him. The old lead cow meandered toward the pasture where the main herd grazed, and Luke only had to urge on the stragglers and make sure they stayed on course.

He heard the bawling of cattle to the east. In a few minutes a group of young steers came into sight moving quickly away from the gray dog nipping at the heels of those in the rear. Jon rode in behind, moving from side to side, keeping the steers from breaking to the right or left. Luke waved, and Jonathan maneuvered his band of steers into the path of the cows and soon both men rode behind the growing herd.

"That'll do, Smoke!" Jon called out. The dog obediently returned to his master, and padded along beside him. "Jest watch 'em now, Smokey."

"He's a real good cow dog, Jon. Did you train him yourself?"

"Naw, Mr. Will helped me, and he had an old dog—we jest put Smoke out with old Traveler when he was a pup, and Trav taught him most things real good."

"What happened to Traveler?"

"He died a few years back. Went to sleep one night and jest didn't get up the next morning." Jon sighed. "He was good dog. He's buried out behind the smithy shed."

"Well, I'd say the way Smokey works those cows is a fine tribute to Trav."

"Thanks!" Jon grinned. "Uh-oh." A steer broke out the left and tried to circle back. Jon turned the bay horse into the path of the runaway then grabbed frantically for the saddle horn as the pony dropped his front end low and snaked his neck out to stop the steer. Before the boy had a chance to recover his senses, Jesse took off again staying in front of the angry black beast, matching him step for step. Luke was reminded of a bull fight he had once seen in old Mexico. Like the matador, Jesse moved with the steer in perfect timing until he was able to move him safely back to the herd.

Visibly shaken, but unhurt and glowing from the experience, Jon rode back to join Luke.

"That looked like quite a ride!" Luke grinned.

"Yeah, real glad I got a hold of that horn, or I'd have been on the ground for sure." Jon shook his head in wonder.

Luke called out, "Hiya, get on, now," slapping his lariat against his leg. Jon whistled and sent Smokey to gather the straying calves. They moved the last of the cattle into the open meadow where they joined the rest of the herd, mingling and beginning to graze. Kate appeared a short time later, driving a small knot of cows and calves before her.

✶✶✶✶✶✶✶✶✶✶✶✶✶✶✶✶✶✶✶✶✶✶✶✶✶✶✶✶✶✶

Jon rode ahead as they approached the sorting corrals. Jake appeared from the barn and took up a position near the gates. The cattle were driven through a wide opening that narrowed into an alley with two gates at the far end. From there they were easily directed into one of the two corrals. The cattle coming in today would be sent into one, and the herd gathered the following day would be sorted into the other pen.

"Where does Kate want these?" Jake called to his grandson.

"The north side."

Jake swung the gate back as the first cows made their way down the chute, bawling their objections even as they passed into the open corral. Once the last steer cleared the opening, he shut the gate, securing it with a wire tie.

Luke and Kate rode into the ranch yard. Kate produced a rag from the pocket of her vest. Dousing it from the canteen hanging near her pommel, she wiped the dust from her face and neck. The cool water ran in rivulets down the back of her shirt making her long for a real bath.

"Good day's work. Hope tomorrow goes as smoothly," Luke said.

"Oh, tomorrow ought to be the fun day, bringing in those longhorns. We got these in before lunch. We'll be lucky if we see the supper table tomorrow." Kate laughed and offered the cool rag to Luke. Reaching out to take the cloth, his hand caressed hers sending a shiver coursing through her.

"Look at all the calves, mama!" Jo shouted, running from the house. With a whoop, she mounted the corral fence and stood with her arms hanging over the top rail. "Nana and I made pies today, and lots of bread. Oh, and I picked all the strawberries I could find, and blackberries, too. Jake churned the butter and dug the pit we need to roast the meat. Oh, mama, I can't wait for Saturday," she sighed.

"Luke, I could sure use your help and Jon's getting this steer butchered," Jake said, joining them in the yard.

"Sure thing, let's get it done now. Then we can clean up and eat a late lunch." Luke replied. "Get down, Kate. I'll put the horses up first."

She swung her leg over the saddle and dismounted in a single fluid motion. Handing the reins to Luke, she paused a moment to stroke Gypsy's velvety nose. "You did real well today, old girl." The mare leaned her head against Kate's shoulder, and Kate gave her a good hard scratching on the neck. "Go on, now, we'll do it again tomorrow," she murmured to the horse.

"Thanks, Luke. I'll go in and help Mrs. Insley with the food and let her know you'll be coming along later. You know how she hates to have her schedule disrupted." Kate smiled as she watched the men head to the barn, talking and laughing over the morning's adventure.

Luke belonged here. She could see it in the way Jake treated him, the way Jon looked up to him. His patience and tenderness with Jo touched her heart, but most of all she felt it within her soul. Why then did thoughts of Tochoway trouble her? The memory of his dark eyes burned within her.

"Come on, mama, I'll race you to the house!" Jo called as she sped by her mother, skirts flying around her pumping legs.

"Hey, no fair! You've got a head start," Kate protested, even as she raced to catch up.

Laughing and out of breath they reached the porch together, collapsing in a heap on the steps.

"You're getting fast," Kate said, tousling Jo's hair.

"I've been practicing," she announced proudly. "Think I can beat Jeremy on Saturday?"

"Oh, I don't know, he's quite a bit bigger than you. I bet you'll give him a run for his money, though."

Jo jumped up and opened the kitchen door.

"Oh, Mrs. Insley, you have truly out done yourself. That smells heavenly!" Kate exclaimed as the scent of fresh baked bread drifted out mingling with the aromas of sweet cherry pies and gingerbread.

"I just hope there'll be enough to feed that crowd on Saturday." Nana scowled at the pot of beans simmering on the stove. "Where are the men? I expect they'll be wanting their lunch about now."

"Oh, I'm supposed to tell you that they'll be coming late to lunch. They wanted to get that beef ready first. What can I help you with in here?"

"You can wash yourself up, get some decent clothes on, and then start in on those vegetables."

"Yes, ma'am," Kate called over her shoulder as she marched off to comply with Nana's instructions.

✶✶✶✶✶✶✶✶✶✶✶✶✶✶✶✶✶✶✶✶✶✶✶✶✶✶✶✶✶✶✶✶✶

Luke sat on his bunk, the dim glow of a lantern holding the dark at bay. His body ached from the day's work, but his thoughts would not be stilled to let him sleep. His mind conjured images of Kate riding with abandon across the deep green sea of the prairie, herding cows, laughing with him. He could see the compelling conviction in her eyes when she spoke of her faith.

"Lord, I am falling in love with her. Help me. How do I become the kind of man that is worthy of her love, or of Your love, God?"

He looked down at the Bible clutched in his hand, and opened it to the sixth chapter of Matthew. He read the familiar words of the Lord's prayer, but his eye was drawn to a verse he had not remembered, *"...your Father knoweth what things ye have need of, before ye ask Him."* Another verse echoed in his mind, and he flipped to the book of Romans, scanning the pages he found the reference in the eighth verse of the twenty-sixth chapter, *Likewise the Spirit also helpeth our infirmi-ties: for we know not what we should pray for as we ought: but the Spirit itself maketh intercession for us with groanings which cannot be uttered.*

Closing his eyes, Luke prayed, "Lord, if ever that were true of man, it is true of me. I have been so lost in this life. Show me, teach me, come and be within me. I need you now. God is it too late?" Hot tears stung his eyelids as he fought the rush of emotion surging within.

"Let go," Kate's words whispered in his mind, "let go of your pride."

✶✶✶✶✶✶✶✶✶✶✶✶✶✶✶✶✶✶✶✶✶✶✶✶✶✶✶✶✶✶✶✶

Luke removed his hat and a ran a hand through his wet hair. They had been chasing wily range cows out of the dense brush for most of the morning. Jon and Smokey had gone to the north and Luke to the south, while Kate worked to hold the main body of the herd together in the large pasture. When Kate had said that today would be the hard work, she wasn't exaggerating. The sun was high and beat down mercilessly on man and beast alike. The cows would dodge and run, and it was all Luke could do to head them off and keep them moving toward the pasture to the east where Kate waited with the others.

He narrowed his eyes, watching a particularly cagey mama cow. She broke hard to the left, attempting to circle back toward the thicket that he had just driven her and several others from. Rio jumped at Luke's prodding and cut the cow off before she managed to make it into the brush.

An hour later they finally had the herd together in the deep green pasture. The three riders stopped in a shady grove to make a quick lunch of Nana's biscuits and bacon.

"Hey, Luke, isn't that where we built the bee gum?" Jon asked, indicating a copse of trees to their left.

"Yep, it sure is. Want to take a look?"

"Bee gum?" Kate asked puzzled.

"C'mon, I'll show you," Jon said. Running ahead, he disappeared into the trees.

Luke stood and reached out to Kate. Helping her up, he drew her close, gazing into the depths of her amber eyes he bent his head and kissed her tenderly. "I think I'm falling in love with you, Kate Shaughnessey."

She reached up and placed a finger over his lips, then tracing the line of his jaw, she nodded, unable to speak.

Taking her hand, he placed a kiss in her palm, and curled her fingers around it. Then he wiped a smudge of dirt from her forehead and laughed, "Only *you* could still be so charming beneath such a thick layer of grime."

"Oh!" Mortified, she reached up and tried in vain to wipe away the dust of the trail, finally joining Luke in helpless mirth.

Leaving the horses to graze in the shade, they walked arm in arm through the dense thicket into the clearing where Jon waited impatiently at the bee gum. "What's so funny?" he asked.

"Nothing," Kate replied dissolving again into a fit of laughter.

Puzzled, Jon looked from one to the other. Realization dawning on him, his face was transformed by a wide grin, but he said nothing.

"Let's see how busy these bees have been." Luke changed the subject. "Stand back, they're apt to be pretty mad."

Kate didn't have to be told twice and moved quickly to the edge of the clearing. Luke loosened the top of the gum, and carefully lifted the lid straight up. Golden combs dripped honey as angry bees buzzed in protest. Kate's eyes were wide in amazement. "What in the world?"

"We built it," Jon crowed proudly.

"We surely did," Luke confirmed, "but it's not quite ready yet. We need to give it a few more weeks to become well established before we take any." Luke replaced the lid in the gum, slapping at a few bees trying to sting his neck.

They hurried back to the horses, and mounted up to push the longhorns on to the ranch. Jon and Smokey worked one side of the herd, keeping the cows and calves from bolting and trying to run, while Luke rode at the rear and Kate watched the other side. They rode at a walk, attempting to keep the cattle calm as they moved them steadily eastward toward the ranch.

Soon the cows seemed to settle in to a measured march in the hot afternoon sun. Luke rode just behind the herd pushing them forward. He could see Kate and Gypsy riding out to the side, keeping them from straying too far to the south. Without warning, a small brown and white calf darted in front of Kate bawling frantically. Luke could see Kate fighting the reins as Gypsy spooked. An enraged bellow filled his ears as the mother cow bolted from the herd. She charged straight for Gypsy, caught between cow and calf. A deadly toss of her head, and five foot horns gored the frantic mare in the side. She reared up too late as her bowels spilled forth. A scream rent the air as the horse crumpled to the earth.

Kate jumped from the saddle as the horse began to fall and landed unhurt beside the dying animal. The cow continued on to the lost calf stopping several yards beyond the woman and her mare.

"No, Gypsy! No, God, no!" Kate's plaintive wail pierced his heart. She knelt beside the mare who had been her friend and companion through the lonely months after Will's death. "Gypsy, oh Gypsy, I'm so sorry." Tears streamed freely down Kate's cheeks as she stroked Gypsy's neck to calm the dying horse. Flecks of foamy sweat stained the soft red coat, and a crimson pool seeped around them saturating the air with the coppery scent of blood. The mare's struggles grew weaker, until finally she lay still, eyes wide, nostrils flaring.

It happened in an instant, no more than the blink of an eye, but the image would be forever seared on Luke's memory. Spurring Rio forward, he stopped hard beside her, swung out of the saddle, and caught her in his arms as she turned to him. Burying her face against his chest, she wept. Her hat had come loose and lay on the ground a few feet away. He stroked her hair, cradling her until at last she lay spent against him.

Her emotions raw, she tuned a tear-stained face to him, "Luke, we have to...I don't think I can...."

"Shhh...I know. I'll take care of her." The mare was dying and in pain. Luke knew that Kate would want her suffering ended quickly. Looking up, he could see Jon, wide eyed and scared, but working valiantly at his post to keep the herd from bolting.

"I'm afraid a shot right now would send those cattle into a runaway stampede. They're already nervous over the smell of blood."

Kate nodded, waiting.

"Take Rio. You and Jon keep them moving on down to the pens. It's not much further. I'll be along."

Staring into his eyes, she nodded silently. Taking the reins, she mounted the large gray gelding. Luke watched as she stoically gathered the errant cow and calf back into the herd, then she and Jonathan moved them over the ridge and down into the hollow where the ranch lay.

✻✻✻✻✻✻✻✻✻✻✻✻✻✻✻✻✻✻✻✻✻✻✻✻✻✻✻

Kate shifted in the saddle, uncomfortable on the unfamiliar horse. She concentrated on the task at hand to block out the pain that suffused her. Though she could see Jonathan stealing glances in her direction, he kept his attention focused on the cattle.

A shot rang out behind them. Kate froze, then let out a long shuddering breath knowing that Gypsy no longer suffered. One of the lead cows bellowed at the sound, but the herd plodded along toward the pens ahead of them.

Jake waited at the gates. Kate could see worry line his face as he realized there were only two of them bringing the herd in. She saw him sit up, looking beyond them. Glancing over her shoulder, she could see Luke walking down the knoll, carrying her saddle.

✻✻✻✻✻✻✻✻✻✻✻✻✻✻✻✻✻✻✻✻✻✻✻✻✻✻✻

Kate stood in the purple twilight leaning against the pasture gate, watching the medicine hat mare graze in the deepening shadows. She heard Luke's quiet step as he joined her at the corral fence.

"Does she ride?" Luke asked.

"I think so."

"You're thinking about using her, aren't you?"

Kate nodded, her gaze fastened on the mare. "Thank you, Luke, for what you did today. You'll never know how much that meant to me."

"Kate, I…" Luke faltered.

"I miss her." A single tear trickled down her cheek. "I miss her kind eye and willing ear. She was always ready to listen to my troubles, never once passing judgement on me." Kate smiled at the memory. "Her presence in my life was a precious gift, and I will always cherish the memories I have."

Luke brushed his hand against her cheek, catching the glittering tear. Cupping her face in his strong hands he gazed into her eyes. Kate's heart raced even as an overwhelming sense of peace flooded her soul. He bent and kissed her, slowly, tenderly. She could feel the awakening of emotions long dormant, and returned the kiss with all that was within her.

CHAPTER XII

"Mama, Mama, wake up!" Jo's voice cut through the sleep-induced haze in Kate's brain.

"What is it?" she asked, trying to focus in the dim room, worry already knotting her stomach.

"It's branding day, Mama, hurry, get up." Jo bounced beside the bed, her bare feet making the floorboards creak and her pale nightdress floating eerily in the shifting moonlight.

"Jo, it's the middle of the night," Kate protested. "You need to go back to bed for a bit."

"Oh, no, Mama, it'll be light soon. I know it will. Can I wear my blue dress, can I, please?" Jo pleaded.

A rooster crowed in the distance, and Candy bounded in adding her barks to the growing cacophony in Kate's room. Peering through the window, Kate saw a faint glow on the eastern horizon. Sighing, she sank back on the pillow.

"Sure. Why don't you go ahead and get dressed, then get your basket and go collect the eggs," Kate said, waiting for Jo's reaction.

"Oh, thank you, Mama." Jo ran to the door. Coming up short, she slowly turned back to her mother. "But, Mama, it will be too dark for me to see the eggs!"

"Really?" Kate feigned surprise. "In that case, why don't you crawl in bed here with me, just until it gets a little lighter."

Laughing, Jo snuggled under the covers with her mother while Candy flopped down beside the bed. Both were soon dozing contentedly. Kate held her sleeping daughter and stroked the soft red hair. Placing a feather light kiss on the tip of Jo's nose, she sighed. Thoughts of the day that lay ahead kept her from returning to the blissful sleep she had been awakened from.

She rose from the warm comfort of the feather bed, donned a light robe and wandered to the window. A faint light in the bunkhouse window told her that Luke was also awake. She smiled to herself as she thought of him. Her feelings for him were new and tender. She was still unsure of herself and of his feelings, though he had told her in no uncertain terms that he was falling in love with her. The memory of it sent a warm tingling sensation coursing through her.

Jon knew. She had seen it in his eyes there at the bee gum. He didn't say anything, but the smile that lit his face spoke volumes. How would Jake react? Or did he already suspect as well? Was it obvious to everyone?

Smiling softly, Kate turned from the window. She dressed in a deep green linen skirt and a fresh white shirtwaist. Running a brush through her thick brown hair, she braided it into a knot, pinned at the nape of her neck. A final glance at Jo sleeping peacefully in the big feather bed, and Kate let herself out of the house.

The warm air caressing her cheeks carried the sweet scent of honeysuckle. Kate breathed deeply, letting the fragrance work its calming effect within her. As her eyes adjusted to the dim light of predawn, she made her way to the barn. Pausing just inside the large doors, she let the familiar sounds and smells wash over her. Raven snorted while doves in the rafters above cooed mournfully. The pungent odor of horse and the rich scent of hay mingled together creating a heady perfume.

Kate reached for the pitchfork resting atop the hay, and forked a pile into the stallion's manger. Leaning against the stall she watched Raven as he munched the hay.

"So, what do you say, old boy, would you like to work today?" she asked.

A shake of his head and another mouthful of hay was her answer.

"Oh, you'd rather eat, would you? Well, I thought perhaps Luke could give you a bit of cutting or roping practice today. I mean, after all, everyone has to earn their keep around here, and while you do make very nice babies, you haven't had a lot of time under saddle lately."

The stallion picked his head up and snorted. Kate turned to see Luke enter the barn from the bunkhouse.

"Good morning. You're up early," he greeted her.

"I had help," Kate said under her breath. "We were just talking about you."

"We?" Luke asked looking around.

"Raven and I," she laughed. "How would you like to use him today for cutting calves?"

"I hear he's a pretty fair cutter."

"Oh, you might say that. Point him at a calf and just hold on," she replied with a mischievous grin.

"How long has it been since he's been ridden?" Luke asked warily.

"A while, but he could use the work."

"Well, maybe I'll warm him up a bit before the men arrive, see how he does."

"Oh that would be wonderful." Kate agreed enthusiastically. "I was just going up to the house to put some coffee on, join me?"

"I'd love to." Luke took her arm to escort her back to the ranch house.

His hand was warm through the thin cotton of her blouse. She could smell his earthy scent. The sound of their footfalls on the dry ground was loud in her ears. Everything seemed so crisp and clear, were all her senses heightened by his mere presence? As they neared the steps, she felt suddenly shy when he stopped and turned her to him. He placed a finger beneath her chin and tilted her face until she was staring into his clear green eyes. She trembled slightly at his intense gaze.

"Kate, I…" he hesitated.

"What?" she whispered.

His eyes clouded and he shook his head slightly, placing a tender kiss on the top of her head. "Lets get that coffee. It's going to be a very long day."

✶ ✶

Luke sat at the rough plank table watching Kate's efficient movements as she prepared the coffee. The kitchen was dimly lit by the light of a single oil lamp. The faint glow of dawn on the eastern horizon cast a rosy hue through the windows, painting the walls with the soft tones of a new day.

Kate placed the mugs of steaming coffee on the table, and took her seat across from him. "Now, what is it you want to say?" she prodded gently.

He took a deep breath and stared into the amber depths of her eyes. "I don't even know where to begin."

"I generally find the beginning is a pretty good place."

"I've been reading the Bible—and praying—since we talked the other day."

Kate's eyes began to glow and a smile played at the corners of her mouth. Luke's heart constricted at the sight, knowing that what he was about to say would take away the joy he saw there.

"Kate, I know you have a small sense of what my relationship with my father has been like."

"Yes," she whispered, a shadow crossing her delicate features.

"There's a passage in Jeremiah –"

"Then shall ye call upon me, and go and pray unto me, and I will hear you. And you shall seek me, and find me, when you search for me with all your heart. And I will be found of you, and I will turn away your captivity, and I will gather you from all the nations, and from all the places whither I have driven you, saith the Lord; and I will bring you again into the place whence I caused you to be carried away captive," Kate sighed as she quoted the verse from memory.

"Yes," Luke nodded slowly.

"When are you leaving?"

"How can I leave here?" his voice was filled with anguish.

"You know you must," Kate replied, fighting to hold back the tears gathering in her eyes. "There are things that we have to do in our lives that are not always easy. God sometimes sets tasks before us that seem impossible. We try and try in our human frailty to go around those things, or to climb over them somehow. But we always fail—until we give up, and let Him take us through them."

"You make it sound so easy," Luke retorted with bitterness filling his soul. "Just give up the things I see here—the love I see in you, give up Jolene and Jon, the thought of having a real family at last? Just walk away, is that it?"

"Until you do, what you *think* you've found here will only be a shadow of what could be."

Luke stared at Kate, anger and fear filling him at the thought of losing her. He slammed the empty cup down and strode out into the emerging dawn.

✳✳✳✳✳✳✳✳✳✳✳✳✳✳✳✳✳✳✳✳✳✳✳✳✳✳✳✳✳✳✳

The first wagons began to arrive less than an hour after sun rise. Kate watched their approach from the porch. Mrs. Insley bustled about the kitchen preparing biscuits, bacon and coffee. The aromas drifting through the open door churned Kate's stomach, as thoughts of Luke's impending departure tormented her.

A pair of high-stepping black mules pulled a buckboard into the yard, driven by a strong young man. Children tumbled from the back laughing. The oldest boy reached up to help their mother from the soft nest of hay she had been riding in.

"Greta, how are you?" Kate called warmly to the woman surrounded by children. "Come sit down. I heard you were expecting another child, but I had no idea how far along you were."

"Oh, I'm fine, Kate. Where's Mrs. Insley?"

"In the kitchen, where else?" Kate laughed, forgetting her own worries in the joy of seeing old friends.

"Aaron, Ross, you carry that food into the kitchen. Kathy, get your apron, and go help Mrs. Insley. I'll be along shortly, I just want to talk with Kate a bit."

"Yes, Mama," replied a shy girl with soft blonde curls, as the boys carried brimming baskets from the wagon.

"Jeremy? Jeremy?" Greta called. "Where is that boy?" she asked searching the yard.

"Greta, look," Kate said, pointing to the corral fence in the distance. Jeremy and Jo stood together on the bottom rail, arms hanging over the top watching Luke ride Raven among the cows.

"Oh, that boy," Greta said shaking her head, "he can get away faster than a greased piglet."

"He'll be fine. Jo will be thrilled with the company."

"I just hope they don't get into too much mischief," Greta said with a sigh.

Two men on horseback approached from the lane.

"Oh, good, Mike and Jeffery weren't far behind after all," Greta said. "They stayed behind to tend our stock, figuring they'd want their horses here anyway."

"I was just about to ask you where they were."

"Kate! Your men up to the sorting pens?" asked a dark man with an engaging smile.

"Yes, Luke and Jonathan are already up there," she replied. "Would you like some biscuits and bacon or a cup of coffee?" Kate couldn't help smiling at the man. She had always liked Mike and Greta Hall and all their children. Their's was a home filled with love and laughter and boundless energy.

"Yes, ma'am, a cup of coffee would just about do me right," he smiled.

"How about you, Jeffery?" Kate asked the quiet young man riding beside his father.

"Yes, ma'am, and could I have a splash of cream, if it wouldn't be too much trouble to ya?" he asked ingenuously.

"Of course you can," Kate smiled.

Kate and Greta entered the kitchen and returned with two steaming tin mugs, one with a splash of cream. The men took their coffee and rode on to the pens, ready for the day's work.

"He sure is growing into a fine young man. How old is he now, thirteen?" Kate asked.

Greta nodded as she watched her husband and their son ride off. "And Aaron is sixteen, and needs to be off to work himself. Where did he get to?"

"I think he's in the kitchen eating a bite," Kate replied. "Will he need a horse to use today?"

"I don't think so. I believe they plan to let Jeffery and Aaron switch off on that old brown mare." Greta said as they walked up the steps into the kitchen.

Aaron and Ross sat at the table devouring biscuits with jam and thick slices of bacon. The older son was an image of his father with black hair and dark eyes in a clear, open face. The younger boy, Ross, was more like his mother and sister, blond and soft spoken. At only nine, he would be staying with the younger children and women today, though he was pleading earnestly with his older brother to be allowed to help with the branding.

Overhearing her son, Greta chided, "Now, Ross, you know what your father said, perhaps next year. For now, I'll need your help down here. It's just as important a job as any other."

"Awww, but Ma!"

"Ross, I'll bet Jake could use your help with the roasting today. He thought he'd have to do it all himself, but I'm sure he'd welcome a strong worker like you!" Kate offered.

"Really?" he asked, eyes shining.

"Really," Kate replied. "Why don't you run out there now. He's got the fire just started, I'm sure he'll have plenty to keep you busy."

Ross jumped up and ran outside as Greta shot a grateful smile at Kate.

"Are the Kellys here yet?" Aaron asked.

"No, you're the first to arrive, but I expect they'll be along soon." Kate said, glancing out the window as a buggy and two more riders appeared on the hill. "There's Lars and Martha now, and it looks like Bert Hanneman with them."

"You just get your hide on up to work. The Kellys will be here soon enough." Greta prodded her recalcitrant son in the side.

"Yes'm, I'm going."

"What's that all about?" Kate asked puzzled.

"Ruth Kelly, " came the terse reply.

"Oh," Kate said with a knowing smile. Ruth was the Kelly's sixteen-year-old daughter, who as Kate recalled, was blooming into a striking young woman.

"I've already got one grandchild on the way, I'm not needin' any more right now."

"You do? You mean Michael married?" The Hall's eldest son had left the farm a few years earlier.

"Yes, and in a hurry, too, that baby'll be here 'fore I know it."

"Is he still running the store in Kingfisher?"

"Yes, and doing a right good job with it, too. He bought old man Huckaby out, and Michael is the proprietor now," Greta said with a note of pride in her voice.

"You must miss him, being so far away," Kate sighed, wondering how she would respond when the time came for Jo to leave her.

"Oh, I do, but he's a grown man now, making his own way. He never did like the farm life much, but he's found his calling in town."

"So, who did he marry? Anyone I know?"

"Oh, no, she seems a right nice girl, though. She's from down south of here, little town called Rush Springs. I've only met her once. She's tall, quiet—stately I guess you'd call it, but she takes real good care of my Michael, and that's a good thing." Greta said.

"Hello, everyone!" Martha breezed in, depositing a crate filled with food on the already laden table. "I've sent the men on up to get a job done, and I'm ready to work. Where do I start, Mrs. Insley?"

"Well, it's about time somebody was ready to work around here, rather than jest stand around jawing all morning!" Nana replied, handing Martha an apron and a pan of beans to snap.

"Oh, guess we've been caught out," Greta said with a twinkle in her eye. "What do you want us to do?"

"I'll need that big table set in the yard, but you're in no shape to be totin' that."

"Greta, why don't you snap these beans? Martha and I can see to the table," Kate decided, taking the pan and apron and handing them to Greta.

"Hey! How come I have to do the hard work?" Martha protested laughingly.

"Well, I could give you the dish rag, but it looks like Kathy has that well under control," Kate retorted. The pretty blonde girl blushed and ducked her head back to the dishes piled before her. "C'mon, let's get that done before the real heat sets in."

They headed out to the yard, where they were met by the Kelly's wagon pulling in. Jim Kelly rode to the corrals, while Lila and Ruth pitched in to help prepare the lunch.

✶✶✶✶✶✶✶✶✶✶✶✶✶✶✶✶✶✶✶✶✶✶✶✶✶✶✶✶✶✶

"Kate, were you expecting anyone else today?" Martha asked setting the heavy clay pitcher down on the table.

Kate glanced up, following Martha's gaze to see two riders coming in from the main road. Frowning, she placed the pies she was carrying in the center of the table, and wiped her hands on her apron as she watched their approach. Worry began to gnaw at her as she recognized the bay colt and the man riding him. What was Matt Johnson doing here?

"I'll be in the house if you need me, Kate," Martha said, watching the men.

"Don't go far."

"I wouldn't dream of it."

"Will you tell Jake they're here before you go in?"

"Of course." Martha hurried off in the direction of the roasting pit.

"Matt," Kate greeted him as they drew closer.

"Kate, I heard you were branding today. I've come to offer my assistance." Matt Johnson dismounted smoothly. Dropping the reins, he took Kate's hand and kissed it warmly.

"Matt, I think we need to talk."

"Of course we do, so many plans to make, so much to do," he smiled at her. "I fear I have been quite remiss in coming to call over the past weeks, but then neither of us are in our first bloom of love, ours will be a marriage of convenience and maturity, will it not?" His hazel eyes shone with a possessive light as he put an arm about her waist, steering her toward the garden.

"Matt, I..." Kate began to protest.

"Dick, you head up to the corrals to lend a hand. I'll be along shortly."

Kate's heart froze at the mention of the name. She looked at the man now riding away from her. He was small, nondescript, wearing a dark jacket even in this heat, and riding a roan horse.

"So, my dear, have you considered a date yet? Perhaps September might be a good month for a small wedding."

"No!" his question brought her attention abruptly back to him. "I—I mean, no, I haven't thought about it. Matt, I can't—"

"Oh, that's all right. I fully understand, what with spring planting, calving, and now the branding, of course you haven't had the time to think about it." He turned to her, "That's why I've made arrangements with Reverend Watterston in Guthrie. I thought I'd leave the exact date up to you, but do make it in September. I'm having the house there redecorated. You can begin moving your things up there anytime you wish. I'm sure you'll be relieved to get away from all this drudgery out here."

Her heart sank. She dropped her gaze to the ground, searching for the words to make him understand. "Matt, I can't marry you."

"Don't be silly, of course you can. A woman cannot manage a ranch like this alone." His voice was hard, his grip tightened about her. "Right now, I'm going out to oversee the branding. When I return, we'll announce the happy news to all our friends here." He tilted her head up to meet his eyes, "I really don't think you have any choice, do you?" The veiled threat sent a chill through her and she shivered in spite of the heat.

✳✳✳✳✳✳✳✳✳✳✳✳✳✳✳✳✳✳✳✳✳✳✳✳✳✳✳✳✳✳✳✳

Luke focused on a small brown and white calf. He could feel the powerful black horse beneath him tense as Raven picked up the calf and began cutting him slowly from the herd. Luke marveled at the natural talent and ability of the horse. The calf ducked back and tried to turn, Luke grabbed the saddle horn and held on as the stallion's lightning quick moves mirrored the calf, moving him away from the herd and toward the branding fires.

Jim Kelly sat on his sorrel gelding with his lariat loosely coiled, ready to rope the calf as he ran past. Once roped and down, one of the boys quickly tied his legs while a second brought the hot iron to sear the Providence brand onto the left hip. Bert Hanneman worked deftly with a sharp knife to castrate the bull calf.

Luke's ears rang with the bawling of calves, snorting irate cows, and the shouts of men at the fires and on horseback. The acrid stench of burnt hair and hide mixed with the coppery scent of blood permeated the air, and the dust boiled, settling in thick layers on man and beast alike.

Luke rode over to the corral fence where Jonathan waited with a canteen of fresh spring water. Taking off his hat, he wiped a dusty arm across his brow.

"Give me that, will you?" Luke asked shortly.

"Sure thing," Jon replied. "It's not too cold, but it's wet enough."

"Right now, that's all that counts," Luke said, taking a long drink. He felt the water slide down his parched throat and was thankful for the cooling refreshment it provided.

"Someone's coming," Jon said, indicating a lone figure approaching the far corral.

Luke watched for a moment unconcerned, until a flash of memory pictured a roan horse through a thicket of green shrubbery. Taking a closer look, he recognized the dark coat and the rifle holstered on the saddle.

"Mike, take over the cutting here for a minute, would you?" Luke called. At a wave from Mike, he handed his reins to Jonathan, "Stay here."

Luke approached the stranger, eyeing him warily. "Can I help you?"

The man sat stiffly in the saddle, returning Luke's gaze with lazy, indolent eyes. "Just here to lend a hand," came the drawled reply, though he made no move to work.

"Roping or branding?" Luke asked, keeping his voice steady.

"Believe I'll wait till the boss gets here. See where he wants me working."

"The boss?"

"You know, Matt Johnson, man who's marryin' old lady Shaughnessey. He'll be takin' over here and callin' the shots 'fore too long," the man said obviously baiting and watching for Luke's reaction as he began to dismount.

The bald-faced statement hit Luke like a gut punch. Marrying Kate? Why hadn't she said anything? A blind rage overcame him as he grabbed the man by the shoulder, jerking him roughly from the saddle. "What are you talking about?" he asked through clenched teeth.

The stranger winced in pain as Luke's hand clamped down. Realization swept through him. He pulled the jacket and shirt back roughly, exposing a crudely bandaged shoulder. "Do you want to explain that," Luke asked harshly.

A small knot of men had gathered, watching the confrontation from a short distance. "And while you're at it, you might try explaining what you were doing on this ranch shooting at the owner and me a few days ago," Luke raised his voice. A murmur ran through the gathered men.

"I don't know what you're talking about," the man countered, trying in vain to escape Luke's iron grasp.

"What's going on here," a sharp voice commanded their attention.

Luke turned to meet hazel eyes glowing with hatred beneath the low brim of a dark hat.

"That's what I'd like to know," Luke answered, undaunted. "This man took a few shots at us earlier this week. Trouble is, I shot back, and there's the evidence."

"Dick, what's the meaning of this?" Matt turned to the cowering man.

"But, boss, you know…" he began feebly, faltering under the baleful gaze.

"If you're back to your rustling, Dick, I have no further use for you." Matt said, his eyes never leaving the man still held firmly in Luke's unyielding grip.

"But, Mr. Johnson…" Dick started to protest.

"Get on your horse and get out of here. If I ever set eyes on you again, I'll have the law out so fast you won't know what happened." Matt spoke harshly, but something in his demeanor caught Luke's attention, making him wonder at the validity of the words.

Dick West grabbed the reins of his horse and mounted, glaring at Luke, and casting a questioning glance at his erstwhile employer. At a subtle nod from Johnson, West turned the horse, spurring him harshly, he disappeared over the rise.

A bitter gall rose in Luke at the exchange between Johnson and West, and he could hear the men muttering among themselves.

"…not enough law in this territory."

"Only the federal marshals…too few and far between."

"That's why we need statehood, we need organized government to run this country right."

"Well, it ain't likely to happen any time soon, and you know it."

Luke caught snippets of the conversation, but his attention was focused on Matt Johnson.

"You must be Josey," Matt said, his eyes narrowed.

Luke remained silent barely acknowledging the statement.

"I believe the show's over men. You'd best get back to work. Those cattle aren't going to brand themselves." Matt Johnson spoke in a commanding tone, yet the men remained, looking to Luke for direction.

Luke's gaze locked on Johnson, unwavering. "He's right, men, Kate needs a job done. Let's get it finished."

✻✻✻✻✻✻✻✻✻✻✻✻✻✻✻✻✻✻✻✻✻✻✻✻✻✻✻✻✻✻✻✻

Kate stood silently, her heart filled with loathing as she watched Matt Johnson ride toward the branding pens. Fear crept through her. What had he meant by saying she had no choice? Her mind raced, searching for answers. Overcome by the shock, she turned and fled up the path to the lone willow, collapsing in tears at the secluded cemetery.

"Lord, oh Lord, what am I going to do?" she prayed. "I can't marry him, I can't, I won't!" she grew desperate, fear building within her until she felt as though it was pouring forth from her soul in great waves of anguish. Her heart raced, her breathing became labored.

"I will love thee, O Lord, my strength. The Lord is my rock, and my fortress, and my deliverer; my God, my strength, in whom I will trust," she repeated the familiar Psalm again and again until the words brought a peace to her heart.

Sighing, she sat up and wiped the tear stains from her face. Kate knew that the strength to face Johnson would come only through her faith.

"Help, mama, somebody please help me!" Jo's plaintive wail reached Kate's ears faintly, borne on the breeze beginning to stir the still heat of the day.

"Oh, Lord, what now?" Kate cried, racing toward the yard.

✦ ✦

"Kate, there you are!" Martha called. "Come quickly, it's Jo."

"What is it? What's happened? Is she all right?" Kate scanned the yard looking for her daughter.

A timid voice caught her ear, "She's up there, ma'am."

Kate glanced down into the terrified face of Jeremy Hall. He was pointing to the windmill. Shading her eyes with one hand, Kate could just make out the small form of her daughter clinging desperately to the wooden framing, her blue dress billowing in the light breeze.

"Jake's gone to fetch Luke." Martha said.

Kate picked up her skirts and ran to the base of the windmill tower, followed closely by Martha and Jeremy. Several women and children were already gathered there, some calling encouragements to the stranded girl, others wringing their hands.

Nana stood apart, hands firmly planted on her hips, "What were you thinking, Jolene Rose Shaughnessey?" she scolded. "How could you have done such a thing?"

"I'm so sorry, Nana, I'll never do it again," Jo cried. "Just please get me down, I'm so scared!"

"Jolene, hold on, don't move, Mama's here now. Luke's coming." Kate called.

"I'm sorry, Miz Shaughnessey, it's all my fault," Jeremy cried, tugging at her skirt.

"Jeremy, what happened?" Kate asked, her gaze fastened on Jo.

"We was just playin', but I beat her racing, and she said she could climb a tree faster'n me, so I said bet I could climb all the way to the top of the windmill, but she said she could go higher and faster. Then 'fore I knew it she was above me, but now she can't get down. Every time she tried, her skirts went all gollywampus and she kept getting her foot caught, and she got scared," he paused for a breath, tears streaming down his ruddy cheeks. "Ah, gee, I'm so sorry!"

"Jeremy, it's going to be all right, Luke's coming, he'll get her down, I know he will." She knelt before the trembling boy and gathered him in her arms. "It's not your fault, Jeremy, do you hear me?"

He nodded, sniffing, his blue eyes swimming with tears.

Kate's heart went out to him, even as she turned her gaze back to her stranded daughter. *Lord, protect these children. They are wholly Yours, take them in Your hand right now, and protect them with Your love and grace,* she prayed silently.

✳ ✳ ✳ ✳ ✳ ✳ ✳ ✳ ✳ ✳ ✳ ✳ ✳ ✳ ✳ ✳ ✳ ✳

"Kate, what's going on?" Luke's angry tone rose above the hum of voices. He strode into the yard followed closely by Matt Johnson, Mike Hall and Jonathan.

"Oh, Luke, thank God you're here," she cried, her eyes pleading with him. "You've got to get her down. I don't know how much longer she can hold on."

The look on Kate's face tore at his heart. Wresting his eyes from hers, he glanced up to where Jo clung to the tower. Fear tried to overwhelm him, but he fought it down, knowing that he would need to stay calm in order to get her down.

"Jo, honey, you hold on tight. I'm coming to get you," he called to the frightened girl.

"I'm trying, please hurry." Jo cried, fear and exhaustion evident in her faint voice.

"Jake, get me that rope from the barn, the long one we were using last week. Jon get that wagon and team over here. Mike, clear everyone away from this area." Luke barked the orders and the men jumped to respond.

"Just exactly what do you think you are doing?" Matt asked in a steely voice.

"I'm going to get that little girl down. What do you think you're doing?" Luke returned evenly. "If you have any ideas, let me hear them. Otherwise, stay out of my way."

Johnson gazed at him with flinty eyes, pausing for an instant, he turned and strode away to stand near Kate. At the sight of the two of them together, Luke closed his heart and turned to the task at hand.

Jake returned with a long, coiled rope. Gauging the height of the tower with a practiced eye, Luke could see Jo clinging to the structure about forty feet from the ground. He cut off a length that was just less than twice the distance. With one end tied securely to the wagon, he tucked the free end through his belt. "Mike, you and Jon are going to take the team out till the rope is just about taut, as I climb up, back the wagon with me to feed it. I'm going to take it up there, throw it over the beam, and tie it around her. As we start down, keep backing the team as we go. That way if she should slip, the rope'll keep her from falling on down."

"Got it. Jon, you drive, I'll give you the cues," Mike said.

"Hold on just a little longer, Jo, I'm coming up." Luke called as the wagon lurched forward, taking out the slack.

Grabbing the rough timbers, Luke tested the first cross beam with a booted foot. It gave slightly, but held his weight. Taking a deep breath, he began the long climb up, hand over hand, testing each foothold as he went. Keeping his eyes fixed on Jo, he was soon beside her.

"Oh, Mr. Josey, I'm so scared!" She clung tightly to the splintered boards, her eyes shut tightly against the dizzying height. Luke could hear the creak of the blades turning lazily over the platform a few feet above their heads.

"Jo, listen to me. I'm going to put a rope around this beam and tie it under your arms. Hold on just as tight as you can while I do that. Do you understand?"

She nodded.

Tossing the rope lightly over the timber with one hand, he caught it and pulled his weight against the wooden beam, it creaked but held fast. With his right arm hooked over a cross bar, and his legs wrapped around a tower post, he passed the end of the rope around Jo's small chest and knotted it securely beneath her arms.

Finding a footing as close to her as he could, he grasped her firmly about the waist with one arm, "All right Jo, I want you to let go of the tower and put your arms around my neck."

Her lip trembled, her arms quivered, "I can't," she gasped, "I can't let go."

"Yes you can, Jo, you've got to!" he commanded sternly.

"I can't, my arms won't move," she wailed as tears began to stream freely down her cheeks.

"Jo, listen to me. With this rope on, you can't fall. C'mon now, let's get down from here." Luke watched her fingers intently, finally they twitched, then in one enormous burst she was wrapped around him, clinging with arms and legs, nearly throwing him from his precarious perch.

Regaining his balance, he grabbed the tower again with both hands. Slowly he began the descent, searching blindly for each step below, checking the rope for tautness. He could make out the wagon, moving slowly back with his descent, one agonizing step at a time. Jo clung to his neck, burying her small face in his shirt. He began to pray fervently for their safety. Looking down he realized there was less than twenty feet to the ground. Breathing a sigh of relief, he picked up his speed, longing to feel the earth beneath his feet.

The relentless rays of the of the burning sun sent sweat streaming into his eyes, the salt stung, momentarily blinding him. His hand moved instinctively to wipe away the irritation, giving up the secure hold. Even as his foot found the next rail, the sound of splintering wood filled his ears and he felt himself falling, reaching out in desperation to grab the tower, but finding only air. Jo screamed as he was torn from her tight grasp.

Pain coursed through him as he landed on his back in the dry dust at the base of the tower. Gasping for breath, a moment of panic seized him before the air rushed back into his lungs. Gulping in great drafts of air filled his throat with dust. Coughing it out, he rose to his elbow slowly, the pain retreating as he searched for Jo. She was dangling above the ground slowly descending as the mules backed the wagon a step at a time under Jon's careful guidance. He tried to rise, but Kate was beside him, her eyes filled with fear.

"I'm all right, get Jo," He managed to gasp, waving her away. Kate nodded, turning just in time to reach up and ease the girl into her arms.

"Mama, oh Mama," Jo cried.

"Hush, it's okay, now, Jo, you're safe," Kate crooned to the girl, stroking her hair and rocking her gently.

"Luke's dead and it's all my fault," Jo continued to wail.

"Well, for a dead man, I'd say I was feeling pretty good," laughed Luke, standing and patting the distraught child on the back. "A little sore, but all in all, not bad for someone who's dead."

"Luke! Oh, Luke, you're not dead. I was sure you were dead. You fell so far. I'm so sorry I did that, I'll never do it again, never." Jo, still held firmly in Kate's grasp, reached over and threw her arms around her hero. Luke returned the embrace, including Kate within the circle of his arms. He could feel the tension leave her body as she rested her head against his shoulder. Glancing over Kate's head he met the hate filled gaze of Matt Johnson.

✳ ✳

"Well, what a cozy tableau this is, my fiancé in the arms of another man."

Kate could feel the rage rising within her at the insinuation in Matt's words. Handing Jo to Luke, she squared her shoulders and faced him. "Mr. Johnson, I am not now nor have I ever been your fiancé. I'm sorry if you had that mistaken impression." Kate struggled to remain calm. She was keenly aware of the gathered crowd, and thankful for their presence. "I appreciate the kindness you have shown to me and my family in the past, and your concern for my present and future well being, but I cannot marry you," she continued in a strong, clear voice.

Matt's countenance grew dark; he took a step forward, "I would urge you to reconsider that position, ma'am," he said in a low tone.

A murmur rose among the crowd, tension filled the air. She felt Luke's hand on her arm as he stepped beside her. She glanced at him, her eyes pleading silently with him to allow her to finish this. He nodded. Their friends and neighbors gathered behind them, leaving Matt Johnson alone and unprotected.

"No," she shook her head firmly. "My home is here, this is my family and my land. The Lord has provided for us, and I have full faith that He will continue."

"Kate, you don't know what you're doing." Matt's tone was threatening.

"I believe she does," spoke the normally taciturn Lars. Kate glanced at him in surprise and flashed him a grateful look. Others voices spoke up in agreement.

"I'm thinkin' perhaps it would be best if you left about now," suggested Mike Hall.

Matt glared at Lars and Mike, then turned his venom on Luke, "I'd watch my step if I were you." With a final dark look at Kate, he strode past them and mounted. Spurring his horse roughly, he disappeared quickly from their view.

"Well, good riddance, is what I say!" Nana pronounced sternly.

Kate sighed as the tension began to ease. Taking Jo's hand, she turned to Martha, "Let's feed these hungry people, shall we?"

The table was set and women carried heaping platters from the kitchen and the roasting pit, while the men took turns at the well sloshing water over dust grimed faces. Children scurried about chasing dogs away from the food, and laughing at the antics of their elders that day. Soon all were gathered around the large plank table in the yard, waiting expectantly for Jake to ask the blessing on the meal. The old man walked to the head of the table, hats were removed and hands folded, a hush descended upon the gathering.

"Our Father, we come humbly this day in thanks and praising Your name. We thank You for the bounty You have provided, the friends You have blessed us with, and most especially, Father, for returning Jo to us safely. Bless now this gathering and this food so lovingly prepared. It is in Jesus' name I ask this, Amen"

The amen was echoed quietly about the table. Kate looked up in time to see a tear slip silently down Jake's leathery cheek. Excusing herself from the group of women gathered about her, she hurried to him, slipping her hand into his as she had so many times in the past. Then she was seeking his comfort, now she longed to comfort him. "It's been a long day, Jake."

"That it has, that it has," he sighed.

"Are you hungry?"

"Not really," he replied shaking his head.

"Then will you sit with me a while in the shade?" she asked.

He nodded, and they wandered over to sit in the shadows of a spreading oak. The grass was cool and thick beneath the boughs thick with leaves that sighed in the gentle breeze. Kate spread her skirt about her as she sank to her knees in the welcome shade.

Jake sat slowly with a grimace. "I guess these old bones are getting a might creaky on me," he said.

"It wouldn't hurt you any to slow down a bit, you know," Kate admonished him gently.

"Ha, slowing down these last few days is what caused these creaky joints! I need to keep working, keep everything tuned up, or this old body'll just up and quit on me."

"Oh, Jake, sometimes I wish I could just build you and Nana a big house and give you everything you deserve in life," Kate sighed. "But you know, I believe you're right. I don't think either one of you would last six months if you had to live a life of leisure." They laughed together with a feeling of camaraderie that Kate realized had been missing these past weeks.

Sitting together in companionable silence, they watched people heaping plates of food and juggling cups filled with water or lemonade as they found seats together in small groups. The drone of conversations punctuated by guffaws of laughter floated lazily on the warm summer air. The scent of smoke from the roasting fire clung to Jake's clothes. The aroma made Kate's stomach growl, but glancing at Jake, she decided staying by him was more important than food just now.

"Are you going to marry Luke?" Jake asked presently.

"He hasn't asked me to."

"He will."

"Perhaps," Kate mused, plucking a fat blade of grass and examining it minutely.

"Well?"

"Well, what?"

"Do you plan on marrying him, or what?" Jake asked in an exasperated tone.

Kate turned to face him squarely. She searched his face for a moment before replying. "Jake, I don't know. I think I'm falling in love with him—no, I *know* I'm falling in love with him, but I'm afraid." She paused, looking for a way to explain the fears that filled her. "I know so little about him, except…"

"Except what?" Jake prodded.

"I think he's leaving, Jake," she spoke quietly, her gaze cast down, avoiding Jake's scrutiny.

"Leaving?"

Kate nodded, "His past is haunting him. If he doesn't find his peace there…" she lifted her face to him. "Jake, what if he doesn't come back?"

"Does he love you?"

She nodded, "I think so."

He studied her face. Reaching out a weathered hand, he smoothed her hair and cupped her chin, "He'll be back," he said firmly.

"Who'll be back?" came Luke's voice from behind them.

Startled, Kate looked up to see Luke trying to balance three full plates of food, forks sticking out of his vest pocket at odd angles. "Oh, my!" she gasped, jumping up to relieve him of his burden.

"I thought you two might be hungry, sitting over here all by your lonesome." He handed one of the plates to Jake, "Mind if I join you?"

"Sit down, young man. The more, the merrier, I always say."

Luke sat, and for a moment no one spoke as the three of them enjoyed the savory roasted beef, fresh bread with butter, applesauce, beans, and fried potatoes.

"Do you really think he'll be back?" Luke asked between bites.

"Huh, what? Oh, Matt Johnson!" Kate said, even as she felt the heat rise in her cheeks. "I hope not. Surely that last was a show to cover his wounded pride."

"I wouldn't be so sure, Kate. He doesn't strike me as the type to make idle threats," Luke said. "What do you think, Jake?"

Jake pushed his potatoes around for a moment, lost in thought. "Johnson's been around these parts a long time. He ran cattle here when it was still Indian Territory. He was one of them that didn't take too kindly to the government openin' this area up to settlement, and he's never been real choosey about which side of the law he was on.

"Course he did help us out in the beginning. Him and Will even made a few drives together. I always believed then that he had some other reasons for all that, other than just bein' neighborly."

Jake paused in his narrative, his eyes seemed fixed on a vision of the past. He shook his head, "I don't know. I just rightly don't know. Appears to me like he's gotten worse in the past months. He's got a look in his eyes now that gives me shivers when I think of it."

✶✶✶✶✶✶✶✶✶✶✶✶✶✶✶✶✶✶✶✶✶✶✶✶✶✶✶✶✶✶✶

After the midday meal, Kate helped the women clean dishes and pack wagons while they gossiped and chatted and watched the children. The men returned to the branding corrals amid good-natured shouts and laughter.

"Walk with me, Kate?" asked Martha.

"Sure, let's head up to the corrals. I want to see how it's going up there."

The two women set off at a leisurely pace. The freshening breeze that held so much promise earlier had died, and now the warm, moist heat was growing oppressive. Martha carried a damp rag, running it over her flushed face every few minutes. "I swear I don't know how you do this day after day, Kate," Martha complained. "I would melt, working out here in this heat. At least I have the cool shade in the store."

"Oh, I suppose it's like anything else," Kate laughed, "you get used to it or die." Though even she could feel the sweat running in warm rivulets between her shoulder blades, and the once crisp white shirt she wore was clinging to her damp skin.

"Luke is riding Raven!" Martha exclaimed as they approached the nearest branding pen.

Kate smiled as she saw the powerful black horse. Luke handled him skillfully, and she realized they made an efficient and handsome team. Resting her arms atop the wooden fence, she watched them approach the herd quietly, though every muscle was tuned and ready. Luke pointed Raven at a calf, and the horse dropped his head to begin the process of cutting the small black bull from the herd. Kate marveled again at the agility and cow sense that the horse exhibited. She could almost believe that Raven enjoyed the work, displaying an air of proud accomplishment when the calf finally turned and ran toward the ropers at the far end of the pen.

"Luke!" Martha called, waving to him.

He rode to the women, smiling warmly into Kate's eyes. "Hello, Martha," Luke said, though his eyes stayed on Kate.

"Well, hello to you, too, but I'm over here." Martha laughed. "Are you men nearly finished up here?"

"Just one more to go after that bull calf there."

"Luke, tell them not to cut him. That's the one I wanted to leave a bull, I think he's going to be a good replacement for Casey." Kate said.

Luke nodded and urged Raven to the branding fire. After a brief conversation, he returned to the rail where Kate and Martha watched the proceedings.

"We're going to mother these up as soon as we get that last calf branded, then push them back out to pasture. Did you want to turn Casey out with the Angus cows first, or the longhorns?" Luke asked as he rode up alongside the fence.

"I want him with the Angus. Mike says he has a new Hereford bull that he'll loan me to try on the longhorn. I'm curious what kind of cross that will be." Kate replied. "He said he could drive him over in a couple of weeks. What do you think?"

A slow smile spread across Luke's sun warmed features as Kate waited for a reply. He sat quietly smiling at her and gazing into her eyes until finally she couldn't stand it, "What?" she asked, puzzled.

"Do you realize that's the first time you have ever asked my opinion when it comes to the ranch management?"

"That's not—well, I mean—I just –" Kate stammered, even as she felt the heat rising within her cheeks.

Martha smiled, thoroughly enjoying her friend's discomfiture. "Feels good, doesn't it, Kate, having a man around to ask?"

"You stay out of this, Martha Louise Jansen," Kate said in frustration, but Martha only continued to smile in a knowing way.

"Actually, I think the Hereford would make an excellent cross on the longhorns, only thing I'd worry about are the heifers. The calves might be a bit big for those first timers," Luke continued. "We could get around that by cutting the heifers out and keeping them down here with your old longhorn bull for their first calves, and turning Mike's bull out with the older, bigger cows. I think that might be a workable solution."

"You're right. Will you take care of cutting the heifers out and sending the rest back to pasture?"

Luke nodded, and with a brief tip of his hat to Martha, he turned Raven on his haunches and loped back to the working fires.

Martha flashed a smug, knowing grin at Kate.

Kate sighed. "You're right. It does feel good to have someone I can intelligently discuss the day-to-day management with," she said earnestly. Then with a wicked gleam in her eyes, she added, "A good ranch foreman comes in handy for that."

"Oh! You are so exasperating, Kathleen Shaughnessey!" Martha stomped her foot, raising a small cloud of red dust. "When are you going to give up and admit to me that you're falling for him?"

"When the moon turns to blue cheese and that cow there jumps over it!"

Chapter XIII

Kate breathed in the rich scent of sun-warmed earth as she picked through dark leaves, finding the yellow squash below. Snapping them from the vine, she placed them in a basket rapidly filling with ripe produce. Cucumbers, tomatoes and squash jumbled together in colorful profusion. She and Nana would be busy the next few days canning, drying and preserving the bountiful harvest to see them through the winter. Jo worked nearby, pulling carrots and chatting to her doll who rode along in the small wagon groaning beneath its succulent orange burden.

Jake had left that morning to inspect the fields planted in corn and oats, and the hay meadows to the east. Jonathan worked in the barn making sure the hay mow and the rakes would be ready to begin the cutting that was rapidly approaching. Luke rode the fence lines and managed the herds, already beginning the selection process of two and three year old steers, aged cows and weaker heifers to be sent to market in the fall. Keeping the herds viable and managing the growth of the herd in relation to the available grazing land was a vital concern in the management of the ranch.

Kate sat back on her heels with a sigh, stretching her aching back and wiping the sweat from her brow. Even as she longed for the cool days of autumn, to see the changing color of the leaves that signaled the approach of colder months, she was struck by a pang of sorrow, knowing that Luke would be leaving then.

He carried a burden that went deeper than his relationship with his father, Kate was certain of it even though he never mentioned it. They had developed a deep friendship in the weeks since the branding. Riding together in the early mornings, or sitting alone on the porch in the evenings after a late supper, they talked of many things, the ranch and its needs, their pasts, their families. Kate had learned much about this man who had entered her life, but she sensed there was more, something held deep within, a scar so painful that he would not let go of it to her or even to God.

She thought of her own scars, physical scars, painful and hidden in shame. What would Luke think if he saw the disfigured flesh of her arms? Were his emotional scars any less painful? Lost in thought, Kate was startled by a shout from Jo.

"Mama, Mama, look! Someone's coming."

Kate stood, shading her eyes against the midday glare of a relentless sun. She saw two riders approaching from the south, red dust billowing around them in a great cloud. As they grew closer, she realized they were driving an enormous red bull with a white face, short horns and a ring through his nose. She smiled and waved at Mike Hall, gesturing toward the corrals, where they could safely pen the Hereford until Luke's return.

"Jo, run and tell Nana to get some lunch ready for Mike and whoever is with him. We'll be down in a few minutes."

"Yes, Mama," Jo answered and scurried off to find Nana.

Gathering up her skirts, Kate hurried to the corrals. Mike was just closing the gate as she arrived. The bull snorted a few times then dropped his head to graze on the sparse grass.

"That is a fine looking animal, Mike," Kate said.

"He does real good for us, and if you like what he produces for you, I've got a son of his out of a good Hereford cow that I could make you a real good deal on," Mike offered.

"I may just do that," Kate said appraising the massive creature before her. Turning to the other rider, Kate exclaimed, "Michael, it's so good to see you! I thought you were firmly ensconced in your business up at Kingfisher. Look at you, all grown up and married, too, or so I hear!"

"It's good to see you, too, Mrs. Shaughnessey." The Hall's eldest son smiled broadly.

"What brings you down this way?"

"I just wanted to bring my Annie down to see the home place and meet the rest of the family," Michael replied.

"I understand congratulations are in order for you two." Kate smiled.

"Yes, Ma'am, the little one should be here early this fall," Michael replied. Kate sensed a note of pride, but thought she saw a momentary shadow pass over his features.

"Well, I guess that makes you a grandpa, Mike, and a new one of your own coming as well." Kate shook her head as she turned to Mike, who was beaming with pride. "How about some lunch? Mrs. Insley should have a little something ready at the house."

"That sounds like just the thing."

"Why don't you put your horses in the pen on the other side of the barn. There's water and hay there," Kate suggested, "then come on down to the house."

"We'll be there shortly," Mike said taking the reins of his horse and heading for the barn.

✳✳✳✳✳✳✳✳✳✳✳✳✳✳✳✳✳✳✳✳✳✳✳✳✳✳✳✳✳✳

Stopping at the garden to retrieve the basket of vegetables, Kate continued on to the house. Nana had adorned the porch table with a fresh white cloth. Pewter plates were stacked neatly to one side while platters of bread, smokey sliced meats, bowls of curded cheese, relish and fresh fruit vied for attention in the center. Jo was busy spreading muslin cloths over the platters to keep away the ever present flies, and Nana carried a pitcher of milk from the spring house. Kate marveled again at the bounty the Lord continued to provide.

"Hi, Mama, who's here?" Jo asked brimming with curiosity.

"Mr. Hall and his oldest son, Michael. They brought the Hereford bull that he promised to loan us," Kate replied.

"Oh, I can't wait to see Michael. I haven't seen him since I was just a little girl. He'll be surprised at how big I've gotten, won't he Mama?" Jo chatted incessantly, continuing to flick at the droning flies with a horse-hair switch. "Jeremy said that Michael got married and his wife is gonna have a baby. Does that make Jeremy an uncle? I wish we had a baby, then I could hold it and rock it, and sing songs to it. I do that with my doll, but I think it would be better with a real baby." Jo paused, a frown creasing her brow. "You have to be married to have a baby, don't you, Mama?"

"Well, yes, that's the way God intended for families to be," Kate said finding a niche for her heavy basket in the cool dark kitchen. "Why?"

Jo heaved a weary sigh, "I just wish you could have a new baby for us, but…."

Kate smiled at the wistful tone in Jo's voice. Returning to the sunlit porch, she gathered Jo up in her arms. "Honey, God has so richly blessed our lives already, maybe someday He'll see fit to bless us in that way, too."

Jo threw her arms around her mother and buried her face in Kate's neck. "I'm gonna keep praying for that."

"Look. Here come the Halls," Kate said setting Jo down.

A flash of petticoats and red curls bolted down the stairs as Jo launched herself into Michael's arms. "Oh, Michael, it's so good to see you again. I bet you don't even recognize me, do you?"

"Could this my wild Irish rose all grown up?" Michael asked swooping her up in a warm embrace.

Jo beamed from ear to ear, her fiery hair and petal soft pink cheeks echoing the bloom for which he named her.

"Hello, Jo, been climbing any windmills today?" the elder Hall asked her.

"Oh, no sir, I'll never do that again," Jo replied earnestly, earning a hearty laugh from them both. Michael set Jo down and she ran off looking for her pup.

"Nana Insley!" Michael called to the frail woman fussing over the table.

"Well little Michael Hall, as I live and breathe!" Nana exclaimed as she all but disappeared in his massive arms. "Only you aren't so little anymore," she said, regaining her composure.

"Nana, it looks as though you've out done yourself again," Mike commented, casting an appreciative eye over the lunch table.

"Oh, you know how 'tis, cooking for all the hungry mouths around this place, a body just does what she can," Nana replied as she wiped at a spot on the table that only she could see.

"Shall we eat?" Kate asked. "I expected Luke back by now, but maybe he's been detained." She sighed, scanning the horizon for any glimpse of him.

"Luke?" Michael asked.

"Sort of a foreman Kate hired a while back," Mike filled his son in.

"Anyone I know?"

"He's not from around here," Kate supplied. "He drifted in early last spring, and Martha Jansen thought he'd make a good hired hand for me. Seems I was having trouble keeping on any local help." Kate smiled wryly.

"Well all this jabber isn't getting you men fed," Nana complained. "Let's eat!"

Mike asked a blessing upon the meal and those assembled, then the men fell to filling their plates and discussing the weather.

"Does it seem like a hotter summer to you, Mrs. Shaughnessey?" Michael asked between bites. He was sitting in a straight-backed chair, balancing a heaping plate on his broad lap.

"Won't you please call me Kate?" she asked with a grin. "Mrs. Shaughnessey seems so formal now that you're all grown up."

"I don't know, might be kind of hard to get used to."

"You'll manage. And yes, it does seem like an unusually hot summer. Good thing we had some rains early on, but we could sure use some more." Kate wiped her face with the edge of her apron before picking up her plate and finding a comfortable spot on the stairs to eat.

"Looks like your garden and fruit trees came on fine this year. Greta's did right well, too. How're Jake's crops doing?" Mike asked.

"He's out checking them now, but so far they seem to be doing fine. I believe he's going to start harvesting the corn this week. And I think we'll be cutting hay here real soon, too."

"Kate, I have a favor to ask of you," Mike said, his voice taking on an earnest tone.

"Mike, you know I'd do just about thing for you. What is it?"

"Greta's time is comin' real soon, I'd be obliged if you'd come on out to midwife for her."

"Well, of course I will, but she's never had any trouble before, has she?"

"No, but she's not as young as she was, and she's been a bit weak these last few weeks."

"You just send one of the boys out here in time to fetch me, don't wait too long! I'll be there for her." Kate reached over and laid a reassuring hand upon his arm. "What about your Annie, Michael? How is she doing with her first one?"

"Can't rightly say. She doesn't say much about it, but she sure looks pale and sickly these last months. That's one of the reasons I brought her out here, Mrs.—I mean, Kate," Michael paused. "I thought Ma could give her some encouragement or something. I mean after all, she's been through it a few times herself."

Kate laughed, "That she has, but I'm not sure it's encouragement she needs right now. Has she been seeing a doctor at all?"

"Yes ma'am, back in Kingfisher, we have a real good doc. He says everything is fine, and she should have no reason to worry."

"Well, Michael, it is a scary thing for a woman to face, especially the very first time. Will you both still be there when Greta has hers?"

"I've got to get back to the store, but I'm trying real hard to convince Annie to stay on here. I think she'd be better off here with ma to look after her. I can get down to see her from time to time, and once the baby's here and they're both well, then they can come back home with me."

"That actually sounds like a good plan to me. What does Annie think?"

"She hasn't said too much one way or the other, but I'm thinking she'll probably stay."

"That's good. Your mother could do her a world of good."

"Yes, ma'am, she sure could."

A movement along the ridge caught Kate's attention. Shading her eyes with one hand, she could make out the gleaming coat of the buckskin colt. The form took shape as horse and rider came closer. Kate smiled at the sight. Luke had done a fine job with the young horse, and he was quickly becoming a sound, reliable mount.

"Looks like Luke is headed in for lunch. You'll get a chance to meet him after all," Kate said watching their approach.

Luke rode into the yard. Swinging down from the buckskin, he loosened the girth, removed the headstall and turned the colt loose to graze. He paused at the pump in the yard long enough to splash water over his face and hands, then turned and strode to the porch.

"Luke, Mike brought the Hereford over this morning," Kate called to him.

"Thought he must have. I saw the bull up at the corrals. Good looking beast, Mike," Luke said, helping himself to a plate and heaping it with food.

"Thanks. Do you need help driving him out to pasture?" Mike asked.

"Nah, we can handle it tomorrow."

"Luke, I want you to meet Michael, the Hall's oldest boy," Kate said turning to the young man at the far side of the table. The look in Michael's eyes sent a chill through Kate. His jaw was clenched, his eyes cold. A shiver of fear shot through her, and she turned, puzzled to Luke. He stood rooted to the rough wooden planks of the porch. Kate thought she saw a flicker of pain before an inscrutable mask descended over his handsome features.

"Michael," Luke rasped.

"Luke Josey," Michael replied, clenching his fists tightly at his side.

An awkward silence ensued punctuated by faint laughter drifting from the garden. A dog barked joyously, and soon running feet announced Jo's arrival.

"Hello, Mr. Josey," Jo laughed, grabbing him about the waist in a warm embrace. "Are all the cows doing well today? Did you check the bee gum? Are we going to have honey soon? Look, the Halls have come, and they brought a big bull with them."

Luke closed his eyes briefly, then set his plate on the table, and tousled Jo's hair with a faint indulgent smile. "I'm suddenly not very hungry. If you'll excuse me, I have work to do." He strode to where the colt grazed, startling the buckskin with his abrupt approach. The horse snorted and backed up, but stood quietly while Luke bridled him and tightened the saddle. Mounting, he turned the horse out of the yard and they rode swiftly away.

"What's the matter with Mr. Josey, Mama? Did I do something bad?" Jo asked with a frown.

"No, honey, you didn't do anything wrong," Kate reassured the small girl. As Jo's lip began to quiver, Kate gave her a quick hug, patted her back, and placed a light kiss upon her furrowed brow. "Now, why don't you go in and help Nana clean up theses dishes, okay?"

"Yes, ma'am," Jo said, though Kate could tell she was not thoroughly convinced.

As Jo disappeared into the kitchen, Kate turned a questioning look on Michael, "I take it you two have met before?"

"Briefly."

"Do you want to tell me about it?" Mike asked his suddenly taciturn son.

"Not really. He was a friend of Annie's brother, Joe." Michael continued to stare in the direction Luke had taken. "Unless you need me here, I'm going to head back." Without waiting for a response, Michael left, heading for the barn where his horse was corralled. Moments later Kate saw him ride in the same direction Luke had gone.

"Mike?" Kate asked, searching the face of her friend for answers.

Mike shook his head and shrugged, "I don't know Kate. I honestly don't know."

✶✶✶✶✶✶✶✶✶✶✶✶✶✶✶✶✶✶✶✶✶✶✶✶✶✶✶✶✶✶✶✶✶

With a heavy heart Kate tucked the faded quilt snugly around Jo's small body. "There you are, sweetheart," she said, placing a tender kiss on Jo's tear stained cheek. "Sleep well, I'll see you in the morning."

"But Mama, why did he go? I want Luke to come home," Jo sniffed.

Kate sighed as she stroked the curls that lay spread upon the muslin pillow. "Honey, I don't know why he left the way he did. I pray that he'll come home, but I don't know, I just don't know." The emptiness Kate felt was mirrored in Jo's eyes. She gathered the forlorn child in her arms and rocked her until exhaustion overcame grief and Jo slept fitfully.

She laid the sleeping child upon the pillow, arranging the light covers. Picking up the oil lamp from the bedside table, she made her way down from the tiny loft. The Insleys had left early this evening, dismayed over Luke's disappearance. Jonathan, vowing to ride out after him, had been firmly dissuaded by Kate.

Drifting through the dim room her thoughts focused on Luke. Where is he? What is his burden? As much as she found herself drawn to him, loving him, she knew that until he exorcized the ghosts of his past, there could be no future for them.

She tried to read, but the words would not conform to any sense upon the printed page. Her mind wandered. Turning to prayer, she implored the Father to watch over Luke, give him the peace he so desperately sought. She prayed for Greta and Annie and the innocent souls they carried within them, and finally she prayed for herself, asking her Father for the courage and strength to face an uncertain future.

Knowing the Lord had heard her prayer, but unable to deny the gnawing angst within her, she rose and paced the length of the small room. Passing the window, her eye caught a hint of movement beyond the shadows of the dogwood trees. Impatiently tossing aside the sheer lace curtains, she gazed into the gathering darkness, as though willing Luke to appear before her eyes. The flicker of movement came again, and Kate could just make out the silent, swift flight of a night owl honing in on his evening's prey. Moments later, a haunting screech lent credence to the vision. Sighing, she let the curtains fall as she turned from the window.

Running her fingers through her hair, she removed the ribbon and the few pins holding it in place. Kate shook her head and let the gleaming curls fall loose as she brushed it vigorously. She felt the grief within her as though an invisible hand laid hold of her heart, bearing down inexorably until she was certain that the very life would soon be wrung from her.

In an attempt to escape the crushing burden, she slipped into the soft darkness of the night, with only the lamp to light her path. The warm air enveloped her, caressing her skin like a lover's embrace. A thousand cicadas sang an evening chorus accented by the deep baritone of bull frogs, with the soft hooting of an owl adding the woodwinds. Kate stopped, letting her senses absorb the rich tapestry of life abounding in the night. The orchestra was brought to a crescendo and suddenly stilled by the mournful howl of a lone coyote. The plaintive wail awoke a stirring within her soul echoing the lonely sound. She closed her eyes as the cry died, and the symphony of the night began to play once again.

Kate found herself drawn to the barn. She pushed open the small side door, letting the lamp cast its glow ahead of her. The ever-present rodents scurried away before the sound of the intruder. A soft thud and a muffled squeal revealed the presence of the ginger tabby responsible for controlling the vermin. Breathing in the rich scents of the barn, she made her way to each stall, seeking reassurance in a familiar nuzzle or the sound of a soft nicker.

The door to the bunkhouse beckoned to her from the far side of the barn. Maybe Luke had returned after all. He could have slipped in under the cover of night. The buckskin might be grazing in the pasture even now. Her heart thudding, she approached the door. Swallowing her fear, she knocked softly upon the rough-hewn timbers. There was no answer.

"Luke?" she asked tentatively."Luke, are you in there?"

Her query met by silence, she turned to go.

Go in.

Stopped by the insistence of the command, she shook her head to clear her thoughts. She could not go in and invade the privacy of another. Kate held the oil lamp high, to light the path that would lead her home.

Go in.

Instead of the path toward home, the glow of her lamp illumined the latch of the bunkhouse door. Without willing it, her hand reached out, almost caressing the smoothly worn peg. Her heart tripped as the latch gave and the door swung slowly inward. Shadows danced upon the walls, showing chinks in the plaster where the logs had settled. Books lay scattered upon the low table, shirts and a vest hung from hooks. Kate felt a sense of life interrupted as she gazed about the room.

An errant shutter banged against the window frame as the evening breeze blew soft across the night, startling Kate from her reverie. Her eyes were drawn to a scrap of paper peeking from beneath the washstand. Crossing the dark room, she cast her light upon the paper, revealing a handbill with the word "Revival" printed in large type across the top.

Kate set the lamp down on the table beside the bed and pulled the handbill from beneath the porcelain bowl. Scanning the paper, she recalled the women at the branding speaking of a large tent revival to be held in Guthrie in September.

Where had Luke gotten a flyer advertising the revival? She sat on the bunk, holding the paper close to the lamp. Her eyes traveled over the words in the dim light, locking on the phrase "the Reverend Daniel Josey." Luke's father. He was to preach at the revival. Why hadn't he told her? Did this have anything to do with his disappearance?

Lost in thought, she jumped when the door opened. "Luke," Kate cried, turning toward the sound of footsteps, but the features emerging from the shadows were dark, with piercing eyes that brought a scream to her lips.

✦ ✦

The fiery ball sank below the western horizon, painting the azure palette with vivid hues of red and orange. The colors seemed to reflect the feverish burning within Luke's soul. He sat on the buckskin colt holding a loose rein, letting the horse pick his path carefully along the ridge, and watching the blazing sun cast its final light across the deepening violet of the night sky.

Seeing Michael Hall at lunch had jolted Luke from the dream he had been experiencing the past weeks. Living in Providence, Luke had almost come to believe that God would forgive him. The image of Christ, torn and bloody, hanging on a rough wooden cross, dying to pay the debt for his sins had seemed tangible and real when he and Kate talked about it. She had begun to make him see the God of love and the forgiveness available to him, so unlike the picture of the wrathful, avenging God his father always preached. He had almost reached out and grasped the love, claiming the promise for his own. Until today. The face of the man on the porch had been vaguely familiar, raising an uneasy feeling within him. Then Kate had introduced him; his name brought the memories flooding back.

Annie and Michael were together at a barn dance the night Joe and Luke had ridden into Rush Springs the first time. Lanterns swung from the rafters, boughs of holly, pine and mistletoe adorned the posts, and an old black iron stove glowed with radiant heat in a vain attempt to keep the cold at bay. A young girl, not more than thirteen, perched precariously atop a hay bale sawing at an old fiddle, it's rich finish glowing warmly in the flickering light. She played a lusty tune, and the dancers' feet kept up a lively step as they whirled about in colorful profusion.

A woman with ebony hair and flashing eyes stood near a table laden with pies, cakes and a bowl brimming with cider. A small boy with the same dark locks clutched the woman's woolen skirt in one chubby fist, the thumb of his free hand planted firmly between bow shaped lips.

"Zora!" Joe called across the crowded room. The woman turned, her face alight with joy.

"Daddy!" The cherub beside her loosed his grasp running full speed into Joe's waiting arms to be tossed high in the air, dissolving in a fit of giggles. Catching him neatly, Joe tucked the child into the crook of one arm, and with the other, he caught Zora in a passionate embrace.

"Oh, mi Amor, I have missed you," Zora murmured against his shirt.

"And I've missed you!" Joe answered, kissing her raven hair. "And you, Sam! How much have you grown in the past couple of months, pardner?" Joe asked the squirming bundle, now fighting to get down.

"Me growed up," Sam said pausing in his struggles. "Mama make me new shirt," he said puffing out his little chest to show off the new prize.

"So I see. Quite handsome, too," Joe said, setting the boy down. "Guess what?"

"What?" Zora and Sam asked in unison.

"I'm gonna get to watch you grown up some more, Sam." Turning to Zora, Joe continued, "I've got some time off between drives. We're planning' on bunking here till after the new year."

Zora's face was a strange mixture of joy and sorrow. Joy at having her husband home for any time at all, sorrow at the prospect of him leaving again so soon.

"Aw, c'mon, honey. You know I have to do this. It's the only job I know." He tilted her head up. "Let's make the best of our time together, huh?"

"Sí, mi corazón, the very best." Her eyes glowed, and the softly accented voice could not disguise the love she felt.

Luke watched the small family with a stab of envy. Would he ever know that kind of love? He cleared his throat, looking pointedly at Joe.

"Oh, sorry! Zora, this is Luke, he's a buddy of mine, kind of hopin' he could stay with us till we have to leave out."

"Pleased to meet you ma'am," Luke said, taking off his dusty hat.

"And I you, sir. Of course you will stay with us. Mi casa es su casa."

"Thank you, ma'am, but if you have a barn or something, I'd be just as comfortable there."

"But, no, you may sleep with Sam," she smiled. "Our house is small, but there is always room for friends."

The sincerity in her eyes silenced any further protest he was about to make, and he simply nodded, "Thank you, ma'am."

The music ended, dancers erupted in applause. A tall woman with auburn hair and luminous green eyes approached them followed by a large young man in a dark suit.

"Joseph!" the woman exclaimed.

"Annie!" Joe cried embracing her.

"Luke, this is my sister I was telling you about," Joe said turning to Luke. "Annie, I'd like you to meet Luke Josey, son of a preacher, but cowboy to the core."

"It is indeed a pleasure, sir," Annie said, extending a slender white hand.

"The pleasure is all mine," Luke replied taking her hand, unable to tear his gaze from hers.

"Annie," the young man beside her spoke possessively, "aren't you going to introduce me to your friends?"

"I'm sorry, Michael," Annie replied turning reluctantly to her escort. "Joseph, this is Michael Hall, he owns the mercantile in Kingfisher. Michael, may I introduce my brother Joseph."

"So you're the trail boss that Annie has told me so much about." Michael extended his hand.

"I am," Joe replied, eyeing the young man.

The fiddle began a lilting waltz. Michael reached for Annie's arm escorting her to the dance floor where they joined in the graceful rhythm. Luke continued to watch for glimpses of the captivating woman among the ebb and flow of the dancers until Joe grabbed his arm indicating it was time to leave.

Michael left for Kingfisher the following day, and over the course of the next few weeks Luke and Annie spent many stolen moments together. One bright December morning found them alone in the small barn behind Joe's place. The smell of fresh hay hung in the frosty air like the clouds of their breath. Dust motes danced in the sunshine forming a golden halo around Annie's dark hair. Luke reached out tentatively, tracing her full lips with the tip of a finger. Bending his head to hers, he kissed her, tasting for the first time the sweet nectar of forbidden fruits.

The buckskin stumbled in the gathering darkness, jolting Luke abruptly back from the past, the bittersweet memories burning within him. Glancing around the unfamiliar landscape, he realized they had wandered into unknown territory. With the approaching night, Luke decided to find what shelter he could, and face the future with the coming dawn.

✶✶✶✶✶✶✶✶✶✶✶✶✶✶✶✶✶✶✶✶✶✶✶✶✶✶✶✶✶✶✶

Stifling the scream with a closed fist, Kate shuddered with relief when Tochoway stepped into the small circle of light cast by the flickering lamp. Her beating heart rang loud within her ears.

"What are you doing here?" she asked.

Without answering, Tochoway took the paper from her trembling hand. His eyes hardened as he glanced over the words. Placing the paper on the table, he stepped beyond the edge of light into the murky shadows. As he stood gazing at the night through the curtained window, Kate could see the tension in his body, the dim light played against the bronzed planes of his rough-hewn face.

"Things are not well here," he stated.

Kate shook her head, fighting the tears that threatened to slip down her cheeks.

"A man rides a pale horse upon the ridge to the south. He is searching," Tochoway said in a low voice.

"But for what? Everything he needs is here," Kate said in anguish.

"No. The peace he longs for can only be found in his Creator." Tochoway turned to face her, his eyes penetrating. Kate glanced down to avoid the intense gaze.

"He will return," Tochoway continued. "You must listen. Do not judge, that is not your place."

"How do you know?" she asked, wanting desperately to believe. "How do you know he'll be back—what's in his heart?"

Tochoway was silent for a moment, his eyes set upon a distant scene that only he could fathom. In the glow of the oil lamp, Kate saw his face soften, a rare smile tugged at one corner of his mouth. Her heart quickened as she gazed upon the stoic man before her. A peaceful calm began to spread its soothing warmth through her in the hushed serenity. What was it about this man that touched her innermost being? A coyote yipped in the distance, the cicadas serenaded, and Kate became acutely aware of the night around her.

"He is a man," Tochoway said. "He will come for you, but he must find his God, and his peace, only then can he truly love you."

Kate sighed, frowning. She plucked at a fold of her skirt, wondering how best to ask the questions that buzzed through her mind. "Tochoway, you know God, don't you? I mean genuinely know Him."

"Yes. He is here," Tochoway placed two fingers beside his brow, "and here," the fingers moved to hover above his heart.

"How?"

Tochoway studied her for a moment. Then as though reaching a momentous decision, he picked up the small leather bag that hung at his waist. Loosening the drawstring, he produced a worn, leather volume.

"The night grows old. I must leave now. It is safer for me to travel beneath the cloak of darkness." Taking her hand he pressed the small book against her palm. His warm hand brushing against the cool flesh of her wrist, he murmured beneath his breath, "Puha."

He was gone as quickly as he had come, melting into the shadows of the night. No sound lingered to tell of his passing. Kate shuddered as she recalled the dangers he faced traveling away from the reservation without permission.

The small volume felt unusually heavy in her hand. Glancing down, she realized that it was a New Testament. The pages fragile from use, she opened it with great care. Faded writing covered the front flyleaf. Holding the page closer to the glowing lamp, she was able to make out in a neatly written script, "Walker Indian Mission, Rev Jonah Walker 1876," then below that, in a different hand, "Rev Daniel Josey 1882."

Chapter XIV

A spasm of coughs stopped Kate in her tracks. The dust coating her parched throat made every breath an agony. She leaned heavily against the handle of a razor sharp scythe as the unmerciful sun hung motionless in an azure sky. Kate straightened, placing a gloved hand in the small of her back as she stretched her aching muscles. Sweat soaked the shirt she wore and streamed down her face and neck in salty rivulets. Looking behind her at the fallen grass, and ahead to the tall stalks spreading out in a green-gold sea, she sighed. To the west she could see Jake urging the draft team on, pulling the hay mow, as row after row of grass lay in undulating ribbons behind them.

The areas she and Jonathan worked were too narrow or rocky for the large team and mow to cut, but the grasses here were too abundant to ignore. They worked with the scythes, swinging in rhythmic motion as they progressed slowly over the ground. Glancing at the cloudless expanse above, she said a brief prayer of thanks for the dry weather, which gave the hay ample time to cure before raking and stacking the golden harvest.

For three days they had been working in the hay pastures. Each morning she woke sore and bruised, her hands blistered and raw, even with the thick leather gloves she wore, but she was thankful for the agonizing labor, as she rarely had time to think about Luke, or wonder where he had gone and why.

Taking a deep breath, she set the scythe and began once again the long sweeping strokes that sent the blades of grass flying, separated neatly from their rooted home. The blade whispered over the grasses as they fell and she stepped on to the next sweep. Arms aching, breathing labored, sweat streaming from her brow, stinging her eyes, she focused only on the next cut, the next step.

Drawing her arm back for yet another swing, she choked back a scream as a hand grasped her wrist. Heart racing, Kate turned to find herself staring into a deeply tanned face with unfathomable green eyes.

"Luke!"

Without a word he took the blade from her hand, positioned it over the row and began cutting, moving away from her with every sweep. Stunned, Kate stood rooted to the ground, unable to move. She wanted to run after him, demand to know where he had been, why he had returned so abruptly.

Do not judge, it is not your place. Tochoway's words echoed through her mind.

✶ ✶ ✶ ✶ ✶ ✶ ✶ ✶ ✶ ✶ ✶ ✶ ✶ ✶ ✶ ✶ ✶ ✶

"So you've been to Guthrie?" Jonathan asked between bites of the hearty lunch Nana had packed.

Luke nodded, savoring the good home-cooked food.

"But why? Why did you go without saying *anything?*"

"Jonathan, let the man alone," Jake said, though Luke knew that Jake was as curious as his grandson.

Luke chewed on a biscuit for a moment before answering. "There was some business I needed to mull over. Still haven't come to grips with all of it." He paused, looking toward the homestead, just visible in the distance. "I did find a ready market for the cattle. I'll need to talk that over with Kate, sort of figured she didn't want to go with Johnson this year," he added with a wry grin.

Jake smiled ruefully, nodding in agreement. "Jonathan, go hitch up the team, time we were after it again."

"Yes, sir."

Luke watched the boy stand and stretch in the patch of shade they shared beneath the lone oak. Reluctant to leave, Jonathan lingered over packing the remains of lunch. Smokey lay at the edge of the shade like a grey shadow, watching covertly, muzzle resting on outstretched paws, his eyes following every move Jonathan made. With nothing left to occupy him, Jonathan shot one last look at Luke before he headed off to hitch the team.

"Well?" Jake asked as soon as Jonathan was out of ear shot.

"What?"

"Are you here to stay this time, or is this just another resting spot between your escapades?" Jake wore an ominous expression.

"I thought you knew me better than that," Luke said, though he didn't blame Jake for feeling that way.

"I thought I did, too, until you up and disappeared. I will not stand by and see my girl hurt like that again," Jake glanced obliquely in Jonathan's direction before continuing. "I really thought you were different, someone she could depend on, build her life back with." He shook his head. "You've got a lot of proving to do." Without waiting for a response, he stood and joined Jonathan, helping position the traces, and tightening the last of the buckles.

Luke felt the burden of Jake's words, and for the thousandth time he wondered if returning to Providence was the right thing to do.

✶ ✶

Kate watched the team approaching from the west, as the sun cast its final red light behind them. Jake drove while Jonathan and Luke walked slowly behind the mow.

"Are they coming yet, Mama?" Jo called from the kitchen where she was helping Nana put the finishing touches on supper.

"They're on the way now," Kate called back.

A lightening blur ran past her. "Oh, I wanna see!" Jo strained her neck as she stretched tall enough to see over the rise. "I see him, I see him!"

Kate sighed and shook her head at her daughter's exuberance. She wished she could feel Jo's unabashed joy at seeing Luke again. In Jo's mind, Luke had simply been gone on a short adventure. All the fretting and grieving Jo had done the last few days had been wiped away when Kate made the simple announcement, "Luke's home."

Mother and daughter returned to the kitchen to set the table and prepare for the evening meal. Jo's incessant chatter and optimistic view of Luke's return soon grated against Kate's already strained nerves. Closing her eyes, she took a deep breath, *Lord, give me patience, I don't want to lose my temper, but I feel it coming.*

"I helped Nana bake a fresh apple tart for desert tonight," Jo said, her little arms straining against the weight of a stoneware jug filled with fresh milk.

"Jo, watch out..." Kate warned just as Jo stumbled on her way to the table. The pitcher crashed to the floor in a jarring lurch, pottery shards and creamy milk covering the rag rug and plank flooring. Jo stopped in her tracks, eyes wide, her mouth a small oh of dismay.

"What do you think you're doing?" Kate snapped. "Get a rag and clean up that mess."

"But, Mama, it was an accident," Jo cried, trembling.

"You weren't paying attention to what you were doing, and you made a mess. Now get it cleaned up," Kate said sternly.

Tears welled up in Jo's blue eyes, her cheeks paled, then turned scarlet as a voice from the door spoke quietly, "Let me help with that. Somehow, I feel I may have been the cause of these troubles."

"Luke, oh, Luke," Jo cried, running into his arms and weeping against his broad chest.

Kate set her jaw, raging with barely controlled anger and an unexpected stab of jealousy at seeing her daughter comforted in the arms of a virtual stranger. "Supper's ready. You may come to the table as soon as the mess is cleared," she said in a cold, even voice.

Jake and Nana exchanged a surprised glance. Nana shrugged her shoulders.

The meal was a quiet affair. Conversation was strained and trivial. Even Jo sat quietly subdued, though Kate noticed the little girl glowed with adoration every time Luke happened to glance at her.

"Jo, honey, if you're done with your tart, then you need to go up and get ready for bed, okay?" Kate said gently, sorry for her outburst earlier.

"Yes, ma'am." Jo excused herself, and climbed down from the bench.

"I'll be up in a minute to tuck you in." Kate smiled as Jo scurried from the room, catching one last glimpse of Luke, as though to assure herself that he was really there.

Nana stood to clear the table. "I'll just get these cleaned up, then Jake and I are gonna turn in for the evening. Jonathan, you run on home now, we'll be along shortly."

"Mrs. Insley, I'll clean up tonight," Kate offered. "You all have been putting in some mighty long days, and I got an unexpected break today. Tomorrow is going to be another long one."

Nana considered this for a moment, glancing between Kate and Luke, before nodding in agreement. Carrying the plates she had already gathered to the sink, she set them beside the pump, took her shawl from its peg, and gathered her basket from the bench by the door. "Come along then Jake, I'll fix you a nice cup of tea at home."

As the Insleys left, Kate began clearing the remaining dishes from the table, wondering if Luke would stay or leave.

"Why don't you go see to your daughter? I'll take care of these," Luke said, his voice gentle, yet distant.

Kate realized these were the first words he had directed to her since his return. She nodded without looking at him, and hurried from the room. Pausing at the foot of the ladder leading to the small loft, she gripped the rung with an intensity that surprised her. Determined to calm her surging emotions before climbing up to see Jo, she closed her eyes and began breathing deeply. Even here the smell of fresh mown hay clung to her skin and clothes. She tried to empty her mind of thoughts and feelings by focusing on these senses, the feel of the wooden rung beneath her calloused hand, the warm breeze stirring the curtains, whispering past her cheek. She felt her heartbeat slow, and finally loosened her grasp and began the short climb to Jo's loft.

Jo lay nestled against the feather pillow, a riotous mass of red-gold curls dwarfing her pale face. Huge blue eyes stared somberly up at Kate. Candy lay nearby on a small rag rug, her tail thumping a steady rhythm as Kate approached. Kneeling beside the bed, Kate took Jo's hand in hers, marveling again at the absolute perfection of God's creation.

"Honey, I'm sorry I snapped at you earlier."

"That's all right," Jo replied. "Mama?" she asked, her gaze fixing on Kate. "Yes?"

"Aren't you glad Luke's home?" she asked. "I missed him so much, and I worried about him, but now he's home, and it feels so right, and I'm ever so glad," Jo paused. "I really like Luke, Mama, and I thought….." her voice trailed off as she glanced away.

"You thought what, sweetheart?" Kate asked, filled with trepidation.

"I thought you liked him, too."

Kate searched her daughter's face, not knowing how to respond. Placing a tender kiss on Jo's forehead, she whispered, "Let's pray for Luke, and for us, and see what plans God has, okay?"

"Okay," Jo replied as she snuggled deeper into the pillow, her doll tucked securely under one arm. The sound of murmured prayers filled the quiet loft and filled Kate's heart with a renewed sense of peace.

Picking up the small oil lamp that burned on the bedside table, Kate scratched Candy behind the ear, and made her way down from the loft. Pausing at the bottom of the ladder, she could hear Luke scraping plates in the kitchen, then the sound of the pump arm being primed and soon water sluicing into the sink full of dishes.

"Wash or wipe?" Kate asked walking into the kitchen and grabbing a towel from the sideboard.

"I'll wash, you dry," Luke answered, sending her a sidelong glance.

Kate began methodically wiping the pewter plates as they came dripping from the water basin, stacking them in the open sideboard as she finished each one. They worked in silence for several minutes. Kate obliquely studied the man beside her. Luke had been good to them, he was diligent and worked hard. He had even risked his own life for them on more than one occasion. She once thought that he had been in love with her. Had she foolishly returned that love? A man in love does not ride away without so much as a word, she fumed.

Do not judge.

"I went to Guthrie." His voice cut into her thoughts.

"Did you?" she asked, remembering the handbill in his room, but the revival was more than a month away.

"I talked to some cattle buyers there. One from Chicago made a real good offer, if we can get the steers to the railhead in Guthrie," Luke said, wiping down the counter around the wash basin.

"Really?"

"With your approval, of course," he added hastily.

"What is he offering?"

"Going market rate, about seven cents a pound. I figure we can send at least forty steers, and there's twelve or fourteen older cows that you have heifers to replace that could go, too, though he'd offer a bit less for them."

Kate made some quick mental calculations. Assuming the steers weighed in at around a thousand pounds each, and the cows besides, that would be well over three thousand dollars.

"Are you sure about this?" she asked.

"I have his card. He said he'd meet us at the yards anytime the last week of September."

She nodded, "I guess we'll be going on a cattle drive, then. Won't Jonathan be thrilled?"

Luke smiled. Their eyes met, Kate felt her heart skip a beat in spite of her misgivings, before an awkward silence fell between them.

"Do you want some coffee or something?" Kate asked to break the stillness.

Luke shook his head. "Will you take a walk with me?" he asked.

Glancing toward the loft, Kate nodded, knowing Jo was sound asleep with Candy on guard.

The night was warm, but a gentle breeze stirred the leaves and ruffled Kate's hair. The sweet scent of honeysuckle wafted from near the spring house which was covered in the deep green vines. They walked past the garden fence, toward the apple trees in the distance.

Stopping beneath the spreading branches, she reached up and picked a reddish fruit, still slightly green beneath the ripening hue, firm and fresh. Kate could almost taste the tart-sweet fruit. She would have to help Nana and Jo harvest the apples soon and begin the drying and canning process.

Luke stood a few feet away, his back to her, staring at the silver crescent moon hung against the black velvet sky where a sprinkle of stars glittered like diamonds. Where were his thoughts just now, she wondered. Were they here at Providence, or did they soar above, winging their way to lands unknown? Could a man like Luke Josey ever be truly happy tied to one place? Kate sighed, realizing she still knew so little of him.

"Have you ever made a mistake?" he asked suddenly, still contemplating the vast heavens.

"Well, yes, of course I have," Kate answered, puzzled.

"A mistake that hurt innocent people?"

Kate was silent.

"How can God forgive me, when I can't even forgive myself?" Luke asked, anguish beginning to seep into his voice.

"Luke whatever it is…."

"No, you don't understand!" He turned, his eyes held hers, filled with torment and rage.

All the anger she had held in check suddenly filled her. "Then tell me! Make me understand," she raged back at him. "You come in here, turn our lives around, tell me you love me, then you vanish without a word!" Kate paused, "What is going on? Make me understand."

She saw his jaw tighten. A tremor twitched above his left brow as he fought to control the emotions held so tightly in check. His eyes grew darker as the rage surfaced. The dam broke, the words spilled forth, sweeping Kate along in a torrent of passions and emotions as the story unfolded.

"So the baby Annie carries is mine." he finished brokenly, the storm spent. "How many lives have I ruined? How many innocent people have I hurt? Three? No, more than that—now you and Jo, the Insley's, and it just goes on."

Kate closed her eyes, numb from shock. Whatever she had expected, it wasn't this. Pain flared within her as the truth of his confession pierced her heart

Listen to him. Do not judge.

Tochoway's words resounded through her mind like a chant. Opening her eyes, she saw before her a man, a fellow being unworthy of God's compassion and forgiveness, yet the recipient of them through God's grace nonetheless. Could she do any less?

She took both of Luke's hands in hers. Closing her eyes, she began to pray, "Dear Lord, show this man Your grace, Your mercy, Your love. Protect him, build him up in Your way.

"Build a hedge of thorns about the unborn babe, who bears no part in the sin of his parents. Be with the mother, Lord, in this time of fear that she faces, and Lord, smile on Michael, the man who is the true earthly father to this precious babe of Yours. We give you these lives, Lord, that only You can heal. In Jesus' most holy name we pray these things, Amen."

Looking deep into his eyes, she held his hands a moment longer. Releasing him, she returned to the house alone.

✦✦✦✦✦✦✦✦✦✦✦✦✦✦✦✦✦✦✦✦✦✦✦✦✦✦✦✦✦✦✦

Tendrils of light painted the eastern horizon. The deep black canvas of night gave way to rosier hues, extinguishing the stars one by one. Luke sat with his back wedged against the gnarled trunk of the apple tree watching the unfolding dawn of God's creation. Fatigue invaded his bones, his muscles screamed in protest as he tried to move. He felt like Jacob of old, wrestling with God throughout the night. But was it God or the devil he had fought?

He stood, stretching his aching body, and headed to the bunkhouse. Stopping at the pump, Luke splashed the icy water over his head and face. The bracing cold struck him full force, casting away the hazy dreams of night. Filling a bucket with the frigid water, he entered the small room. A brief glance in the mirror revealed his haggard expression and the filth of days on the trail. He removed his woolen vest, stripped away the dingy muslin shirt, his nose wrinkling at the stench imbedded within the fabric. Sitting on the bunk he grunted, struggling with the heavy boots, pulling them off and dropping each one with a dull thud against the wooden floor. The Levis came away, slick from wear, dust adorning every crease. Begrimed cotton under drawers and socks joined the steadily growing pile.

As he removed the layers of filthy clothes, Luke felt a burden cast away with every garment. Taking a clean white towel from the shelf, he immersed it in the water. He brought the rag dripping from the bucket and scrubbed himself. Feeling the external cleansing power of the water, he longed to feel the same internal cleansing of his soul.

Closing his eyes to the filth about him, he prayed, "God, if you are the God of grace and mercy that I have been led to believe, I stand here today covered in my sin and shame, repentant, seeking Your compassion once and for all. Take my life, Lord, lead me, use me. God show me, show me what I need to do."

He opened his eyes to the morning sun streaming through the cracked window, pooling in golden light all about him. A renewing energy began to flow within him, as he dressed for the day ahead.

Jake and Jonathan were coming down the path toward the barn when Luke emerged from his room.

Jake stopped, studying Luke for a moment through narrowed eyes. "Well, if I didn't know better, I'd say you looked something like a new man today. Get a good night's sleep?"

"Not exactly," Luke answered, slapping Jake on the back. "Let's get to work. What are we doing today?"

Jake continued to watch Luke with a bemused expression before answering, "We're going to rake and stack that last field today, probably won't finish, but I'd like to get as much in as we can today."

"Did I see a dump rake behind the barn?" Luke asked hopefully.

"Yep, goes a might faster than the old days." Jake said with a twinkle in his eye.

Luke nodded, remembering the raking days of his youth. He, his mother and sister would take the long hay rakes, turning every blade of cut grass in the field, then going back and pitching it into long rows that would be forked into the bed of a hay wagon pulled by a team. It meant days of arduous work in the blazing sun. With a mechanical dump rake pulled by the horses, a field could be turned and raked into neat rows in one continuous process, reducing the manual labor to almost nothing, until it came time to pitch the hay into the wagon.

"I don't suppose you have one of those new stackers hiding around here somewhere?" Luke asked.

"Nope, not yet. Will bought the mow in Missouri before we came down to the Territory," Jake explained. "Those first years, we hand raked the fields. After the first good steer sales, Will managed to buy the rake from a boomer that went bust for next to nothing. He always planned to get a stacker, but—well, things don't always go the way you plan, do they?"

"No, they sure don't," Luke agreed.

✶✶✶✶✶✶✶✶✶✶✶✶✶✶✶✶✶✶✶✶✶✶✶✶✶✶✶✶✶✶

Kate stabbed the tines of her pitchfork into the ground with a satisfied grunt. The last forks of green-gold hay had been pitched into the wagon now sagging beneath the stacked tonnage.

She had worked side by side with Luke the last two days, sweating beneath the same burning sun, covered in hay and dust, but able to laugh at his antics when a spider crawled up his pant leg. Their relationship was forever changed, she knew that. He had been kind and solicitous, even friendly during the haying, and she was seeing something new within his character. It was as though they were starting anew, getting to know one another all over again. Hope dawned within her as she began to see the man he was meant to be.

"Whoa, Goldie, slow up there, Rosey," Jo chanted, pulling against the reins with all the might her small arms could muster. The obedient mares stopped, standing quietly between the traces. The harnesses jangled as the horses stomped or twitched their backs in an effort to rid themselves of the ever-present flies.

Bringing in the hay pressed everyone into service, even Jo was able to help by driving the team slowly along the rows as the rest of them walked beside, gathering the hay into the tines of the forks and pitching the heavy loads into the bed. Nana drove the buggy back and forth, carrying water and food. The work went on until it was too dark to see, and began again the next morning at the first light. Everyone heaved a sigh of relief seeing the last of the harvest safely in.

"Well, I say we have us a good rest for an hour or so, something light for supper, and I believe there may be enough ice left down in the spring house to make us some ice cream to celebrate with. How does that sound?" Kate asked the tired crew.

"Ice cream? Yippee!" Jo shouted.

"Who's cranking?" Jake asked.

"I'll crank," Luke offered, "as long as we can have some of Nana's good strawberry preserves over the top."

"I reckon I could scrounge up a jar of preserves," Nana said.

"It's settled then. Let's get this last load put up in the loft." Kate tossed her pitchfork beneath the seat of the wagon. "Scoot over, Jo, I'm driving."

The men clambered aboard the wagon, Nana took up the reins in the buggy, and Kate slapped her team, "Let's get up, girls, we're headed home."

A few hours later, the pulleys squeaked beneath the weight of the last of the harvest as it was hoisted by the draft team into the loft through the high, open doors. Kate coughed from the choking dust, and waved a tired hand shooing the incessant gnats from before her face.

"You look tired, sure you're still up to a celebration?" Luke asked.

"I couldn't possibly look half so bad as you!" Kate laughed, plucking a stray tuft of hay from his vest.

"Ha!" rejoined Luke, reaching out to extricate several blades of grass from Kate's hair.

"Perhaps, but, *I* wear it well!" Kate realized it felt good to laugh again. The hay was in, a market had been found for the cattle, God's providence at work once more. She wondered just what His plan was for them. Kate turned her face to catch the glorious last rays of the dying sun. *Thank you, Lord, but just once couldn't You give me a little hint about what the future holds? Oh well, I guess that's what faith is all about, isn't it?*

"What are you thinking about?" Luke asked.

"The substance of things hoped for, the evidence of things not seen," she replied cryptically. "I'll see you all at the house in an hour or so. C'mon, Jo, I'll race you home!"

✳ ✳

Kate filled Jo's pitcher from the pump in the kitchen and carried it to the loft. "Wash up as best you can, honey, and get those filthy clothes down to me. Nana plans to wash tomorrow."

"Ugh! Do I have to help with laundry?" Jo asked wrinkling her nose in distaste.

"Yes, of course you do, but then so do I," Kate sighed, rolling her eyes. Laundry was the dreaded chore in the Shaughnessey house.

"I'd rather be doing hay than washing."

"I don't know, right now, I think I'd even take the laundry if it meant I didn't have to go back into that hayfield again," Kate decided. "I'm going to wash up, too, then get some sandwiches made if you want to help."

"Okay, Mama, I'll be down quick."

Kate descended to the kitchen, filled her own pitcher, and went to her room, closing the door behind her. She cherished these few moments of solitude. Pouring the water in the basin, she dipped her fingers in grimacing at the chill. There just wasn't enough time to heat any right now, the cold would have to suffice. She sat in the hard chair near the window, and tugged off her boots, then slipped out of the shirt and pants she wore, shaking out enough hay and weeds to start a small meadow in her room.

Approaching the basin of frigid water with a clean rag and a bar of lye soap, she glanced longingly at the small copper tub sitting in the corner of her room. She couldn't remember the last time she had a good long soak in there. Soon, she promised herself, *I am going to fill that old black kettle, boil the water scalding and sit in there until it's cold.* Kate could almost feel the soothing warmth radiating through her, perfumed water wafting a gentle aroma and pure soft soap to caress her skin.

She had a sudden inspiration. Tossing aside the rough cake of lye in her hand, she knelt beside the trunk at the foot of the bed. Rummaging through the camisoles and petticoats, she found what she had been looking for, the box from Martha. Had it really been over three months since the trip to Fallis? Selecting a lavender scented beauty bar, Kate decided she might not have a hot bath, but she didn't have to smell like a farm hand tonight.

Kate scrubbed her skin until it glowed pink, and all she could smell was clean, fresh lavender. She brushed her hair with vigorous strokes, shedding the dust and hay. Soon it was gleaming mass of curls again, caught up in a ribbon at the nape of her neck. Selecting a rose colored calico dress with delicate white edging, she dressed with a delight she hadn't felt in ages. Sighing at the callouses on her hands, she tugged the long sleeves snugly down over her wrists, but like the scars, the callouses represented a sense of honor.

Satisfied with the transformation from farm urchin to respectable member of society once more, she returned to the kitchen to prepare a light supper for the others.

"Oh, Mama, you look beautiful!" Jo clapped her hands in delight as Kate entered the kitchen.

"Why thank you," Kate replied crossing the room to Jo.

"And you smell good, too."

"I'll second that," Luke spoke from his seat in the corner.

Kate whirled around, "You startled me. I didn't see you. What are you doing here already?"

"You said dinner in an hour, didn't you?"

"Has it been an hour already?" Kate asked in alarm.

"Hour and ten minutes to be exact," Luke said. "But then, who's counting?"

"Oh, no, the Insleys will be here any minute, and I don't have a thing done."

"Where's the ice cream freezer?" Luke asked.

"In the shed by the smokehouse, why?"

"You get the ice cream mixed up, and start on the sandwiches. I'll get the freezer and the ice, and I can be cranking while you finish up dinner," Luke said, hurrying out the door.

"Jo, can you get the cream from the spring house?"

"Yes, Mama."

The fast approaching dusk cast purple shadows through the kitchen. After lighting the lamp, Kate built up the fire in the stove, measured sugar, set out vanilla and separated the eggs beating the yolks into the sugar. When Jo returned, they carefully scalded the thick cream, stirring in the yolk and sugar mixture along with a generous dollop of vanilla.

"We'll let this cool until Luke gets back with the freezer," Kate said. "Let's get the rest of supper ready."

"I can slice some bread," Jo offered.

"All right, but be careful, that knife is sharp."

"I will."

Kate set out jars of pickles, jams and corn relish, a stack of plates and some forks.

"Are there any apples in the larder?" Kate asked searching through the cupboard.

"I think Nana and I used them all for the tart."

"Well, I've got to get some meat from the smokehouse, I can gather a few apples on the way," Kate decided. "Are you finished slicing the bread?"

"Uh-huh," Jo answered. "Here you are."

A loud clatter on the porch took them by surprise. Opening the door, Kate saw Luke struggling with the freezer, a stool and a large block of ice wrapped in a piece of canvas.

"Wouldn't it have been easier to chip the ice at the spring house? There's a pick, and you could have put it in the freezer there," Kate laughed.

"Oh, sure, now you tell me! That would have been just too easy," Luke said depositing the unwieldy block on the porch.

"Is that the last of the ice?" Kate asked.

"There's one more small block, don't know how much longer it'll last."

Every winter they froze large blocks of ice and packed them underground in layers of insulating straw. During the warm summer months, the ice cooled the spring house enough to store some perishables for short periods. They used the precious ice for rare treats like ice cream or lemonade.

"Oh, well, winter will be here before we know it," Kate sighed. Picking up a basket from the nearby bench, she continued, "Jo can get the ice cream mixture for you whenever you're ready. There's rock salt in the pantry. If you wouldn't mind lighting the lantern, I'd sure appreciate it, it's already starting to get dark. I'm going to the smokehouse to get some venison."

Luke nodded as he set about chopping the ice into small enough chunks to fit in the freezer.

✷ ✷

Jo brought out the bowl with the cream and a box of salt. "I love ice cream, don't you, Luke?"

"It is indeed a treat."

"My mama makes the very best ice cream. She uses five eggs, but just the yolks. She says it makes it richer." Jo wrinkled her nose in thought. "Luke, how can ice cream be rich? It doesn't have any money, and eggs aren't money. Well, I mean, mama sells eggs for money sometimes, is that how it makes it richer?"

Luke laughed out loud. "Jo, in this case 'rich' isn't anything to do with wealth, it just describes how something tastes. I guess you could say it has better taste than another kind, so that makes it richer in flavor."

"Oh, I see." Jo watched in fascination as Luke placed the chunks of ice in the outside freezer, poured the ice cream mixture into the container, and fitted it down into the ice, making sure the lid was secure. Then he added the rock salt over the ice, placed the handle in its slot and began turning the crank.

Kate returned carrying the basket laden with smoked venison and fresh apples picked along the way.

"Aren't the Insleys here yet?" Kate asked with a note of concern in her voice.

"No, as a matter of fact. It's not like Nana to be late, is it?" Luke said. Not liking the worry he saw on Kate's face, he quickly added, "Though they were pretty tired after all that work today."

"Look, here comes Jonathan," Jo chimed in.

"Jon, what is it, what's wrong?" Kate asked.

"Nana's had a spell," Jon said, his face ashen. "Papa put her to bed, and he's sitting with her. He said to go ahead and have our party, anyway."

The stricken look on Kate's face tore at Luke's heart. "Well, if they can't come to the party, maybe we can take the party to them," he said cheerfully.

"Oh, that's a great idea," Jon said. "Surely that'd perk her right up."

"I don't know," Kate's voice trailed off.

"Please, Mama?" Jo pleaded.

"You could take your medicine bag," Luke added in a low voice.

"You're right," Kate said, relief flooding her face. "I'll pack the food."

"I'll carry the freezer."

Kate packed the sandwich makings, fruit and her bag of healing herbs in a large basket, covering it all with a large cloth. Headed for the door, she stopped and returned to the pantry, searching the shelf. The jar of strawberry preserves was tucked in a corner. Grabbing it, she placed it gently in the basket and rearranged the cloth. Within minutes the small party set off toward the Insleys' cabin.

Jon walked ahead carrying the lantern high to light the well-worn path. Jo skipped along beside him chattering about the hay, ice cream and bemoaning the laundry day ahead of them. Luke struggled with the freezer now laden with ice and the cream mixture. Kate walked along beside him carrying the basket of food.

"Has Nana had these 'spells' before?" Luke asked.

"Twice. The doctor says that her heart is weakening. He gave her some medicine for it last time. Luke, it scares me so. I don't know what I'd do if I lost Nana or Jake." In her pale countenance, Luke could see the struggle she faced to keep her fears in check.

As the children entered the cabin, he set the freezer down and turned to Kate. "Will you pray with me right now for her?"

Kate stopped, the amazement written plainly over her features dissolving in a soft radiant smile. "I'd like that," she whispered, reaching out to take his hand.

Her hand was small within his. He could feel her warmth, smell the faint soothing scent of lavender emanating from her. Closing his eyes he began, "Lord—dear Lord, I—we ask that you protect and heal our Nana. Um, well—and be with us tonight, Ah—in Jesus' name. Amen."

"Amen," Kate echoed.

"Sorry, I'm not real good at that yet."

"You will be," she said her amber eyes glowing softly in the shadows. "Thank you."

The love he thought had been lost forever flooded over him in a palatable wave. The emotions that filled him were pure and strong with their roots in a source beyond himself. "Thank *you*," he whispered, placing a gentle kiss above her brow. *And thank you , Lord,* he added silently.

Picking up their burdens, they hurried into the Insleys small soddy. Nana lay propped on pillows, covered in a faded quilt, a cool damp rag folded across her forehead. Jake sat beside the bed holding her hand, his face a mask of worry. Jo took Kate's basket to the table while Kate hurried to Nana's side.

"How is she, Jake?"

"I'm right here, you could ask me you know," Nana barked irritably.

Jake shrugged and rolled his eyes, as Kate tried to hide a smile.

"Then, how are you, Nana?" Kate asked.

"I've been better."

"Did Jake give you the medicine the doctor left from last time?"

"He did, nasty stuff," Nana said, struggling to sit up.

"Now, Nana, you just lay still there," Jake ordered.

The old woman settled back, taking the cloth from her head. "Here, this isn't doing anybody any good," she said handing it to Kate. "I want a cup of tea."

"That I can do," Kate answered.

Luke was busy cranking the freezer, as Jo made sandwiches for everyone. Kate set the kettle to boil on the stove, and retrieved her herbs from the medicine bag. Selecting chamomile and adding a pinch of valerian, she placed the concoction in a tea ball as she waited for the water to heat.

"Would you like honey in your tea, Mrs. Insley?"

"That'd do right nice, and maybe just a slice of bread with butter, Jo."

"Yes, ma'am," Jo answered.

As fast as the supper materialized on the table, it was devoured. Luke and Jonathan ate heartily, Kate snatched a bite here and there as she made sure Nana drank the tea and ate something light. Assuring himself that his wife was in good hands, even Jake ate two of the smoked venison sandwiches.

"Who's ready for ice cream?" asked Luke.

"Oh, I am." Jo clapped her hands in delight.

"I'd sure take a scoop," agreed Jon.

"I think you can make it unanimous, except for Nana," Kate said, smiling tenderly at the woman now fast asleep. The herbs had done their work, and Nana slept peacefully.

"Is she going to be all right?" Jake asked.

"We need to make her rest for a few days, then just ease her in to some light work, but I think she'll make it," Kate replied.

"Nana's tough as old shoe leather," said Jonathan. "How do you think we're going to keep her from doing too much?"

"I guess we could always hog tie her if we have to," Kate said with a grin, taking her bowl of ice cream dripping with strawberry preserves. "Mmmm, doesn't that look wonderful."

"What about laundry tomorrow, mama?" Jo asked. "If Nana's sick, I guess we'll just have to wait."

"Oh, I think you and I can manage just fine. That laundry needs to be done, and I don't want Nana fretting about it when she gets well."

Luke had to turn away to hide his amusement at the look on Jo's face. "Kate, I was wondering if you wanted to ride the herds early tomorrow?" he asked between bites of the delectable treat. "We haven't been out for quite awhile now, but if you're going to be busy –"

"Oh, I'd like that," Kate interrupted. "We'll do it early. I'll have plenty of time to get back and do the wash with Jo."

"Will you be riding the medicine hat?"

"Yes, she's turning into a pretty good mount."

"I'll have them saddled at first light then," Luke said with a nod.

"As nice as the evening has been, I guess we really need to get back," Kate sighed. "Nana should sleep through the night, but if she needs me, please send Jonathan, won't you, Jake?"

"That I will," he answered, gazing at his sleeping wife.

"Jo, you carry the lantern. I'll get the basket if you can manage the freezer, Luke."

"I've got it. Jake, I'll see you tomorrow. Are you going to start harvesting the oats?"

"That was the plan. Jon and I usually do it, but I could sure use the extra help if you're offering."

"I am. I'll meet you there after we get back from the herds."

"That'd be right fine," Jake said, clapping a hand on Luke's back.

✳ ✳

Kate kissed her sleeping daughter fondly as the faint dawn light played against the window. She had left breakfast laid out on the kitchen table in case Jo woke before their return. In the kitchen, Kate shivered from the cold morning air. The wind had turned to come from the north sometime in the night, bringing with it a taste of the winter to come. She knew the air would warm again before noon, but dug out a heavy woolen vest for this morning's ride. Buttoning the vest, she headed out the door, reveling in the brisk fall like day.

Luke had the horses saddled and ready by the time she reached the barn. Taking the reins she mounted the white mare, who snorted and danced, feeling the weather in her blood.

"Easy, girl, we've got a lot of riding to do today."

Luke mounted the buckskin colt, and they turned to the east.

"How's she doing for you?" Luke asked indicating the new mare.

"I like her. She's smooth and fairly responsive. I wish I had more time to work with her, but so far we're doing fine," Kate said. "How's that buckskin working out?"

"He's great, a little strong minded sometimes, but that's part of being young."

"You want to let these two get a little of this pent up energy out?" Kate asked, fighting to keep Hawk to a walk.

"You're on," Luke replied, loosening his rein.

Kate touched her heels to the mare's sides, moving her rein hand slightly ahead of the saddle horn. An intense surge of power flowed through her as the mare leapt forward covering the ground in long strides. Kate's body moved in rhythm to the undulating gait of the horse as the landscape rushed by in a blur of green, amber and blue. She was vaguely aware of Luke and the buckskin matching them stride for stride. The very energy of life seemed to be caught in that ride, blowing away the fears of the past as the wind blew her hair streaming behind her.

The horses slowed their pace as they crested the rise. Sitting deep in the saddle, Kate reined the mare to a stop. Luke rode up beside her and they drank in the beauty of God's creation. The cattle grazed on the new-mown grass in the valley before them, the homestead lay bathed in mist behind them, the sun just beginning to gild the edges of leaves and buildings in the golden glory of an autumn morn. After the exhilaration of the ride, the peaceful silence descended over Kate like a gentle dew, nourishing her soul and bringing a deep seated joy that filled her completely.

Turning to Luke she saw the same joy reflected in his eyes as his gaze swept over the idyllic scene, then came back to rest on her.

"Kate, will you walk with me a bit?" he asked.

"I'd like that."

They dismounted, dropping the reins allowing the horses to graze.

The sun continued its gradual arc across the eastern horizon, bringing the rich red hues of another dawn and the promise of warmth for the coming day.

"Words just don't exist to describe a morning like this," Kate mused.

They walked a short distance in silence, drinking in the peaceful beauty, then stopped at the top of the rise and stood bathed in the radiant glow of the rising sun.

"Kate," Luke hesitated before continuing, "I'm not a perfect man. You know the sins of my past, yet still you accept me."

"Yes, of course –" Kate started. Luke laid a gentle finger on her lips.

"Let me finish, please?" he asked, taking both of her hands in his.

Kate nodded, her heart pounding.

"I feel a love for you that denies explanation. I believe the Lord must have brought me here even through the circumstances of my sins. I am so sorry for the hurt that I have caused. If there is any way that you can find forgiveness in your heart, accept me for who I am now," Luke paused, his eyes dark with emotion. Taking a deep breath, he continued, "Kate, would you be my wife?"

Searching his face, Kate could find only love there. Sending up a silent prayer, she sought God's will once again. The words of Proverbs 13:12 filled her mind: *Hope deferred maketh the heart sick: but when the desire cometh, it is a tree of life.* Here was her hope and her desire, a life with a man committed to God and to her. Unable to speak for the tightening in her throat, she nodded, tears of joy marring her vision as his lips claimed hers in a kiss that consumed her. She answered his passion, enveloped within his strong embrace, her desires matching his. He covered her face in sweet kisses.

"Kate, oh, Kate how I love you," he whispered against her ear. "As God is my witness, I promise to love, honor and protect you, always."

Drawing back, she tilted her head to gaze into his eyes, and knew that he meant those words.

✶✶✶✶✶✶✶✶✶✶✶✶✶✶✶✶✶✶✶✶✶✶✶✶✶✶✶✶✶✶✶✶✶✶✶

Feeding tinder to the small flame trying to ignite the logs beneath the huge black iron kettle in the yard, Kate could still feel the tender promises Luke had made early that morning. The emotions taking root and growing strong within her heart were new as supple green saplings. She wanted to nourish them and see the love emerge in glorious growth like a new spring.

The fire caught; crackling flames leapt forth. Kate jumped back. Even now the radiant heat of a fire brought fear with the memories. Rubbing unconsciously at the scars beneath her sleeves, she went in to help Jo carry out the laundry.

"You seem awfully happy today, mama, for laundry day," Jo said as they piled sheets and petticoats, pants and shirts together on the kitchen floor.

"I am. It's the very first day of a whole new life, Jo!"

"Why?"

"You'll see," Kate replied smiling. She wanted to wait until Luke was there before telling Jo the good news. He had ridden on to check the herds and fence lines while Kate had returned to the house to see to Jo and the laundry. Then he would be joining Jake and Jonathan harvesting the oats. Chances were, he wouldn't be back before supper, but the peace Kate felt didn't require his physical presence. The knowledge of his love ran deep within her.

Jo shrugged, and continued sorting. "I can carry this pile out, it's not too big," she said, completely hidden behind a mountain of sheets, only her legs peeking out below.

Kate laughed, "Let me take some of that, why don't you? We can make as many trips as we need."

They spent the morning hours boiling, scrubbing with soft lye soap, and rinsing clothes until their arms ached and they were both soaked through. Everywhere they looked clothes fluttered in the light breeze, hung to dry on lines, rails and any other available space.

"I'd say we deserve a break right about now. How about some lunch?" Kate asked.

"But there's still those sheets to hang, mama."

"I can do that after we eat. I want you to take a basket up to Nana and check on her," Kate said. "Why don't you slip into something dry while I make lunch."

"Yes, ma'am," Jo replied running into the house.

Kate went in the kitchen and made some sandwiches, packing one away in the basket along with herbs for more tea and the rest of the apple tart still covered in the pantry. Jo returned neatly dressed once again. They ate their lunch and talked of everything and nothing as mothers and daughters are inclined to do on special days.

"Why don't you take your slate and a couple of books with you," Kate suggested handing the basket to Jo. "You can stay and read with Nana, or just keep her company. I'm sure she'd like that. It may be awfully lonely for her there."

"All right. Maybe I can take my doll and we can have a tea party?" Jo asked, the doll already tucked firmly under her arm.

"That sounds wonderful," Kate acquiesced. "I'll try to come down a little later to see Nana. Bye now." Kate kissed Jo on the forehead.

"Bye, mama," Jo called, skipping down the lane.

Kate sighed watching her daughter disappear from sight. She was growing up so very fast, it wouldn't be long before she was a young woman. Kate wondered what Jo's reaction would be to the news of Luke becoming her step-father. She was sure Jo would be thrilled, knowing how her daughter felt about Luke already. Kate smiled and turned back to the laundry waiting to be hung.

Wrestling with the last wet sheet, still dripping and making puddles of mud in the dust at her feet, Kate was startled by the sound of galloping hoofbeats growing ever nearer. Trying to keep the wringing mass of muslin out of the dirt, she tossed it up on the rail, heedless of where it landed.

Aaron Hall rode into the yard on his old brown mare. The horse was covered in foamy sweat, her sides heaved as Aaron pulled her to a stop. "Miz Shaughnessey, ya gotta come quick. Ma sent me to fetch you. The baby's coming, and something's terrible wrong."

Kate's mind whirled. Greta had never had problems before, but every pregnancy was different, and her age could cause complications. "Aaron, do you know if the doc's in Fallis?"

"No, but I'm gonna go see if I can find him."

"Your mare's done in. Go put your saddle on that bay in the corral by the barn. He'll take good care of you. I'll get my things and be on my way to your place as fast as I can."

"Yes, ma'am," Aaron said wheeling his mare around and heading to the barn.

Kate ran in the house, changed out of the suds soaked clothes she wore into a riding skirt and shirtwaist. Filling her bag with everything she could possibly need, she dashed off a note to explain her disappearance, anchoring it to the kitchen table beneath the lamp. Kate saw Aaron through the window as he rode by on the bay heading at full speed for Fallis.

Hawk waited near the garden, tied loosely to the low branch of a tree, still saddled since Kate had planned to ride later to the harvest, taking food and water to the men. Shaking her head, she decided the men would have to fend for themselves as Greta needed her more. Kate strapped her bags behind the cantle, tightened the girth, and swung herself into the saddle. A quick squeeze with her knees, and the mare picked up a fast trot. Reaching the main road they turned south toward the Hall's place.

The first nine miles of the journey were over a well traveled road. Kate paced the mare, alternating between a trot and a lope for much of the distance, slowing to a walk when she felt the mare tiring, then urging her on again in her haste to reach Greta in time. Nearing the turn off to the Hall's homestead, Kate watched for the path she knew led to the southwest. The sun was beginning to sink slowly toward the western horizon by the time she saw the marker.

Breathing a sigh of relief, she headed the weary mare down the narrow trail grown over with trees. The passage through the dense growth kept the pair to a slower pace. It was nearly half an hour before the cabin came into sight. Emerging from the woods, Kate urged the mare into a lope. Arriving in the yard, Kate was met by Ross and Jeremy.

"I'll take your horse, Miz Shaughnessey, ma says to hurry," Ross said, taking the reins as Kate dismounted.

Nodding to Ross, Kate unstrapped her bag from behind the saddle, and followed Jeremy into the dim cabin. As her eyes adjusted from the bright afternoon light, Kate saw Kathy Hall sitting near the large stone fire place holding a whimpering infant, rocking it to and fro, humming a lullaby to calm the baby's fretting.

"Kathy? Where's...." Kate started.

"Kate, I thought you'd never get here, hurry, please," called Greta appearing from the bedroom.

"Greta, but I thought –" Kate said in bewilderment.

"Oh! You thought *I* was having *my* baby." Greta said, realization dawning on her face. "Dear, no, I had my beautiful little girl a week ago now, never a problem, you know me. It's Annie, she's bad off, and I'm worried."

Kate's heart stopped for one paralyzing instant. Annie. Luke's baby. *God, give me the strength to see this through,* she prayed. Following Greta into the dark room, she saw a woman in agonized silence, eyes closed, jaws clenched against the pain, her hands clutching the sheets, knuckles white. Annie's body relaxed as the contraction eased.

"Annie," Greta spoke softly, "Annie, this is Kate. She's come to help you through this."

"No one can help me." Annie's voice was barely audible. Her eyes fixed straight ahead, acknowledging no one.

Greta looked at Kate helplessly.

"Why don't you go tend to your own baby, Greta," Kate said. "You look exhausted, I can take care of Annie now."

"All right," Greta said with a sigh. "There's water in the basin there and more heating on the stove, clean towels and everything else you might need."

"We'll be fine. I'll call you when I need anything."

"I'll send Kathy in with a lamp in a bit. Dark comes earlier now," Greta said as she left, closing the door behind her.

Crossing to the bed, Kate reached for Annie's hand. The pulse was fast but steady, her hand warm, offering no resistance. Suddenly the hand clamped down on Kate's as another spasm racked the tired body. Sweat ran down Annie's temples, soaking the thick auburn hair and drenching the thin muslin gown she wore. She made no sound, though her body was tense, fighting the paroxysm of torture that spread through her.

A minute later, the pain subsiding, her body relaxed, and she began to breath again. Kate took the damp rag from the basin, bathing Annie's forehead as she whispered soothing words.

"Annie, listen to me. The next time a contraction comes, you need to breathe, breathe hard and fast, it will help the pain not to be so bad," Kate said. "This baby needs you to help it, not fight it. Do you understand me?"

Listless green eyes glanced in Kate's direction. "Why?" she whispered.

Taking a deep breath, Kate said, "Whatever you may think, whatever your pain, this child is a gift, it belongs to God, and He has seen fit to give it into your care."

For the first time since Kate had entered the room, a spark of life seemed to ignite the pain racked body on the bed. "A gift?" Annie spat out. "More like a curse."

Kate's heart ached for this woman, as she realized the pain she felt went far deeper than the physical torment her body endured. "Annie, there is no sin in this life that God cannot forgive. You are blessed with a husband who loves you, and who loves this child, no matter the origins."

Annie's eyes held Kate's, "How do you...." the question was obliterated in a scream of pain as Annie grabbed Kate's arm.

"Breathe, Annie, breathe," Kate commanded, gripping her hands in support.

Annie's eyes flew open, staring at Kate with hope, "God forgive me," she gasped, "Help me, save my baby, please." She drew in deep ragged breaths as the spasm began to subside.

Uncertain whether Annie pled with God or with her, Kate resolved to do everything within her power to save both mother and child. "Annie, I'm going to check and see how you are progressing," Kate said. "I'll try not to hurt you, but I need to do this, okay?"

Annie nodded.

Laying aside the muslin sheet, Kate began a brief examination, feeling for the baby's head and position. "Annie, the baby isn't laying the way he should. It's not too bad, but that's why it seems to hurt so much. He's laying face up and I need to get him face down. I'm going to try to get the baby to turn after the next contraction."

Fear shone in Annie's green eyes. "Is he going to be all right?" she asked, her voice hoarse from fatigue.

"If we can get him to turn over, I think he'll just slip right out," Kate said, wiping her hands on a coarse towel.

"Oh, oh, here comes the next one!" an agonized wail escaped Annie's lips before she clamped her jaw shut.

"Breath, Annie, come on, you can do it!"

Annie gasped at the pain, then began breathing in shallow rapid bursts until the contraction subsided.

"Hold on now, honey," Kate said working rapidly to turn the infant within the womb. "There, I think that's better. How do you feel now?"

"Scared," Annie said, her eyes wide. "Where's Michael?" she asked looking beyond Kate.

"His father's gone to fetch him," Greta's voice came from the door. She entered and placed a lamp on the table near the bed. "How is she doing, Kate?"

"I think we're almost there. Can you stay to help now?"

"Of course," Greta answered. "Just let me get the water,

"Annie, with the next pain, I want you to bear down as hard as you can. Do you understand?"

Annie nodded. Kate could see the toll the exhaustion was taking written clearly in Annie's features. "You're almost through now. This baby will be here real soon," Kate said, hoping she was right. Greta returned carrying a basin of warm water and several more clean towels.

"Figured we could use these," she said, placing her burden on the floor near the foot of the bed.

"Good, thank you, Greta," Kate said, watching Annie's tired features. Greta went to Annie's side taking her hand, and stroking her feverish brow. A spasm of pain racked the tired woman, "Push now, Annie, push." Kate said.

"I can't do it, I can't," she screamed.

"Yes, you can, now push! Annie, I can see the baby's head, push."

Kate could see Annie's grip tighten even harder on Greta's hand. Her eyes pressed shut, every muscle taut and straining against the agony. The pain subsided and Annie gasped for breath.

"It's going to start again right away, Annie, take a deep breath," Kate encouraged.

Annie complied, breathing rapidly, then drawing a great breath as the pain came roaring again.

"Now, Annie, use the pain, push!"

The baby's head appeared again, this time emerging from the womb in one great effort. Another brief respite and the next contraction delivered first one shoulder and then the second. The tension in Kate's neck and back began to ease slightly even as her hands trembled feeling the new life. She worked to clear the baby's tiny airways even before the final push delivered the precious infant into her waiting hands. *Oh, bless you, Lord, thank you*, Kate voiced her silent prayer, tears of relief flooding her eyes, even as she worked at tying and severing the cord that held the child to its mother.

"A girl, it's a girl, a beautiful, perfect little girl," Kate said wrapping the baby in a towel.

A thin wail pierced the growing darkness in the room. "I want to see my baby," Annie whispered hoarsely.

Tears flowing freely down her cheeks, Kate looked at the precious child in her arms, then handed the infant to Annie, praying that Annie would accept and love the child, and as God commanded, would put the sin behind her and remember it no more. The look of wonderment that crossed Annie's tired features made Kate's heart soar. This child would be loved and cherished, she could see it in the mother's eyes as surely as she could hear it in Annie's voice when at last she spoke.

"Oh, my daughter, you are beautiful," Annie whispered, closing her eyes and rocking gently, holding the baby close to her breast. A slow smile curved the corner's of her mouth, her features softened, and a look of peace settled over Annie's face.

"Oh, Annie, I'm so happy for you," Greta said. "Why don't you let me get her cleaned up? You can rest for a bit, get cleaned up yourself, and then she'll probably be wanting to eat." Greta took the infant, her own face glowing with a grandmother's special joy. "Do you have a name for her yet?"

"Amanda. If it's all right with Michael, that is." Annie said.

"It's fine with me," came a voice from the front room, deep with emotion.

"Michael," Annie exclaimed weakly.

"You just stay put, young man, until I have your wife looking decent for you!" Kate called, hurrying to put Annie to rights. She bathed her with the warm, soothing water, dressed her in a fresh gown and brushed the damp auburn hair. Greta washed the tiny girl and wrapped her in a soft cotton blanket. As Greta handed the baby to Annie, Kate opened the door to admit the anxious husband.

"Annie?" Michael asked, crossing to her bedside.

Annie said nothing, her tender gaze falling on their daughter. Looking up, her eyes shimmered with unshed tears.

"She's beautiful, our daughter," Michael whispered, "Amanda," reverence filled his voice. A sense of awe crossed his handsome face as he beheld his wife and their child.

Kate motioned to Greta, and they slipped out of the room, closing the door as they left.

"I swear, I have never seen a woman that fearful of havin' a youngun before," Greta said as the door latched behind them. "I do believe that's the first time I've seen her smile in all the weeks she's been here."

"Well, she's going to be just fine now," Kate answered. "And you have a beautiful granddaughter. But I haven't even gotten a chance to see your new little girl!"

Kathy handed the small bundle of sleeping baby to Kate. "Here, you take a turn, I've got to get dinner on anyhow," Kathy said.

Kate looked down into the sleeping face. A stray wisp of dark hair peeked from beneath the blanket, curling against a pale ivory forehead. Her small mouth was the color of wild pink roses, and lay like an exquisite bow beneath a little button nose. "Oh, Greta, she's absolutely breathtaking. What's her name?"

"Rose Marie Hall, after Mike's mama," she said smiling. "Only you won't think she's so very perfect in a few more minutes. She's bound to be wakin' up hungry any time now."

Kate laughed as she handed the child to Greta. Would she ever again know the joy of holding her own child, so perfectly formed, known by the Creator even as it grew within her? A wistful sigh escaped her lips as she watched Greta prepare to feed the baby.

"I figgered you'd be staying to dinner, Miz Shaughnessey, and I can fix up a pallet on the floor if you want to take my bed tonight," Kathy offered.

"Oh, dinner sounds wonderful, but I need to be getting back to Providence tonight. They'll be worrying about me if I don't show up soon," Kate replied.

"Now, Kate, you shouldn't be out travelin' after dark like this, it's just not safe," Greta protested.

"There's a full moon tonight to travel by, and Hawk knows the way," Kate answered. "Besides it's only a few hours, and Jo needs me."

"Well, at least take some food with you. Kathy can make you up some biscuits and ham. You can eat along the way," Greta said. "Ross, you go saddle Miz Shaughnessey's horse for her."

"Yes, ma'am," Ross answered, hurrying out to do his mother's bidding.

"Thank you, all," Kate said accepting the parcel of food from Kathy. "Annie and the baby will be just fine now, but if you need anything at all, please know that you can send for me."

"I know that," Greta smiled. "And I thank you for it."

The door opened, and a weary boy walked in. "Aaron, you look all done in," Greta said, concern flooding her face. "Did you find Doc Horn?"

"No, ma'am, he was away, but I left word at Jansen's store for him." The exhausted lad sank into a chair at the table, and began shoveling biscuits into his mouth as fast as he could. "I left your gelding in the corral where I found him, Miz Shaughnessey," he said around the food in his mouth. "My horse was well enough rested, I rode her back here."

"Thank you, Aaron," Kate said. "Did you see anyone at my place?"

"No, ma'am, funny thing, I figured they'd be in, it was getting well nigh dark when I dropped by there."

"Well, you know how harvesting goes, and I had sent Jo up to the Insleys," Kate said, shrugging off any concern she may have felt. "Nana had another attack last night."

"Oh, dear, is she all right?" Greta asked.

"She seemed to be resting well when I left her." Kate said. "I'm worried, though, I don't know how much more her heart can take."

"Well, I can understand you wanting to get on home then," Greta said. "You just get going, hurry, but be careful along the way." Kissing Kate on the cheek, Greta sent her out the door.

"I will, Greta, you take care of that new family in there," Kate called, waving as she hurried toward the barn.

Mike was pitching hay into the corrals for the horses and Ross was just making the final adjustments to Hawk's saddle when she got there.

"Thank you so much, Ross," Kate said. "She seems to like you, it's not everyone she stands still for like that."

"Aw, I just got a way with critters," he replied, blushing.

"Kate, I need to speak with you for minute," Mike called as she was mounting.

"Sure, Mike, what is it?" Kate asked, stepping down from the stirrup.

"Ross, you go on up to dinner now," Mike commanded.

Glancing from his father to Kate and back, he nodded and headed off to the house.

"Mike?" Kate asked, wondering what was on his mind.

"Kate, first I wanted to thank you for being there for Annie. Michael and I had a long talk about it, and, well, this is hard for me to say—"

"I think I know, Mike."

"The baby isn't Michael's." A look of pain crossed Mike's face as he said those words.

Taking his hand, Kate prayed for wisdom. "I know."

Mike looked deep into her eyes, searching, Kate felt, for answers, something to help him accept and love his grandchild.

"Mike, I'll tell you exactly what I told Annie." Kate paused, gazing at Mike, wanting to give him a peace that he could hold on to, "This child is a gift from God. She deserves the love and respect of her family just as any child would. Michael has *chosen* to love this baby, regardless of the past. I believe he will be doubly blessed by that choice.

"Only you can decide how you will treat this child and her mother, but think, Mike, think what God would have you do." Kate paused, watching Mike's face in the flickering glow of a lantern for any hint of response. Shadows danced over his features, obscuring his emotions within the play of light. After a long moment, he nodded. Kate reached up and hugged him briefly, whispering in his ear, "I know you're going to just love your granddaughter, she's beautiful."

Kate turned to mount the impatient mare who stood pawing the ground and snorting. "Easy, girl, we've got a long ride ahead of us," she said taking up the reins.

Turning to leave, she was stopped once again. "Kate, one more thing," Mike said.

"What is it?"

"Matt Johnson."

Kate's stomach tightened at the mention of the name.

"He came by here a couple of days ago wantin' to buy me out," Mike continued. "I ain't sellin', but he's a hard man to convince of that."

"I know," Kate replied, trying to keep the bitterness out of her voice.

"Well, just so you know, he's still tryin' to buy up just about every scrap of land around these parts, and I don't like the way he's going about it."

"You're not selling so that should be the end of it, right?" Kate said.

"Yeah, well, Selby's weren't selling either, and I heard they lost their barn to fire last week. They can't make the winter, cause they lost their hay with it," Mike's voice was hard. "They're sellin' now. I guess Johnson got himself a pretty good deal on that place."

"I see," Kate said quietly. "Has anyone contacted the marshal's office in Guthrie?"

"How're they gonna prove anything?" Mike asked. "I just wanted you to know so you'll be careful. We'll be all right. Got my boys, and we keep an eye on this place 'round the clock. It ain't easy, but it's better than losing it."

"Thanks for the warning," Kate said. Laying the rein along the mare's neck, she gave a light squeeze and rode into the night.

✶✶✶✶✶✶✶✶✶✶✶✶✶✶✶✶✶✶✶✶✶✶✶✶✶✶✶✶✶✶

Pale moonlight lay like liquid silver along the ground. Creatures of the night skittered away from the woman and the horse traveling unbidden through their domain. Kate rode with a loose rein, trusting the mare to find her way along the unfamiliar trail. Her body protested at the thought of additional hours in the saddle even as her heart yearned toward home and family.

She wondered what Jo was doing now. Had Luke found her note? Were they worried, or had they gone to the Insleys' for the evening. Undoubtedly, they assumed she would be spending the night at the Halls'. Wouldn't they be pleased and surprised when she arrived in just a few short hours? Sighing, Kate urged the mare on.

Emerging from the narrow path, Kate was glad to see the road ahead of them. Turning north, they continued on under the canopy of stars now glittering above. Walking along under the bright moon of a cloudless sky, horse and rider were bathed in the silvery light. Contentment settled over Kate, and the gentle swaying of the horse lulled her into a dreamy repose.

A distant report brought Kate fully to her senses. Her head snapped up, senses crackling as fear filled every pore. Another shot sounded, and Kate felt a sharp blow to her chest. Bringing her hand up instinctively to the wound, she looked at her blood-stained fingers trying to understand what was happening. She began to sway. The mare, smelling the fear and the blood, bolted forward, throwing Kate into the brush beside the road. Still conscious, she listened in desperation to the diminishing sound of Hawk's hoof beats.

Voices drifted to her ears. Fighting the darkness that threatened to envelope her, Kate dragged herself further into the woods, trying to hide from the would-be assailants.

"She's got to be around here somewhere."

"Look!"

"Blood. You must have hit her, boss."

"The horse took off."

"Yeah, but look there, I bet she's dragged herself off into the trees."

Fighting both fear and pain, Kate closed her eyes, feigning unconsciousness. She could feel the muffled footsteps on the dry ground as the men approached. The voices drew closer. Kate's heart beat a loud staccato rhythm in her ears.

"There she is." Came Matt Johnson's unmistakable drawl.

Pain exploded in her chest as a rough booted foot pushed her over. She rolled with the kick, swallowing the scream that tried to escape.

"Want me to finish her off?" The voice was familiar. Kate concentrated on trying to remember where she had heard it before. The solid click of a hammer being cocked echoed loud within her ears. Dick West. His face rose from the depths of her memory.

"Are you insane? Two shots already. We're taking enough chance as it is. Someone hear's that and they'll find us for sure." Matt said. "She's as good as dead. Look at the blood she's already lost. Come on, let's get out of here."

Movement rustled the bushes before a sudden sharp pain flared through Kate's temple as a booted foot landed on the side of her head and blackness claimed her senses at last.

Chapter XV

Luke rode toward the barn in the gathering dusk. Jake and Jonathan had headed home to check on Nana. Luke sighed, anticipating another long day of harvesting on the morrow. Stopping the young horse near the corrals, he glanced down at the house wondering why Kate hadn't lit the lamp or started a fire to warm the house against the inevitable evening chill. Perhaps she was with Nana.

Luke dismounted, and set about unsaddling the colt. As he turned the buckskin into the corral, he saw the bay gelding standing with his head low, dried sweat marring the normally gleaming coat. An uneasy feeling settled over Luke. Frowning, he pitched hay into the horses at the corral and went to check those stalled within the barn. Raven whinnied at him, demanding his supper. It wasn't like Kate to leave the horses untended. He fed Raven and the mares in the pen behind the barn, filled water troughs, then hurried to the house.

Dry laundry fluttered in the evening breeze from every line and rail. Mounting the porch steps in two strides, he yanked the door open. "Kate!" he called into the dim interior. His voice reverberated in the empty rooms. Fighting down the panic that tried to overcome him, he scanned the kitchen for any clue as to her whereabouts. His gaze fell upon a sheet of paper beneath a lamp on the plank table.

Grabbing the note, he strained to read it in the failing light. The words written there eased his mind, and he breathed a deep sigh of relief as he realized that Kate had gone to the Halls' to help with the birth of Greta's child. Sinking into a nearby chair, he felt the adrenalin drain from his body, then let his gaze return to the note to read the last line again; "..don't worry about me, I love you, Kate."

★★★★★★★★★★★★★★★★★★★★★★★★★★★★★★★★★

"Humph! Greta Hall ain't never had no trouble havin' babies. Don't see why she needed Kate this time," Nana complained from her bed.

Jo sat beside her playing with the doll, while the men sat around the Insley's small table finishing the last of their supper.

"Fine lot we make without a woman to cook for us," Jake said, tapping a rock hard biscuit on the edge of the table and wrinkling his nose at the burned bacon and cold tinned beans.

"Well, if you'd let me cook, I could have made you a good dinner," Jo countered from her perch on Nana's bed.

"You're too little to reach the stove," Jonathan observed.

"Ain't neither, mama lets me stand on a chair."

"Quit bickering, you two. We'll just have to make the best of things until Kate gets back," Jake thundered.

Jo sulked, sticking her tongue out at Jon when Jake's back was turned.

Luke coughed to hide his laughter at her antics. "Nana, do you need anything else?" he asked trying to change the subject.

"I'm fine as can be expected, considering." Nana sniffed. "I would take a spot of that tea Kate sent, though."

"Coming right up." Luke jumped up and moved the kettle nearer the heat. "Speaking of Kate's return, when exactly do you think she'll be back?"

"Well, if she's not here by now, I expect she's staying the night there. Can't imagine she'd risk traveling after dark," Jake said.

"I suppose you're right," Luke sighed. "Where is the Halls' place anyway?"

"It's about ten miles south-southwest of here, just a few miles north of the Comanche Reservation." Jake said, eyeing Luke before he decided to continue. "You take the road south out of here, go about eight miles or more, then you'll see a great stone cairn they built to mark the path to their place. Turn back to the west at the marker, 'nother couple of miles and you're there. They've got a pretty good quarter section down that way."

"Humph! Other than being too close to the injuns if ya ask me," Nana added.

The kettle began to whistle. Luke reached for it without thinking. "Ouch!" he exclaimed, dropping the handle and shaking his hand.

"Here's some butter," Jon offered.

Luke shook his head. "It's not that bad." Glancing around, he found a rag to use before picking up the kettle once again and pouring the steaming water into Nana's cup. Carrying the tea to Nana's bedside table, he asked, "Can Jo stay here tonight?"

"'Course she can," Nana replied. "She can have Jon's bed, he'll make do with a pallet on the floor."

"Thanks," said Luke. "I suppose I'll turn in for the night. Goodnight, Jo, you be good for the Insleys," he said scooping her up.

"Goodnight, Mr. Josey," Jo said giving him a hug around the neck.

"Nana needs your help here," he whispered in her ear, "so you do everything you can for her, okay?"

Jo nodded vigorously, "I will, but I miss my mama."

"I miss her, too."

"You do?" she asked, her blue eyes wide.

"I do," he answered solemnly, setting her down again. "Harvesting again tomorrow, Jake?"

"We'll be at the barns early, then head out after the drying starts."

"I'll be ready," Luke said.

Stepping out into the night air, he was struck by the chill already frosting the grass and trees. Dark clouds scudded across the full moon, beginning to obscure its glittering light. Turning his collar up against the stiffening breeze, he started down the path toward the barn.

Closing the door behind him, Luke fumbled for the lamp and matches, his fingers stiff from the cold. Adjusting the wick, the room was soon bathed in a soft glow. This wasn't how he had planned on spending the evening. He had looked forward to seeing Kate, and together telling Jo the news. A disquieting feeling settled over him.

Walking to the window he could feel the chill seeping in around the edges of the pane. A fire would be welcome tonight. Luke wasn't even sure the ancient iron stove in the corner worked. He opened the grate to a puff of soot. Digging through the remnants of long ago fires, he decided the old thing could probably be coaxed into lighting. Luke remembered an ash bucket just outside. Opening the door invited a blast of frigid air. He grabbed the bucket and slammed the door shut against the chill.

Cleaning the stove took more time than he anticipated, but an hour later the pot bellied furnace was empty, the flue was opened and rammed clean, and Luke's face was a black mask of grime. Grimacing, he wiped his hands and face on an old rag. All he needed now were some logs and kindling. The woodpile was near the kitchen porch. Buttoning his jacket against the night, he picked up the lamp and a canvas tote and stepped out into the dark wind.

The moonlight faded in and out between the blowing clouds. Glancing at the sky, Luke didn't think rain was likely, just a good blue norther. A sound from behind made him whirl around, senses keen. In the shadows near the front of the barn, Luke could just make out a large shape. Holding the lantern ahead of him, he walked toward the noise. The clouds cleared momentarily allowing the moon to shine against the white coat of a horse. Hawk!

"Kate?" Luke called. "Kate, where are you?"

The mournful whine of blowing wind was his only answer.

Reaching the horse Luke's fears mounted. The reins were loose, the torn bridle hanging low on her brow. Mud and briers dulled the normally bright coat. Her right front leg was cut and badly swollen. Gathering the reins and grabbing a handful of mane Luke led the limping horse into the barn. As he set the lamp on a barrel, he adjusted the wick to cast a brighter light. In one swift movement he removed the badly damaged headstall and bit, noticing as he did the swollen bars of her mouth. Loosening the girth, he saw the blood. Dried brown spots covered the pommel and marred the white mane.

Great waves of fear crashed upon the shores of his mind. Breathing rapidly, Luke tried to calm the angst. Think, he told himself, How am I going to find her? How long has she likely been out there? What do I need? Even as his mind whirled, he automatically put the mare in a stall, checking the hay and water as he did. Grabbing a halter from the hook on the wall, he slipped out to the corral, and haltered the startled buckskin.

In a moment he had the horse saddled and ready to go. Setting his foot in the stirrup, he stopped, returned to his room, and came back with a bedroll that he strapped on behind the cantle. There was a blanket, hardtack and jerky, and some first aid supplies rolled up in the oiled canvas. Pulling his hat low over his brow, he turned out the lamp, mounted the colt and set off down the lane leading to the road south.

Luke fought the bile that rose in his gorge. Fear was a palatable presence, riding beside him. He fought the urge to hurry, afraid that he might miss something along the road. The colt snorted and pawed impatiently as Luke scanned every broken branch, scouted every side path. Where was she?

An hour of agonized riding and still there had been no sign. Was the search futile? The full moon cast a glow over the landscape that aided the process though the clouds still obscured the moonlight from time to time, causing him to pause and wait for additional light. Every rustle tickled the hollow of his ear, urging him to peer deeper into the bushes. The night sounds became a haunting chorus, taunting him with the promise of finding her just over the next rise, around the next bend, but still he could find no trace.

Voices. Reining in the colt he listened. Surely he had heard a voice off to the left. Staring transfixed into the trees, he waited, stilling his very breathing, he listened. The soft hooting of an owl, the scurry of a rodent in the brush, only the night sounds surrounded him. Expelling his breath in a rush, he urged his horse on yet again.

How many miles had he come? Jake had said it was nearly eight miles to the marker. He had covered perhaps half that distance. The pale light of the moon was coming more from the west with every step. A permanent chill had settled in his bones, fear permeated every cell, his head pounded, fingers numb, still he rode on, searching.

Blood. A small pool of blood lay before him on the road drying and clotting in the moonlight. Streaks of brown and red gore showed plainly where the victim had crawled or been dragged off the road to the west. Shredded leaves and mangled branches gave their own mute testimony to the passing.

Swallowing the fear that rose within his throat, Luke dismounted in one swift, fluid motion. The buckskin followed Luke into the trees reluctantly, snorting at the coppery scent of blood, eyes wide with fear. Not fifteen feet from the road, they emerged into a small clearing.

She lay sprawled beneath a scrub oak, blood soaking the jacket and trickling from her mouth. Dried gore matted her hair. She made no movement, no sign of life was evident in the still form. A moment, frozen in time, Luke's heart stopped in paralyzing fear. The colt behind him, already filled with a sense of panic, sat back on his haunches at the sight of her body, jerking the reins through Luke's hand. The sudden movement jarred him from his dazed stupor.

"Whoa, boy, whoa," he said to the quaking horse. Picking up the reins he looped them securely around a stout tree. Turning to Kate, he knelt beside her lifeless body. Her skin was cool, but still held the resiliency of life. Placing his fingers on her neck in a feather-light touch, he felt for a pulse. Barely breathing, he waited, moving his fingers as he sought the artery near the side of her neck. There, it was there, he could just feel the blood still pulsing faintly beneath her skin.

Now what? What could he do here, in the middle of the night, in the cold? He knew so little about healing. He had dug a slug out of a cowboy's arm one rainy night years ago. But this was the woman he loved, her lifeblood seeping from her in an inexorable tide. Panic began to overcome him. He was going to sit here and watch her die, there was nothing he could do. Luke had never felt so utterly alone and helpless in his life. The fear held him in iron bands, constricting his chest, binding his heart.

Breathing in deep ragged breaths, he closed his eyes and turned his face to heaven. "God, oh God, why? I am coming to You, broken, helpless, humble. There is nothing I can do. Only You can cleanse me, Lord. Only You can heal her. She has been Yours for so long, and only now do I truly realize what that means. To be wholly yours, I have to sacrifice every earthly desire, trust You, stop relying on my strength and allow You to work through me. God, save her, save me."

The shriek of a night-hunting hawk rent the air. Luke's eyes flew open. A man stepped from the shadows, his dark gaze searching Luke's face before falling on the woman still motionless on the ground.

Luke's hand reached instinctively for a gun he no longer wore.

"She lives," the man pronounced.

Luke nodded. Though wary of the stranger, something about him told Luke that he meant no harm.

"Tochoway?" Luke whispered.

The man nodded. "She has spoken of me."

"Yes."

Tochoway knelt beside Kate. Removing his woolen jacket, he placed it over her cold body. Gentle fingers probed the wound on her head, then moved to her chest. Lifting her slightly, he explored her back. Nodding, he turned his gaze on Luke.

"How bad is she?" Luke asked.

"The bullet has gone through. That is good. She has lost much blood, and is too cold. We need to move her to shelter now."

"Bullet? But who would..." Luke trailed off, realization dawning, anger rose to replace the fear

"The blood still flows," Tochoway observed, waving off Luke's concern. "We must stop it."

Jolted into action. Luke unstrapped the bedroll from the buckskin, still pawing the ground where he was tied. Opening the roll he retrieved several cotton rags and a thick green blanket.

Tochoway took the rags. Folding them into tight bundles, he placed them over both entry and exit wounds to staunch the flow. Luke laid aside his jacket and removed his muslin shirt. The icy wind raised chill bumps along his exposed skin. Ignoring the cold, he tore the shirt into long strips to bind the makeshift bandages into place. Working together the men shifted her enough to get the strips bound tightly around her, stemming the flow of her blood.

Tochoway raised his head, listening to the wind. "Come."

"How?" Luke asked. "She'll never survive the ride all the way back to Providence."

As they rolled Kate gently into the relative warmth offered by the blanket, a groan escaped her.

"Shhh, it's going to be all right. You're going to be fine," Luke whispered to her, not knowing whether she heard or not. His heart ached, but he knew they had to work quickly in order to have any chance of saving her.

Tochoway picked up the limp form, cradling her within the shelter of his arms. With no more than a glance toward Luke, he set off through the trees. Luke untied the reins of the colt and followed behind.

The man ahead of him traveled swiftly even with the burden he carried. Luke was hard pressed to keep up, and more than once thought he had lost him. Each time, Tochoway paused and waited for him to reappear.

After an hour of travel this way, Luke found himself in a valley, surrounded on three sides by rocky canyon walls. A lake shimmered with
ethereal beauty under the waning moonlight ahead of them. Tochoway
stood before the door of a simple log cabin, all but hidden in a copse of
trees. Tying the colt to a fence rail near the cabin, Luke hurried over to
open the door.

Pushing through the door, Tochoway laid Kate on the rough bed
occupying one corner of the small room. A stove glowed in the opposite
corner with the fading radiance of banked coals.

"Build the fire up. We will need water heated." Tochoway said.

Luke complied, finding the wood and kindling near the door of the
cabin. A kettle stood atop the stove, already filled with water. As the fire
caught and began to warm the room, Luke moved the kettle over the
heat and waited, watching Tochoway minister to Kate's wounds.

"The bleeding has slowed, perhaps stopped, but the wounds are bad.
There is a woman in the village skilled in healing. I will bring her."
Before Luke could respond, Tochoway vanished.

Luke poured warm water from the kettle into a basin and carried it to
the bed. He set the bowl on the floor, and retrieved one of the two chairs
from the table, which along with a chest and one wall cabinet, made up
the only other furnishings within the austere cabin.

Tochoway had left a cloth over her forehead. Taking the rag, Luke
dipped it in the water and wrung it out. He daubed the wound on the
side of her head, cleaning away the blood and dirt to reveal a small cut,
some minor swelling and bruising. Another rinse in the soothing water,
and he began to wash the dirt from her face. Her eyes fluttered, opening
for a brief moment, but unable to focus, they closed again. She moaned
in pain, trying to get up.

"Shhh, Kate, lie still. You're going to be all right," Luke said, pushing
her gently down.

She collapsed back on the bed and lay so still that a moment of panic seized Luke, until he saw the gentle rise and fall of her breast with each shallow breath.

The chill in the cabin slowly dissipated as the fire warmed the air. The stars still twinkled through the window, though the eastern sky was beginning to lighten. The Insleys would be waking soon. What would they think? Jake would find Kate's horse in the barn and Luke missing. Worry began gnawing at him even as he bathed Kate's face.

The sound of horses approaching stirred him from his reverie. Moments later, the latch moved, and the door swung in. Tochoway was followed by a woman bundled in a bright blanket and two or three shawls. Her black hair was streaked with silver, but her bearing was erect, her eyes bright and clear.

A few phrases were exchanged between Tochoway and the woman in a language Luke could not discern. As the woman removed her outer garments, Tochoway returned to Kate, watching her shallow breathing with an immutable gaze.

The Comanche woman paid scant attention to Luke as she checked the kettle on the stove, removed a bowl from the cupboard and began measuring out herbs from a pouch at her waist. Luke watched in fascination and growing concern as the woman poured steaming water over the concoction and took it to Kate's bedside. A few more words were exchanged, and Tochoway motioned Luke to follow him from the cabin. Glancing at Kate and the woman standing beside her, Luke reluctantly followed Tochoway through the narrow door.

Gray skies lightened the eastern horizon as a bleak dawn approached. The clouds lay low in the sky, and a damp chill penetrated even through Luke's heavy jacket. The two men stared at the lake, as ripples blown by the wind washed the silver shore.

Luke watched the light play against the waves in the pale dawn of morning. Tochoway stood at the rail, gaze fixed on a distant point. In that instant, the realization struck Luke fully.

"You're in love with her," he stated flatly.

Tochoway made no answer, but a tremor ran through his jaw as it tightened, and his focus remained fixed for a long, tense moment.

"Why?" Luke asked. "Why haven't you told her?"

Drawing a deep breath, Tochoway began to speak in a quiet tone, "There is a Comanche legend. A small girl, She-Who-Is-Alone, lost both parents in a great famine. The rains did not come, the people were afraid. The only thing she had left was the beautiful cornhusk doll made by her mother and decorated by her father with the beautiful blue feathers of the jay.

"The medicine man prayed to the Great Father to send the life-giving rains, but still they did not come. She-Who-Is-Alone told her precious doll that all would be well, surely the medicine man would know what to do.

"Finally one day the medicine man went alone to the mountain. He fasted and prayed and sought the will of the Great Father. When he returned, he told the people that they were becoming selfish and forgetting the bounty was provided by the Great Father. They were to sacrifice their most valuable possession in a fire, repent of their selfish ways, then the rains would come.

"The people grumbled among themselves. 'Surely, he does not mean my bow,' said the warrior. 'How then would I hunt to provide meat?' And the maiden said, 'I must have my blanket to stay warm. He could not mean for me to give that up.' So the people drifted off, saying that tomorrow was another day.

"She-Who-Is-Alone looked down at the wonderful doll in her hand, the only thing she had left in the world. 'It is me, I must do this,' she said to herself. With tears in her eyes, she gathered some small sticks, took a burning ember from the village fire, and began the long walk to the mountain alone.

"There she built a pyre, laid her precious doll atop, and with a trembling hand, laid the fire brand against the dry sticks. She watched as the doll burned in a swirl of blue smoke. Then, exhausted, the girl fell asleep upon the mountain.

"When she awoke the land was covered in a carpet of beautiful blue flowers the very color of the jay feathers, and the rains came." Tochoway turned toward Luke. "She-Who-Is-Alone did not want others to endure the loss she had suffered. The Heavenly Father sent a son, knowing that he would die in agony, so others could be spared the pain of eternal death. My sacrifice is a small one, knowing the prejudice she would suffer as my wife or my lover. I have endured the heartbreak of being caught between two peoples, I will not ask that of her."

Howling winds died with the coming dawn, stilling the turbulent lake. The rising sun broke through the gray clouds, sending shafts of radiant light to illuminate the peaceful waters. The ensuing silence was broken by the soft rustle of a woman's skirt as the cabin door opened. Tochoway and Luke turned expectantly, and the dark-haired woman stood aside as she motioned for them to enter.

The cabin was warmed by the glowing stove where a kettle simmered, wafting a soothing herbal fragrance into the air. Tochoway strode across the room to gaze upon the woman laying still upon the bed.

"Weakeah?" he asked.

"She sleeps now. Perhaps she will live," Weakeah answered in softly accented English as she busied herself at the table folding cloths and sorting herbs into her deerskin pouch.

Luke approached the bedside. Kate's pale face was clean, all traces of blood wiped away. The wound on her temple had been skillfully cleaned and covered with a light bandage. She was covered by a colorful woolen blanket that rose and fell with her steady breathing. Her clothing lay in a pile at the foot of the bed, dried blood crusting the jacket and blouse.

Finished with her tasks at the table, Weakeah walked over to retrieve the clothes, and disappeared through the cabin door.

"Weakeah will clean and mend them if she can," Tochoway said.

Luke nodded, numb not only from the shock and cold, but from Tochoway's revelations as well. Would he ever be the man Tochoway was? Did he even deserve a woman like Kate? She had said she loved him, would marry him. Was it really only yesterday they had watched the sun rise over Providence together and the future had held such bright promise?

Kate moaned softly from the bed. She became restless, trying to throw the covers back. Tochoway reached out a hand to stroke her hair, calm her, then glancing at Luke, he stepped back with an indication that the rightful place did not belong to him.

Luke knelt beside the bed reaching for her hand as it flashed from beneath the blanket. "Kate, hush now, you need to rest. I'm here. You're going to be all right now," he comforted her. As he spoke, she grew still, her eyes flew open, searching, wary, unfocused. Kate's head turned from side to side as she fought toward consciousness. Closing her eyes with a deep sigh, she sank back upon the bed into a fitful sleep.

Luke stroked her hand and arm now laying atop the blanket. Puzzled as his fingers felt the unfamiliar scarring he glanced down at the bare skin of her forearm. Normally hidden beneath the long sleeves she always wore, the livid scars ran from a few inches behind her wrist to just before her elbow. Luke stared at them intently, wondering where they had come from, and why she never mentioned them. Did she think he would be repulsed by them?

"Puha," Tochoway said in a low voice.

"What?"

"Puha," Tochoway repeated. "I cannot find a way to say it in your tongue. It is a Nuumu concept for great personal honor, bravery and healing power."

Luke nodded, still looking at the scars. "But, how…"

Tochoway shook his head. "She has suffered much," he continued, his voice deep with emotion. "Yet she is strong, brave, ready to face any challenge life may have for her. Through faith, she has found peace, and an inborn willingness to serve others. Now she deserves happiness."

Luke turned to face Tochoway. In his eyes, Luke could see the love this man felt for Kate. In that instant, Luke resolved to honor the sacrifice and all it meant.

✶✶✶✶✶✶✶✶✶✶✶✶✶✶✶✶✶✶✶✶✶✶✶✶✶✶✶✶

Cold, she was so cold. Why wouldn't the cold go away? The swirling darkness came again enveloping her brain in a foggy haze. She had to— had to—what? There was something very important she had to do, why couldn't she focus? The pain, that was it! If the pain would just go away, she could think. A voice! Luke! Yes, it was Luke. What was he saying? Praying? Why? They had to find Jo and tell her the news. Jo would be so happy. Kate tried to rise, but the pain came again. Darkness.

She moaned softly as she realized the cold was no longer so intense. She was moving, cradled against someone warm. She felt safe, so safe now. The scent of leather and male sweat filled her nostrils as she tried to breathe deeply, but the pain struck again as her lungs filled with air. Black hair brushed her face as her savior bent his head to quiet her. Tochoway? Where was Luke? She knew she had heard him, where had Luke gone? Struggling to see and understand, the pain overwhelmed her and the dark haze claimed her senses again.

She fought through the black void as though it were a tangible foe. Luke was stroking her head, she felt him, heard him, she was sure it was Luke. If only she could tell him she loved him. Willing her eyes to open she saw blurs of light, but the pain was too intense. Her eyes closed. Trying to speak, the only sound that escaped was a gasp of pain.

"Shhh, Kate, lie still. You're going to be all right." Luke's voice penetrated through the haze of pain clouding her brain. Claiming the words as a promise, Kate lay back, giving herself over to the darkness, no longer trying to fight it.

Kate coughed as the bitter herbal drink trickled down her throat. A firm hand held her head up while another poured the warm concoction into her mouth. Forcing her eyes open, Kate could see the soft, dark features of an Indian woman. Her liquid brown eyes held tender compassion. Kate nodded, finished drinking the tea and slipped again into a restful sleep.

The heat was suffocating her. Too hot—fire, get away from the fire. Kate fought to throw off the confining weight of the covers. Why couldn't she move? Why was it so hot? Groping with her hand, she tried to get away. Voices, Luke?

"Kate, hush now, you need to rest. I'm here. You're going to be all right now." Once again his voice had the power to still her restless mind. She wanted to see him, to know that he was here. Willing her eyes to open, she searched for his familiar face. There it was. She wanted to reach out, to feel his firm jaw beneath her fingers, but she was too weak. A movement behind Luke caught her eye. Dark haunted eyes in a sun-bronzed face appeared from the shadows. Her heart beat faster as she saw the longing in Tochoway's face, a yearning for something that could never be. Closing her eyes, she sank into the pillow and surrendered to a fitful sleep.

Kate's slumber was filled with dreams of voices, white horses disappearing in a silver mist, the agonized wail of a hawk who's breast is pierced by an arrow shot from a bow she found in her own hand. During brief bouts of wakefulness, the Comanche woman tended to her needs, fed her strong broths and herbal teas. At times she was aware that Tochoway sat beside her. Other times she would awake to find herself utterly alone.

Gradually, she became aware that she was in Tochoway's cabin. Her faithful companion was named Weakeah, and she now knew that she was gaining strength rapidly.

"Tochoway?" Kate said.

"You are awake."

"Yes," she answered. "How long have I been here?"

"A little more than a week." Tochoway said.

"Luke was here."

"Yes," he nodded.

"Where is he?"

"He returned home, to let your family know you are safe."

"Oh," Kate said, struggling to sit upright.

The door opened and Weakeah entered carrying wood for the stove. Kate smiled at her, wanting to get to know this quiet women better.

"You are Weakeah, aren't you?" Kate asked. "Thank you for seeing me through this."

"You heal well," Weakeah answered.

"Only from all your good medicine." Kate smiled. "Can you tell me what some of those herbs are?"

Weakeah smiled as she stacked the wood. Retrieving her deerskin bag she carried it over to sit beside the white woman and show her the secrets it contained. The women sat together with their heads bowed over the treasures displayed from the bag as Tochoway returned to the leather he was working.

✶✶✶✶✶✶✶✶✶✶✶✶✶✶✶✶✶✶✶✶✶✶✶✶✶✶✶✶✶✶✶✶✶

The morning dawned with a promise of warmth. Kate sat in the bed gazing out the small window watching for Weakeah to appear. She drummed her fingers against the woolen blanket impatiently, knowing that the day had finally arrived when Tochoway would take her home to Providence. She was still weak, but Weakeah and Kate both knew that Kate's heart was with her child and her family. Her strength would grow more rapidly there, surrounded by those she loved. Her wounds were healing well, and she had managed to eat several small meals over the last two days. It was time to go home.

The door opened, Kate turned in surprise. Tochoway entered carrying a small bundle.

"Is Weakeah not coming?" Kate asked.

"She will come," Tochoway answered, setting the package on the table. "Are you hungry?"

"Not really, but I suppose I should eat something." Kate smiled.

Tochoway nodded, turning to the stove and dishing up two small bowls of the venison stew Weakeah had made the evening before. Handing a bowl to Kate, he retrieved two spoons from the cabinet and sat at the table facing Kate. As Tochoway asked the blessing on their small breakfast, Kate added her silent thanks for the care and comfort she had received from these wonderful people.

As she was finishing the stew, Weakeah came in. Tochoway spoke to her in their native tongue, then left the room abruptly. Weakeah shook her head, and began cleaning up the dishes. "Your clothes are clean. The blouse could not be well mended, but there is another shirt there for you to wear over it if you like," Weakeah said, indicating the bundle Tochoway had placed on the table.

Kate walked to the table holding the blanket around her as she had for the last two days when Weakeah would let her stand and move about. Taking the clothes, she unfolded her riding skirt and drawers, both clean and fresh. Her jacket was next, washed but still bearing the telltale rust colored stains of blood. The white shirt had been washed and mended, but had been so shredded by her ordeal that even with Weakeah's careful attention, it was little better than a rag.

At the bottom of the pile lay a pale, creamy leather blouse. Kate's fingers ran over the deerskin, marveling at the soft texture. Holding the shirt up, Kate's breath caught in her throat. The front of the butter-soft leather blouse was intricately beaded with brilliant blue beads and ivory quills in the shape of a jay's feather. The work was skillfully crafted, and matching fine leather fringe draped from the shoulders and sleeves.

"Weakeah, this is so beautiful. Did you make it?" Kate asked.

Weakeah shook her head. "Tochoway."

As though summoned, Tochoway entered the cabin. "I'm sorry. I thought you would be ready. I will be just outside, waiting for you," he said as he disappeared again.

"I can't accept this, Weakeah, he's already done so much for me," Kate said.

"You must, it is our way," Weakeah said, taking the blanket and holding Kate's underwear out to her.

Kate dressed, wincing at the pain as she pulled her own tattered muslin shirt on before taking the beautiful leather blouse and slipping it over her head. The soft leather fell in graceful folds over her body, the blue beads glittering in the morning rays. Weakeah brushed Kate's hair and tied it back with a matching leather thong, fixing two perfect blue feathers at her temple.

"I will miss you, Weakeah."

"Do not be sad. You will always carry a part of me in your heart, as I will carry your memory with me."

Kate hugged Weakeah, and hurried from the room.

Tochoway stood outside holding the reins of a sorrel and white pony. His face softened at the sight of her. Kate smiled, lifting her arms so he could see the beautiful shirt, the fringe blowing gently in the morning breeze. She walked over to where he stood holding the horse.

"I don't know how to thank you," she said.

"It is my wedding gift to you."

Kate's eyes filled with tears at the plaintive sound in his voice.

"Come, it is a long ride," he said gruffly.

Tochoway lifted Kate onto the pony, who wore only a blanket. Kate had never ridden a horse bareback before and the feeling was a bit insecure at first. Mounting skillfully behind her, Tochoway reached around, holding her securely as he took the reins and urged the pony toward the north.

They traveled at an easy walk through country unfamiliar to Kate for over an hour. Tochoway's arms holding her securely, the warm sunshine upon her face, and the gentle swaying of the pony combined to work their lulling charms on her tired body and she dozed intermittently.

Starting awake, Kate's heart leapt within her as she recognized the road they traveled. Tilting her head back and to the side, she smiled into Tochoway's eyes. He dropped his gaze to her, his eyes smiling softly. Here and there among the green leaves Kate saw flashes of red, amber and yellow as the leaves responded to the shortening days and the cooling temperatures. Squirrels chattered and dashed from branch to branch, busily storing away their bountiful harvest of pecans and acorns. A distant honking alerted her to vast flocks of geese winging their way toward southern climes. She could feel Tochoway look to the skies as the trailing vees of plump grey and white birds filled the blue expanse, and thought of roast goose dripping fat over an open fire.

As they approached an open meadow only a few miles south of Providence, Kate felt Tochoway's arms tighten around her, his gaze urging her attention to the west. Looking in the direction he indicated, Kate caught her breath at the sight of a small herd of bison grazing in the golden sun. Perhaps fifty cows and half as many calves shuffled through the deep grass. A great bull lifted his head and stared at them, his horns curving in a graceful, deadly arc above his head, a massive hump rising from his shoulders covered in tattered shreds of brown wool. Most of the vast herds were gone now, only scattered remnants traveling in family bands like this one still remained on the southern plains. Kate's heart ached for the vanishing life and the lost culture of the people left behind.

By midday, they crested the rise that brought Kate's home in sight. The carved wooden sign rocked in a gentle breeze on its posts above the road. The house lay in the distance, blue smoke drifting lazily from the chimney. As they rode on, the sound of voices carried on the breeze made her heart race. Rounding the bend, Kate saw Luke chopping wood in the yard while Jo played with her pup near the garden. Before they were sighted by the family, Tochoway reined the small horse to a stop, and Kate slid to the ground. Still holding Tochoway's outstretched hand for support, she gazed into his dark eyes looking for some way to express the depths of her gratitude to this man who had touched her life in such a profound way. In another time, could things have been different for them? A single tear slipped down her cheek. Tochoway brushed his hand across her cheek, catching the glittering tear, and brushing it away to the wind.

"Do not mourn, I will be with you always," he said, touching his hand to his breast. "Here will I carry your spirit."

Kate nodded, unable to speak past the swelling in her throat.

"Your home is there. Your daughter needs you, and there is a man that loves you well. Go."

Turning away, Kate went home to Providence.

✶✶✶✶✶✶✶✶✶✶✶✶✶✶✶✶✶✶✶✶✶✶✶✶✶✶✶✶✶

From his vantage point, Tochoway watched as the little flame-haired girl ran toward her mother, nearly bowling Kate over in her joy. Luke dropped the axe near the wood pile, and gazed at Kate as though he had never seen anything so beautiful in his life. The blue feather so painstakingly sewn on the white leather tunic sparkled in the sun. Tochoway saw Luke's eyes drawn to the symbol, then look up, searching the horizons.

Raising his arm in a final farewell, Tochoway turned the pony to the south.

EPILOGUE

"Mama, Mama, wake up." The insistent voice cut through the hazy dreams in Kate's mind.

"Jo, what is it?" Kate asked, opening one eye, annoyed to be awakened in the predawn chill.

"It's Christmas morning, you've got to get up," Jo said, jumping up on the big feather bed. "C'mon, Daddy, wake up!"

"Huh! What? What's wrong?" Luke bolted upright.

"It's Christmas morning, dear," Kate said with a wry grin.

"Well, so it is!" Luke exclaimed. "Let's go make your mama some coffee, maybe then she'll be more cheerful."

"Oh, yes, and see if there are any gifts in our stockings!" Jo added.

"I can't believe you two," Kate said. "It's two hours till the sun will even be up."

"But Grandpa Josey will be here soon,"Jo reminded her. "He promised he'd be here in time for breakfast on Christmas morning."

"So he did," sighed Kate. "You know I still don't think he's forgiven me for wearing my leather tunic when he married us in Guthrie."

"Oh, I admit, he thought it was a bit heathen," Luke agreed. "But I think you won him over, when he realized it was because of you 'I finally repented of my sinful ways, and fell on my face before the Lord! Hallelujah Brother!'" Luke spoke in perfect imitation of his father from the pulpit. Jo dissolved in a fit of giggles.

Kate punched him playfully on the arm. "You oughtn't to joke like that, Luke Josey!" she admonished.

"And why ever not, Mrs. Josey?" he teased.

"Well, it has to be sacrilegious, don't you think?" By now they were all laughing so hard, Kate knew they would never go back to sleep. "Well, as long as we're all up, let's get breakfast going so Nana doesn't have so much to fuss over when she gets here." Kate said. Swinging her legs over the side of the bed, she was overcome by a wave of nausea so strong she grabbed for the chamber pot resting nearby.

"Kate, what's wrong?" Luke asked, worry creasing his brow.

Swallowing hard as the nausea passed, she shook her head. "Nothing really, this just confirms my suspicions."

"Your suspicions?" Luke asked in a puzzled voice. His eyes grew huge as a look of joy and surprise suffused his features. "You mean…."

Kate nodded, smiling.

"Yippee!" Luke shouted, pounding his fist against the pillow.

"What?" Jo asked perplexed, looking from her mother to Luke and back again. "We're going to have a baby?" She asked, eyes as wide as saucers.

Kate smiled, placing her hand over her mid section, feeling the first joys of new life.

Printed in the United States
128208LV00002B/445-486/A

9 780595 197804